The Legacy of Lillian Parker

LESLIE HOLDEN

HARVEST HOUSE PUBLISHERS
Eugene, Oregon 97402

Scripture quotations are from the King James Version of the Bible.

THE LEGACY OF LILLIAN PARKER

Copyright © 1986 by Harvest House Publishers
Eugene, Oregon 97402

Library of Congress Catalog Card Number 85-081934
ISBN 0-89081-517-8

Printed in the United States of America.

The Legacy of Lillian Parker

CHAPTER ONE

A gun and a Bible.

How pathetically ironic, thought Lillian.

To think that her father, the fabulously wealthy J. J. Parker II, president of Michigan Technologies, could secretly have been so in debt that the only two possessions he would leave his daughter would be a gun and a Bible!

She glanced again at the newspaper's headlines: PARKER ESTATE LIQUIDATED TO PAY CREDITORS. Beneath it was a photo of her father—so distinguished, so confident-looking, so maturely handsome. *Incredible! He just couldn't be dead!*

But he was. In fact, it had been six months ago to the day that the funeral had been conducted. And just two days later, still numbed with grief, Lillian had been given the equally shocking news that she had inherited more than three million dollars in corporate and personal debts which her father had accumulated.

She shook her head in amazement even now as she recalled it.

No wonder her father had kept a well-worn Bible and a shiny new revolver here in his office desk! He probably had spent many an afternoon wondering if he should expect a godly miracle to end his problems or if he should end them himself by committing suicide.

The poor misguided man, thought Lillian. He knew nothing about guns and even less about the Bible. Maybe it was best that his dilemma had been solved for him. His cause of death had been listed as heart attack due to adverse tension and stress. *Small wonder*, mused Lillian.

A tap at the door interrupted her thoughts. She quickly scooped the gun and the Bible into her purse.

"Mind if I come in?" asked Roderick Davis, entering without waiting for an answer. "I thought I'd find you here. Getting one last look around, are you?"

Lillian turned her cheek to Roderick as he bent toward her. She accepted his perfunctory kiss and then watched him as he sat near her at the desk. She sensed some tension in his behavior. He did not look at her as he opened his briefcase and began to remove papers.

"I came to clean out Daddy's desk," Lillian explained. "Here are some client profiles and a few copies of contracts."

She pushed a small stack of files toward Roderick, who eagerly grabbed them. He began a brief survey of each one. His business-first attitude bothered her. She decided not to tell him about the gun and the Bible that also had been in the desk.

She watched him closely. In many ways he was like her father had been. He wore conservative three-piece suits, dark ties with subdued patterns, and long-sleeved dress shirts even in the summer. His hair was flawlessly styled to accent the random flecks of gray that showed prematurely at the temples. His black shoes were buffed to a high gloss.

Yes, Lillian determined, *he was handsome. Very handsome indeed.* His tan skin was so smooth that she wondered if he shaved more than once a day. Probably so. After all, everything else about him revealed a sense of image—manicured fingernails, evenly capped teeth, tinted contact lenses. He was more image-conscious than anyone else she had ever known. But his image seemed to work on people. It had on her. Seven months ago she and Roderick had announced their engagement.

"Everything in order?" she asked.

Roderick glanced up. "What? Oh. . .oh, yes, of course. Sorry."

He quickly shoved all the papers, except for one envelope, back into his briefcase. His eyes again avoided hers. His movements were awkward. Something *was* wrong.

Lillian reached across and touched Roderick's hands. He flinched instinctively, then tried to relax. He forced a smile.

"Hey!" said Lillian. "Don't let this office spook you. Daddy's dead. I've accepted that, and you must too. Sure, you were one of his closest advisers for years, but he's gone now. And we've got to go on."

Roderick cleared his throat. They sat in silence.

"It's not that, is it?" she said after a pause. "Something else is bothering you. What is it?"

Roderick stood slowly and walked to the window. He watched

the city traffic below. Finally, with his back still turned toward Lillian, he spoke.

"The property liquidation was finished today. The board of directors met this afternoon to review the proceedings."

"I know that," said Lillian. "I helped to arrange things, remember? It had to be done. So now it's done. The bonds and stocks and estate are all gone, but at least Daddy's debts are paid and the company is secure. All's well that ends well."

Roderick turned around and eased his hands into the pockets of his suitcoat. "Not quite," he said softly.

Lillian looked puzzled. "What do you mean by that?" she asked.

"I'm afraid the board of directors feels that the repayment of company funds is not the total solution to the company's public relations problem," said Roderick. "The stockholders were stunned by your father's...uh, carelessness. Before they will start to reinvest in the company, they're going to have to have some assurances that this sort of thing could never happen again."

"My father is dead. What more definite assurance could they want than that?" insisted Lillian.

"Just one thing," said Roderick cautiously. "They want every trace of J. J. Parker purged from the company. Including you."

"*Me!*" said Lillian, suddenly turning white with shock and anger. "*Me!* I'm the director of sales! I know the company products better than anyone! My father saw to that. I'm vital to the operation. Besides, I personally own 16 percent of the company stock. They can't ask me to quit. I refuse. I absolutely refuse. This is ridiculous."

"I'm afraid it's not a matter open for discussion," explained Roderick. "You've been dismissed. Whitfield is being moved up into your job. The board made the decision less than an hour ago. I was told to give you the news."

Lillian's eyes narrowed. She clutched her purse close to her. As if the liquidation of the family holdings had not been enough, now she was out of a job, too. She was outraged. What was that line from the Bible? *The sins of the fathers shall be visited upon the children*...something like that. How true! Oh, why hadn't her father started to read this Bible long ago? It might have made such a difference in the way things turned out.

She stared at Roderick. "You go back there and tell them they can't fire me. I have friends in this company, not to mention a huge block of stock."

Roderick shook his head. "You have neither friends nor stock," he said, sensing the need to be direct. "I was at the board meeting. No one spoke on your behalf—except me, of course. But I can't vote, just advise. You're a Parker and that makes you persona non grata around here. You were dismissed, and by a unanimous vote."

Lillian seemed awestruck. Twice she tried to speak, but the words wouldn't come.

Roderick moved back to her side and continued, "And your stock has been usurped through the use of a loophole in the company's charter. Although you legally own your shares of the company, they were bought for you by your father before you were of legal age. Because of that, he had to sign for them as custodian and co-owner. So, technically, he was also an owner of your shares."

"So?" asked Lillian.

"So the company charter says that whenever a board member dies, all of his stock must be made available for purchase by the other board members should they wish to buy it. Since your father was a board member, the stock he jointly owned with you became open for sale when he died. And one of the board members exercised the option to purchase just when the company stock hit its lowest ebb just after...well, just after the scandal about your father was publicized."

"This is unbelievable," Lillian whispered, mostly to herself.

"I'm really sorry, Lill," said Roderick, placing one hand on her shoulder. "I know this must be a terrible shock to you."

"How...how much?" she asked.

"Not even 30,000 dollars," he answered quietly. "The check is in here." He picked up the envelope that had not been put into his briefcase. He laid it on the desk in front of her.

"Is there anything I can do for you?" he asked.

Of course there's something you can do for me, she thought. *You can put your arms around me, hold me, say something to encourage me, wipe my tears, tell me you love me. I'm falling apart and you're still playing corporate lawyer. Don't you know anything about people and their needs? Don't you care?*

Roderick cleared his throat again. It was his habitual cue for announcing more bad news. Lillian hated to hear him clear his throat. Why didn't he just *say* what he wanted to say and not precede it with needless dramatics?

"There's also the matter of our delayed engagement," said Roderick, sounding more like a corporate executive than a sweetheart. "I've given it a lot of thought and I see now that you were right."

Lillian opened her purse a crack and found a tissue. "Right? About what?"

"About the need for the delay in our marriage," explained Roderick, speaking in measured tones. "Six months ago, when your father died, I tried to pressure you into a quick marriage. I honestly felt I could be of more comfort and support to you if we were married. But you asked for time to sort out your feelings and to deal with your father's estate. I see now that you were right in your decision."

"I couldn't agree less," she replied softly. "These past six months have been miserable. I was foolish to keep you waiting. I've needed advice and support, and while Pastor and Mom Mead have been wonderful, I really needed you as my husband. I'm not going to make that same mistake twice. I'm ready to marry you, Roderick, I'm not ashamed to say I need a man to care for me. I need you."

Lillian's expression evidenced a blend of forlornness and optimism. Now surely, she thought, Roderick would pull her to him, hold her tightly, and convince her that all was well between them.

But he remained rigid. His brow wrinkled and his mouth turned itself into an odd twist. Love was not on his mind, much less thoughts of marriage. He sat down and pointed toward the envelope with Lillian's check in it.

"You've been given a solid jolt," he said. "This check is the sum and substance of what you are now. And, considering the life you were leading a year ago, that's quite a fall."

He cleared his throat. "Naturally, as far as our engagement is concerned, I'm not worried about your financial standing. Still, I'm sure that you must be in a state of shock over all this. This isn't the time to act hastily or irrationally."

"I love you, Roderick. I don't need more time to realize that. You've asked me to marry you and I've accepted. I'm ready now.

We don't have a fortune, true; but we're young, and we've got each other. Right now that's what I need. When I had money, it didn't make me happy. I've learned that lesson. Now I want something better. I want love."

Roderick stared at Lillian. She was sincere in what she was saying, and he knew it. Such sincerity would be difficult to quell. Still, it had to be done. Marrying the board chairman's beautiful and wealthy daughter was one thing. Marrying a pretty girl with no clout or wealth was something else. Lillian lacked the former appeal she had held for Roderick. She was now expendable.

"You're sweet, Lill. I'm sure we could...well...be happy together—eventually. But so much has happened recently that I just think we should take a few months or a year to assess where we—"

"A year!" she exclaimed. "Roderick! Are you serious? You want to postpone our marriage for a year? What can you be thinking?"

"Only of you, believe me," hastened Roderick. He reached out and touched her hand. This time it was she who flinched. His movement was calculated, his touch cold to her. Lillian had felt similar coldness once in college when she had touched a snake in biology class. She hadn't liked the snake then and she didn't like Roderick's hand now.

Roderick continued, "Just hear me out. Then you can do whatever you please."

He quickly probed into his briefcase and found a travel brochure.

"Look, Lill. It's a flyer about private cabins in the Black Hills of Dakota. You've said a hundred times that your one great fantasy has been to fill your car trunk with novels and go off to a private mountain retreat. Now's your chance."

Lillian shook her head. "Oh, Roderick, be serious."

"I am—I am serious," he insisted. "There's nothing to prevent it. You have no ties here any longer—no father, no job, no family home. Just close your apartment downtown or sublease it and go. The change will be excellent for you."

"No! Don't be silly. I'd be bored to death in less than a week."

"Then take some projects with you," said Roderick. "Write a biography of your father. Or what about that book you were going to write about how to train women executives? You could work on that!"

Lillian offered no reply. None was necessary. For now the idea seemed to be out of the question. Roderick decided to give it one more plug and then let her mull on it for a while.

"You've got enough money to live on comfortably for a year, Lill. Part of that time should be spent relaxing, reading, and reevaluating your goals. If after a time you still want to be married, I'll still be here in Detroit. We can talk more about it then."

Lillian suddenly was very tired. Her neck felt stiff, her arms were tense, and her back was sore. She could feel a headache coming on, too.

"I . . . I just don't want that," she said, half in a whisper. "I want us to be together . . . to help each other . . . to love each—"

Roderick rose abruptly. He patted her hands twice, the way a person would do when saying "buck up." It was both curt and patronizing. Lillian would have been offended by it had she not been so overwhelmingly pained emotionally.

"Come on, come on," said Roderick with mock bravado. "You can handle things. All you need is some rest. You'll be just fine. Here, I'll leave this brochure. I've got to get to a staff meeting right now, but if you need help on anything just call my secretary. I'll check on you soon, okay?"

"Roderick, can't you just stay and talk for a little . . . ."

"Really, Lill, I have to run. But honestly, I'll call you. And remember, let Amy know if you need anything."

He walked hurriedly to the door, then stopped. He hesitated a moment, then slowly turned back.

Lillian looked up quickly and smiled. He had decided to stay with her after all. Her heart leaped. She started to rise from her chair.

"One more thing, Lill," Roderick said without moving toward her. "As long as you're cleaning things out of offices today, you might want to go ahead and get started on yours. Whitfield will need to move in as soon as possible. Thanks. You're a doll."

He turned, grabbed the door handle, and was gone.

● ● ●

Roderick Davis walked the same way he talked—in meandering lines. He bobbed and weaved along corridors, never taking the direct route, never indicating by the glance of his eyes where he was really going. The man was a mystery to everyone except Paul Stattman, his office partner. "Vultures of a feather" they were referred to behind their backs.

When Roderick arrived at his office, Paul was at one of the desks reviewing a ledger. Roderick dropped into a swivel chair and let out a sigh.

"That bad, eh?" asked Paul, smirking.

"Tears and the whole bit," confirmed Roderick. "For a moment I almost thought I might have a breach-of-promise suit on my hands."

They laughed.

"So what's the bottom line?" Paul asked.

"She knows she's lost both her job and stock and that the company has liquidated all her father's property."

"No, no," said Paul, waving his hand. "I mean the situation between the two of you. Did you get the engagement ring back?"

Roderick pulled a hand slowly across his face.

"Well, not exactly," he admitted. "I told her we needed to delay the marriage for a year, and I suggested that she should take a long vacation."

Paul winced dramatically. "Ooooh! I bet that went over well with her. You're all heart, counselor."

"Actually, I made her think it was her idea. After all, she was the one who postponed the marriage after old J. J. kicked the bucket."

"Ah, yes, how well I recall it," said Paul, leaning back in his chair and using his hands to animate his exaggeration of the situation. "Here was the grieving daughter of J. J. Parker II, all draped in black, yet soon to be covered with green. Or so everyone thought. And so the suitors gathered around like jackals waiting to pounce on the defenseless lamb. The smell of money was stong in the air."

"You should know," teased Roderick.

"True, true," confessed Paul, still smirking. "But we were too late. For, by good fortune, just one month earlier you, our dear colleague, Roderick B. Davis, attorney-at-law, had become betrothed to the swimmingly wealthy Miss Lillian Parker of the Parkers of Detroit . . . check page 219 of your current social registry for pedigree, friends, and neighbors."

Roderick laughed out loud at Paul's narrative, even though he knew that in a moment the punch line of the story would be at his own expense.

"To make sure that no one else would take his prize, good ol' Roderick pressed his fiance for an immediate tying of the knot. But, alas, the winsome bride-to-be said, 'Nay, nay, not till father is cold in the ground and I've had time to count the loot.' And try as Roderick might, he could not sway her. But then a new ripple developed in the story."

"Ripple? More like a tidal wave," interjected Roderick.

"Quite," Paul concurred with classic understatement. "A post-mortem of both J. J. and his company books revealed that the old codger was into the stockholders for three million. Ouch! There goes the stock, the mansion, the bank accounts, and the company presidency that our hero Roderick had been coveting. Nevertheless, he is still stuck with the grieving daughter."

"Who, I might add, is still wearing a 7000-dollar diamond ring which I haven't finished paying for yet."

"Ta, ta, Roderick, ol' chump . . . er, chum. Not all investments pan out. You should know that by now. Considering what might have been, you got off easy. Besides, I understand that the new board chairman has a daughter too. There's hope for you yet."

Roderick grimaced. "What I wouldn't give for 200 grand right now!"

"If you're dreaming, why not dream of 200 *million?*" returned Paul. "One dream is as cheap—just as ridiculous, too—as the other."

"No, no, I'm speculating more than dreaming," explained Roderick. "The company is as sound as ever, now that J. J.'s estate has covered his debts. But the stockholders are selling so ridiculously low right now. Before long the word will spread that we're solid again. Prices will rise. A guy who could buy 200,000 dollars of company stock today would control a million dollars in stock a year from now."

"And with a million bucks in stock, that same guy could demand a seat on the board of directors," Paul finished.

"How true, how true," mused Roderick.

"Well, then, I may have some interesting news for you after all."

"What do you mean?" asked Roderick. "Are you going to rob a bank and then make me a loan?"

Paul stood up and came around to where Roderick was seated. He handed the ledger to Roderick and pointed to a line item which had been circled in yellow felt-tip markings.

"See this?" asked Paul. "It's a quarter of a million dollars in insurance left by J. J. to his son Scott."

"Scott? Who's Scott? I never heard of Scott."

"He's never talked about," said Paul. "I didn't know who he was either until I worked on the final audit. Scott was seven years older than Lillian. Eleven years ago he was with an assault unit with the Army in DaNang. Their base camp was overrun one night and Scott was captured."

"Is he an M.I.A. or something?"

Paul lifted his shoulders. "J. J. always believed that Scott was being held as a P.O.W. and would one day come home. After he had been missing in action for seven years, the Army declared him dead and paid his G.I. insurance to the family. But J. J. never gave up hope."

"I never knew any of this," said Roderick.

"From what I gather, J. J. received word that a P.O.W. from another unit in Vietnam saw a soldier named Parker in one of the North Vietnamese prison camps four years ago. J. J. was sure it had to be Scott, but there was no other proof."

"So what happens now that J. J. is dead?"

"The will calls for the insurance money to be put into an account to draw interest until Scott returns home to claim it." explained Paul. "However, since the military has already declared Scott to be dead and since Scott has never come back . . ."

". . . His sister could get a court order to recognize his death and then she could inherit his account," said Roderick.

Paul smiled wistfully. "Tell me, friend: Do you know of a good lawyer I could recommend to Lillian to help her check into this?"

"Funny," said Roderick, "very funny." He hurried to the door.

"Am I still on tap to be best man at the wedding?" called Paul.

But it was too late. Roderick Davis was already weaving his way down the hall to the elevator. He had to catch Lillian before she left.

• • •

Lillian didn't remember much about what she did after Roderick left her alone in the office. Like an automaton, she gathered up her belongings, left her father's suite, and went to her own office. Still dazed, tired, and confused, she took one look at her office and decided she had neither the interest nor the energy to pack her belongings. She instructed her secretary, Susan, to "do something" with her things. She would send for them . . . probably . . . someday.

She rode the elevator to the ground floor. People glancing at her in the lobby saw a smartly dressed blonde businesswoman with glazed eyes and slumped shoulders. There was no smile on her face, no lilt to her walk, no determination in her posture.

Once out on the sidewalk, she turned toward the river. Five blocks, 15 blocks, 25 blocks. Her feet were taking her somewhere, though she was conscious of no specific destination.

Sometimes she jostled along with crowds of people crossing streets. Other times she ambled slowly down sidewalks of nearly deserted neighborhoods.

Faces with grins and smiles of friendship beamed at her from billboards and posters. They tried to get her attention so they could sell her soft drinks, shampoo, luggage, real estate, fried chicken, and school supplies. But she saw nothing. Other signs tried to advise her about what airline to fly, what radio station to listen to, what church to attend. But she saw nothing.

Lillian's senses were turned off. She was numb. Life had dealt her too many blows, too many setbacks, too many disappointments. She wanted no more of it.

Why struggle? Why try? There was no love to be found. There were no people to trust. Daddy was dead. Mother was dead. Scott was gone. Roderick had changed. The money was lost. The career was over.

Just forget it: Life was worse than a joke—it was a nightmare. Daddy was right—death was the only option, the only peace. Death—the sooner the better.

She focused her eyes. She found herself at the East Gate Bridge which spanned the Detroit River. Perfect timing.

She looked around. Traffic was getting heavy, but there was no one else nearby on foot. She would go to the middle of the bridge and jump.

• • •

When Roderick arrived at Lillian's office, he was surprised to see Susan taking Lillian's sales awards off the wall. She was wrapping them in newspaper and putting them in cardboard boxes.

"Where's Miss Parker?" he asked.

"She came in here about 20 minutes ago and told me to pack her things."

Roderick looked concerned. "She didn't stay?"

"No, sir," said the secretary. "She said she wasn't coming back, ever. She just left. To tell you the truth, she didn't look right to me. Kind of sick or upset or something."

"Did she say where she was going?"

"No, sir. She just turned around and headed toward the elevator."

Roderick seemed agitated. "Listen to me. I want you to call Miss Parker's apartment every ten minutes. If you reach her, ask her to call me right away. Tell her it's important."

The secretary nodded obediently and reached for the phone. She was punching digits as Roderick left the office.

He rode the elevator to the lobby and then hurried outside. He craned his neck left and right. There was no sign of Lillian. Where could she have gone? He hailed a cab and jumped in. He would try her apartment.

"Riverview Apartments on Crestmount," he instructed the driver. "Take Devroe to the East Gate Bridge and cross there. It'll be faster. There's an extra ten in it for you if you set a record getting there."

The cabbie made an illegal U-turn and squealed his tires as he darted into traffic.

• • •

A sharp wind was hitting Lillian in the face as she stood in the middle of the East Gate Bridge. She looked down into the water and realized that the drop was not high enough to guarantee her death. Why jump if she would just get wet and embarrass herself? If she could have her way, she would like to be dead before she ever hit the water.

It was then that she remembered it: the gun.

Daddy's gun. She still had it in her purse.

One shot in the head, a topple forward, a plunge, a splash and then silence and peace. It would work. And it would be simple.

She glanced around. No one else was on the bridge. She opened her purse.

• • •

Roderick leaned over the seat. He extended a ten-dollar bill and pushed it into the taxi driver's shirt pocket.

"Come on, come on," he admonished the driver. "Here's the tip up front. Now move it, okay?"

The driver frowned into the rearview mirror.

"Look, Mac, rush-hour traffic is rush-hour traffic," he said. "I've already made a U-turn, hustled two yellow lights, and broken the speed limit. I'm doing what I can, right?"

"Just hurry. It's important."

The lane ahead cleared and the cab driver slammed down hard on the accelerator. The jolt threw Roderick backward.

The cabbie smiled.

• • •

Upon opening her purse, Lillian found her father's Bible atop the gun. Seeing the two items together in her own purse reminded her of the same sense of irony she had felt when she had first seen them in her father's desk. Now, however, the former irony seemed less bizarre. Instead, she somehow felt closer to her father than ever before. Now she understood his frustrations, his mental agony, and his sense of hopelessness.

It seemed silly, but in his memory Lillian decided to hold her father's Bible close to her as she ended her life. Maybe he hadn't been a Christian and maybe he hadn't really read much of this

Bible, but for once, at least, something would help them draw close and completely understand each other.

She grabbed the Bible in her left hand, turned her back to the road on the bridge, and faced the water. She laid her purse on the bridge ledge and removed the gun. She held it close to her so that it couldn't be seen by anyone else. She knew it was loaded because she had examined it at the office.

Instinctively, she bowed her head.

"Oh, Lord," she whispered, "I'm so tired. I can't take any more of life. I'm sorry. I know better than to do this, but I just can't face the pain. I need help, but no one is here for me. Please forgive me. I just don't want to go on any longer."

She cocked the pistol.

"I never developed that inner peace that Pastor Mead told me about so often. I looked for peace. I tried to find it with money, but it didn't work. Nothing did. I kept wanting a sign from You—a lightning bolt. . .a voice in the night. . .a burning bush. . .something! But nothing ever came. So I guess even You don't need me."

She gripped the Bible harder with her left hand. She began to raise the revolver to her temple with her right hand.

Something rubbed against her thumb as it hooked over the binding of the Bible. She paused a moment to look down.

A small bookmark placed in the Bible by her father was sticking out the end.

Her curiosity was piqued. She lowered the gun and flipped open the Bible. The wind was strong, but she was able to hold the book open by spreading her fingers. She found an underlined passage in Second Corinthians: *Our light affliction. . .is but for a moment.*

Lillian reread the underlined words several times.

Was this what had kept her father going, she wondered? Something must have. After all, he had the chance to kill himself, but he hadn't. He had kept his troubles to himself, never complaining. He had been strong right up until the end, just the way Mother had been.

Mother?

She hadn't thought about her mother in a long time. It was painful to recall that last year. The cancer had caused Mother unending agony. Yet she had never complained, even at its worst. She had been strong. The whole family had been strong. Even Scott.

"That's why Daddy used to say that Scott would come back one day. 'He'll survive,' Daddy would say. He's strong. He's a true Parker. We're all strong.' "

All of us? wondered Lillian.

She thought of Daddy, of Mother, of Scott. She recalled her father's strong profile, her mother's calmness, her brother's determination.

"They were strong," she whispered aloud. "We are strong. W-we are a-all strong. The...Parkers...are...strong. I'm a Parker. I-I'm strong."

She lifted the deadly revolver before her eyes.

"No!" she said flatly. Then, more defiantly, she screamed, "No! No! No! No-o-o-o-!"

She drew her arm back and flung the pistol as far from the bridge as she could. She watched it arc, turn over and over, and then drop heavily downward, finally hitting the dark water with a plunking splash.

She smiled as she hugged the Bible close to her. The bookmark was still in its place. She had found her sign.

She turned and walked briskly to the far end of the bridge. She felt good. She felt alive. She wanted to stay alive. And she wanted to talk with other people who enjoyed being alive. *Right now* she wanted to talk to them.

She stepped into a phone booth located at the end of the bridge. She dialed the home number of Pastor and Mrs. Mead.

Behind her, outside, a cab raced by. Neither the driver nor his handsomely dressed male passenger in the backseat gave even a passing glance toward the phone booth.

CHAPTER TWO

Even before she rounded the corner from Maple to Elm, Lillian could smell the chicken broth. Her stomach whimpered in protest. She had grown up with Bea Mead's pungent yellow brew, and after 21 years of progressing from spoon to cup to mug to bowlful, she appreciated its intent more than its taste.

The soup had been present at all traumatic moments of her life, from infant bouts with croup, to the searing sorrow of doomed puppy love, to the hollow hurt of extracted wisdom teeth. It had been on the back burner during her mother's debilitating illness, Scott's disappearance, and her dad's death. Somehow the awful liquid had always soothed, if not erased, the pain.

As she approached the source of the cloying odor—the Meads' tidy bungalow—Lillian marveled at Mom Mead's contentment with the assignment the Lord had given her 30 years earlier. Being the wife of Pastor Charles Mead had been Bea's goal since Bible college, and she was still awestruck at the good fortune of achieving it.

"Luck had nothing to do with it," Bea often said, reverently rolling her eyes skyward. "Credit the Lord, from whom all blessings flow." In gratitude she attempted to repay the debt daily by being the most supportive, solicitous preacher's wife in all of Michigan. And that called for a lot of chicken soup.

"Who knows?" Mom Mead often asked no one in particular. "A hungry indigent or a grieving widow might come knocking at the parsonage door at any time." In preparation for that unlikely event Bea Mead stood ready with ladle in hand. It was a vigil she had kept faithfully for all her married life.

• • •

"Come in, come in, child," said Pastor Mead, fumbling with the latch of the study storm door. "Bea, pour this girl a steamy bowl of your fine gruel." Then he added hastily, "But none for me, Dear."

"No, thank you. Really," insisted Lillian. "I feel wonderful— better than I have in months. That's why I'm here. I wanted to share it with you."

"Congratulations!" exuded Pastor Mead, immediately jumping to the wrong conclusion and hurrying across the room for a quick buss on the cheek. "Lillian and Roderick have finally set the date, Bea," he bellowed toward the kitchen. "Why, if we were drinking folks I'd offer you brandy or champagne. Bea, open that bottle of grape juice we've been saving. This is a real occasion!"

"No, please, you don't understand," Lillian said. "Roderick really has nothing to do with it. In fact, I'm not sure I'll ever see him again. But if you'll just sit quietly for five minutes and let me talk, I'll explain everything."

• • •

Her story took longer, since Bea Mead succumbed to near vapors when she heard about Lillian's contemplated suicide. Pastor Mead felt led to pray over the situation at one or two points and added a lecture on handgun control for good measure. It was only after they had rejoiced in Lillian's newfound peace that he offered her some serious advice.

"I don't approve of Roderick's behavior in all of this, but I agree with him on one thing. I think you need to get away for a few weeks to sort out your feelings. And, if you're really serious about knowing the Lord better, you need time to dig into His Word. Why not do what Roderick suggested and go to the mountains?"

Lillian paused, excited by the suggestion that suddenly seemed plausible because of Pastor Mead's endorsement. "I wish I could leave right now, before I think of a hundred good reasons why I shouldn't. I wish I didn't have to go back to my apartment at all. All those pictures of Roderick and the stacks of business reports—I don't want to face them. I'm afraid the depression will come back and I'll lose this wonderful new feeling. It's still so fragile."

"Then *do* it," urged Pastor Mead. "Bea can loan you some warm clothes, and when you're settled we'll send you whatever you need from your apartment." He could see the idea was catching hold, so he continued his sales pitch. "While you girls are worrying about your wardrobe, I'll be in charge of entertainment."

"Entertainment?"

"Tracts. You'll need lots of tracts to read. And tapes. You have a tape deck in that sporty little car of yours, don't you? Well, throw out all those devil wailings because you won't have room for them once I fix you up with your new inventory." He flipped the controls of his recliner and was ejected in the direction of his bookcases. "Let's see, a few motivational messages, something by the Gaithers . . . how do you feel about the Happy Goodmans?"

Lillian escaped to the couch to prevent being trampled by all the activity. "The Happy Who-mans? I don't think I've had the pleasure . . . ." By now Pastor Mead had his hands full of cassettes, and he looked helplessly around for his wife. "Bea? I need something to put all these confounded tapes in."

"Something bigger than a breadbox?" asked Bea from the kitchen, where she was filling a thermos with chicken soup for the trip.

They were having fun, and so was Lillian. The decision for her to go to the mountains apparently had been made, and although she didn't recall making it, she was excited at the prospect. She felt free and independent. She could go anywhere the Spirit moved her, she giggled to herself. For that matter, her destination didn't have to be South Dakota at all. The Black Hills had been Roderick's idea, and right now his advice carried little weight. No, she would choose someplace else, she decided quickly. Different mountains, perhaps. The Rockies? Too far. The Smokies? Yes, that sounded perfect.

"And I don't have to be Lillian Parker if I don't want to be," she announced to the startled Meads. "I mean, on the trip I could use another name so people won't ask me about Daddy and the company. I'm tired of newspaper reporters and telephone calls and strangers pointing at me and whispering."

"By being someone else perhaps you'll find out who you really are," nodded Pastor Mead, assuming his counselor role. "I like that; let's kick it around some more."

It wasn't until she had retrieved her red Corvette from the

company garage and was wedged behind the steering wheel and held in place by books, pamphlets, and a hamper of food that Lillian realized that her odyssey had progressed beyond the "I wish" stage and was on the launching pad. She started to turn the key in the ignition.

"Rufus!" she gasped. "I completely forgot about Rufus."

Of all the trinkets that Roderick had given her during their courtship, the honey-colored cocker spaniel was the only thing she truly valued. He had been purchased as a watchdog, but to Roderick's dismay he proved to be an utter failure in that job description. Lap dog duties were more to his liking, and Lillian's habit of tying plaid taffeta ribbons in the curls of his long, floppy ears did little to enhance the killer image. Roderick had thrown up his arms in disgust and Rufus had rolled over on his back in bliss.

"We'll take care of Rufus, won't we, Mom?" said Pastor Mead, his asthmatic nose twitching in anticipation. "We haven't had a good watchdog around here since Duke crossed over the bar."

Bea Mead nodded dutifully, removing the last obstacle in Lillian's path. The car's engine roared to life and drowned out the final round of "Goodbye," "I love you," "Be careful," and "Keep in touch." Before turning the corner Lillian glanced at the rearview mirror and savored one final glimpse of her very special friends—Bea fondly waving her hand in the air and Pastor Mead, sneezing uncontrollably, standing at her side. She would miss them, of course, but she suffered no second thoughts as she pointed her car south and opened the glove compartment in search of a map of Tennessee.

• • •

Roderick, reaching his hand into his vest pocket, pulled out the antique watch that once had belonged to J. J. Parker and studied its ocher face. He shook the old timepiece roughly and listened for its tick. The verdict was the same as five mintues ago: Time was passing, all right, but at a snail's pace.

He was tired, angry at himself, and worried that he might not be able to reach Lillian and convince her to marry him as soon as possible. How could he explain his change of heart? He laughed, knowing that this would be the least of his problems, since he had always managed to manipulate her into believing whatever he chose. But where was she now? Why wasn't she home? His only bit of encouragement was located behind Lillian's apartment door in the form of one very hungry cocker spaniel. The fact that Rufus was still there was a good sign, Roderick assured himself. Lillian was crazy about the mutt and would never leave him behind.

He slouched against the elevator frame, closed his eyes, and imagined the dialogue that would be exchanged when he told Lillian he couldn't bear to be separated from her for even a few hours. He would propose a modest wedding, followed by a short trip to the mountains. Surely that would satisfy her.

His thoughts were interrupted by a soft hum and the feeling of vibration against his shoulder. The elevator was in operation and seemed to be pausing at Lillian's floor. Roderick straightened his tie and stepped back to greet the passenger. The doors parted.

"What are *you* doing here?" Roderick asked abruptly.

"I stopped by to pick up my houseguest," replied Pastor Mead pleasantly. He slipped a key into apartment 5-F's lock and then squatted down to accept the wet kisses of a jubilant Rufus.

"Where is she?" probed Roderick.

"Lillian? I honestly don't know. But if you're interested in *how* she is, I can honestly say that she's never been better. That was a fine idea you had, m'boy, to send her away for a few weeks. Or will it be a few months?"

For a moment Roderick considered grabbing the visitor by the collar, but remembering what kind of collar it was, he decided on a different tack.

"Look, I'm sorry if I sounded sharp. It's just that I'm so worried about Lill. I've been waiting here all night just to ask her to marry me."

"What's your hurry, son?" asked Pastor Mead. "Yesterday you told her you both needed more time. This wouldn't have anything to do with the *Wall Street Journal* story, would it?"

"I don't know what you're talking about."

Pastor Mead unfolded the newspaper tucked under his arm and handed it to Roderick. "They were filling the vending machines with these when I came through the lobby. The story on the right caught my eye, so I bought one."

The headline—UPSWING EXPECTED FOR MICHIGAN

TECHNOLOGIES—caused Roderick's face to pale. He quickly skimmed the column to learn the predictions of one of the *Journal*'s most trusted reporters. The trauma caused by J. J. Parker's death and the revelations of his erratic business practices have calmed, said the article. The company seemed to be back on solid footing, and speculators were expected to flock to the fold. Price of the stock already was starting to rise.

"I've got to find Lillian," Roderick said, more to himself than to his kindly companion. "She's at your house, isn't she? She'd never leave town without the dog. All I want is five minutes alone with her."

"Sorry, I can't help you, son. She left us hours ago with her car loaded down with enough clothes and books to last a year. We promised we'd take care of Rufus until she's settled. Can't say where she went. In fact, I'm not sure she knew."

Roderick studied the sweet face of the elderly pastor and decided to believe him. As an attorney he had developed the knack of recognizing an honest answer, and one glance assured him, unfortunately, that Pastor Mead was telling the truth. Without even waiting for the elevator, Roderick turned abruptly and exited by the stairs.

• • •

Paul Stattman was pacing up and down the floor, barking orders at the intercom and eating his third cream horn of the morning when Roderick arrived at the office a few minutes after nine.

"Where have you been? Have you read the story on page 1 of the *Wall Street*—" Stattman's assault of questions stopped mid-sentence when he paused long enough to notice his friend's unusual appearance. The always fastidious Roderick had a day-old growth of stubble on his chin and for the first time in his life looked old.

"Good gosh, Rod," whispered Stattman. "Who let the air out of your face?"

"She's gone," Roderick said dully. "Lillian's gone."

"Where?"

"No one knows for sure. She packed up and left town in the

middle of the night. I waited in front of her apartment until dawn, but she never came home."

"Aw, c'mon. You know her better than she knows herself. Can't you figure out where she'd go? Think, man, think. She must have said *something*."

"We talked about the mountains yesterday. I told her she ought to get away for a while. Maybe the Black Hills. She always said she wanted to go off to some secluded mountaintop with a trunk full of books. But it was sort of a joke. Surely she wouldn't . . ." Roderick paused, uncertain whether to take himself seriously. "No, surely she wouldn't take me up on that idea."

"Why not? She always does exactly what you tell her to do," said Paul. "Sounds like this is all we have to go on," he continued, pressing the intercom button. "Amy, get Triple A on the line. Find out the best route to the Black Hills, and get a list of motels and tourist cabins along the way that are open this time of year."

Roderick knew that Paul was right. Hours had passed since anyone had seen Lillian, and every minute translated into miles traveled and money lost. He sat thoughtfully for a few minutes, then on a whim picked up the phone on his desk and dialed the police station. He recognized the voice on the other end as his friend, Sergeant Barton.

"Terry? Roderick. Remember those eviction papers I drew up to get rid of that old couple in your rental? Well, you might say I'm calling to collect my bill."

He explained his need to locate a motorist heading toward South Dakota in a bright red Corvette with Michigan plates. No, it wasn't a theft or a runaway, he assured the policeman. Then he sheepishly admitted that it was a personal matter. Lillian had been overly sensitive since J. J.'s death, he explained. The tiniest word seemed to send her into either hysterics or a rage. They had had a lovers' spat and she had run off in tears, saying something about going to the mountains. He feared for her safety and her mental stability. No telling *what* she might do, he hinted to his friend. Could the police help?

"Of course," assured Barton. "I'll radio the state trooper posts in Illinois, Minnesota, South Dakota and, of course, here in Michigan. What shall we do when we spot her?"

"Just tell her to phone home. Say it's an emergency. I'll stay close to the telephone for the next couple of days. I'm so worried about her I can't concentrate on anything else anyway."

Paul choked at the remark, but regained control of himself when Amy bustled in with a list of motels along the highways between Detroit and the Dakotas. Roderick studied the names and put check marks beside the most likely choices. He was familiar with Lillian's taste and knew she preferred large, comfortable accommodations with saunas, pools, room service and creature comforts. Although she often expressed a willingness to live a more simple lifestyle, Lillian was, after all, J. J.'s daughter, and J. J. Parker had always gone first class. It was a standard of living that Roderick aspired to since childhood and one he had every intention of attaining.

"You take this half of the list, Paul, and Amy can take the other," ordered Roderick. "Call the desk clerks at each motel and tell them if a Lillian Parker checks in she is to phone home immediately. Say it's a family crisis." He was starting to relax, confident that he was setting up a net that Lillian couldn't possibly wriggle through. Before Paul or Amy could protest, he had started out the door. "I think we've touched all the bases," he concluded. "Between us and the police, we've got people in four states looking for her. I'm going home to take a nap."

• • •

Lillian woke up, flung her arm over the side of the bed, and waited for the familiar nibbles on her fingertips. No Rufus. Confused, she opened her eyes and assessed the simple decor of the budget tourist lodge. Oh, yes, now she remembered. It was Belbrook, Ohio, wasn't it?

She looked at the clock—10 A.M.—and counted backward. Although she only had slept four hours and ten minutes, she felt wonderfully refreshed. She stretched and then began to plan her day. She would need all the energy she could muster, she decided, because she still had many miles to travel before she arrived in Tennessee. What bothered her most was her lack of a definite destination. Originally she was concerned only with running off to the mountains. They seemed so far away that "the mountains" was a specific enough destination. But now she was within one day's drive of them, and she knew she needed a more detailed plan. Should she phone ahead and inquire about cabins? Better yet, if she hurried she could be on the road within an hour and arrive in the mountains before dark. That way she would have time to locate a real estate agent and visit several cottages before making a choice. She wanted to be settled as soon as possible, because for the first time in her life she was on a tight budget, and she had to keep motel expenses to a minimum.

Two cups of coffee later she was on her way, with maps of Kentucky and Tennessee stretched over the dash and the Imperials crooning on the tape deck.

A name, she said to herself. *I've got to think of a good name for myself.* She realized that the chances of anyone recognizing her in the secluded hills of Tennessee were slight, but she didn't want to take any chances. Besides, the trip represented a new beginning for her and she wanted to set aside Lillian Parker's shortcomings, fears, romantic entwinements and opulent lifestyle. *Let's see, it ought to be something very basic. Ethel? No, too basic. Madge? Sounds like a waitress in an all-night diner. Blanche? Nope, definitely smacks of fallen arches. JoAnne?* "JoAnne," she said out loud. "JoAnne Parks. Hello, my name is JoAnne Parks...yes, I could live with that."

She thought of Scott and how as children they each had loved to pretend to be someone else. Scott had been blessed with a wonderful imagination and would concoct scenarios and dramas that occupied them for hours. Since she was seven years his junior, she was his half-pint shadow and did whatever he instructed her to do. If he was Batman, she was recruited as Robin. When he was Robin Hood, she was Maid Marian. On the receiving end of his heroics, she was required to jump from trees, be rescued from burning buildings, and once swing across a creek in true me-Tarzan-you-Jane style. She had adored her big brother, and since J. J. was always preoccupied with business matters, she looked to Scott for direction even in adulthood.

"Oh, Scott, how I could use some of your good advice right now," she whispered. But no, Scott was gone, and it was time she took charge of her own life. She was painfully aware of her tendency to let other people make choices for her. First there had been Scott, then J. J. after Scott had gone into the service, and now she had allowed herself to be passed on to Roderick. Well, finally it was her turn.

She wondered how different her life might have been had she

not always been so willing to do as she was told. She remembered high school graduation, when she confided to her father that she wanted to go east to school and major in English at a small liberal arts college. Although she lacked Scott's imagination, she loved words and wanted to study literature. Perhaps someday, she shyly told J. J., she might try putting her own thoughts on paper. Then she took a deep breath, summoned all her courage, and declared, "Daddy, I want to be a writer."

He had laughed at her. Great loud gales of laughter. She would never forget the sound, or the tears that blurred her vision and spilled over onto her burning cheeks. Seeing her pain, he adopted a more gentle attitude that made her feel even more foolish. He sat her down on the cold leather couch in his den and explained to her why her idea, while ambitious, was neither practical nor possible. Having a fondness for words hardly qualifies her as a writer, he pointed out, and besides, the world had enough starving authors without her joining the ranks. He went on to explain *his* plan for her future. He had spoken with a friend, the dean of the business school at Michigan State, and had arranged for her to enroll in September. Her major would be business administration, but she would take several classes in accounting, statistics, and management. A smattering of computer science would be included too.

She never regretted his intercession. She applied herself dutifully to the course of study he had selected for her, and she excelled. By the time she was an upperclassman it was obvious to everyone but J. J. that Scott would never come home from the war, and that the burden of following in their father's footsteps would fall to her. She accepted the responsibility without question and set about to be J. J.'s most trusted apprentice. The fact that she spent her private moments reading Keats and Lord Byron rather than *Forbes* and *Fortune* was her well-kept secret.

Well, now she could come out of the closet, she thought ruefully. How ironic! Michigan Technologies was the reason she had turned her back on literature, to become a respected member of the business-financial community. Now Michigan Technologies was done with her, and she was finally free to pursue her interest in writing. But it was too late. She felt she had lost the spontaneity to be creative; she was now more comfortable with a calculator at her side and a sales ledger in front of her. She still appreciated the beauty and sensitivity of poetry and literature, but only as an outsider. Her own spark of ingenuity had died, snuffed out by Michigan Technologies.

Deep in thought, it took a sharp toot from the horn of an oncoming car to jolt her back to the present. The motorist blinked his headlights as a suggestion for her to turn on her low beams. The sun had set, the landscape had become a roller coaster of slopes and hills, and the cassette in her tape deck had long since run its course. She realized she hadn't eaten in several hours, and decided to turn off at the Compton Gap exit in search of dinner and directions.

So these are my mountains, she said to herself as she stretched her cramped legs on the dimly lit parking lot of the rural truck stop. Shadows of the Smokies loomed all around her and made her feel very small and insignificant. The neon sign promised homecooked plate dinners and all the coffee you could drink. Apparently inflation had bypassed this tiny tuck in the mountains. She liked it already.

At 7 P.M. the small dining room was cleared of customers. A middle-aged blonde woman was setting each table with placemats that advertised the breakfast menu.

"Am I too late to get a sandwich?" asked Lillian.

"Not if it's ham salad," replied the waitress. "That's all we've got left."

"Okay, I'll have ham salad and black coffee."

The warmth of the room and the soft country music on the radio caused Lillian to slowly unwind. She was tired—exhausted, in fact. Obviously it was too late to talk to a real estate agent about renting a cabin, so it was time to put Plan B into operation. She took note of the waitress's nametag as her coffee cup was refilled.

"Madge, I wonder if you might suggest a motel close by. Something inexpensive."

"Nope, there's nothing between here and Stokes Corner. That'll take you an hour-and-a-half or so. We've got a motel in Compton Gap—the Pine Acres—but it's closed for a couple of weeks." Lillian's disappointment caused the woman to soften. "You look a little frayed around the edges, Honey. Had a bad day?"

"No, just tired. Actually, I'm interested in renting a cabin for two or three weeks, but I guess that'll have to wait until tomorrow."

"Maybe not," said Madge, pouring herself a cup of coffee and sitting down across from Lillian. "Echo Bluff usually has some openings this time of year. You might check with Dave Thompson. He's the ranger up there and kinda oversees the property during the off-season. Too bad he doesn't have a phone; the only way to reach him is to drive up and look for him. Best time to catch him is early in the morning or anytime after supper."

"He'd be there now?"

"More than likely."

Directions were scrawled on the back of the breakfast placemat and a ham sandwich was wrapped in napkins for the trip. *My gosh*, giggled Lillian, remembering the untouched thermos of chicken soup in the car, *I must invite charity.*

Because the road to Echo Bluff was narrow, winding, and poorly lit, she drove cautiously. By the time she turned onto the gravel trail and approached the rustic cabin in the pines, it was almost 10 o'clock. With relief she noticed lights in the kitchen, a sure sign that the Thompson family was at home. The realization that her long trip had come to a safe, uneventful end gave her a fresh spurt of energy. This was the final leg of her journey, and now she anticipated the rewards—a leisurely soak in a hot bath, a warm fire, a comfortable bed, and maybe a cup of chicken soup to take the chill off.

"I'm sorry, ma'am, the cabins are all filled until tomorrow," said the young man at the door. "I've got two families leaving in the morning, so you can have your choice—lakeside or in the woods. Why don't you come back sometime after lunch?"

She tried to hold her tears in check until she could retrace her steps to the car, but her bravado had disappeared. No longer did she feel like the independent young woman who had embarked on a solo junket just 24 hours earlier. She was tired, cold, and homesick.

"Look, on second thought, come on in and get warm before you head back to town," said the man. "We'll have a cup of tea."

She followed him inside and was surprised to find the lodge actually to be one enormous room with a kitchen area occupying one wall and bookshelves lining the other three. A hugh open fireplace was situated in the center, with an overstuffed chintz-covered sofa and matching chair grouped around the hearth. The furniture was in shades of blues and beige, and a thick ring of sunny yellow carpet circled the fireplace. The pine floor underneath was waxed to a glow, and pots of grape ivy and ferns dropped from the ceiling at varying levels to add to the freshness of the room. A small loft overlooked the great room and offered a bathing area and twin cots.

"This is so beautiful!" exclaimed Lillian, sinking into the chair by the fire. "My compliments to your decorator, or is it your wife?"

"Neither. I just put together all the things I like. Glad you approve," said Dave Thompson. He brought her a mug of tea and sat down on the floor, propping his lanky frame against the built-up circular hearth. "You said you're interested in renting one of the cabins, Miss—?"

"Parks. JoAnne Parks. Yes, for a couple of weeks at least," she said. "You mentioned there are two available? I guess I like the sound of the one by the lake."

"Well, it won't be vacant till tomorrow, but we could take care of the paperwork tonight, then I'll give you the key and you can move in whenever you want, without having to track me down." He handed her a simple form to complete and indicated where she should sign. "I'll need to see your driver's license for verification," he said.

Her panicked expression surprised him. "It's just a formality, Miss Parks," he assured her. She opened her purse slowly, reached for her wallet, and handed him the card.

"Lillian Parker? I don't understand," he said, matching the photo on the license with the embarrassed girl sitting across from him. "Are you Lillian Parker or JoAnne Parks?"

The tears started again. "Lillian Parker," she answered. "I'm sorry; I feel so foolish. Please don't make me explain it all. I'm awfully tired. If you could just tell me how to get to the nearest motel I won't bother you anymore."

"I don't know what's going on here," replied Thompson, his thoughtful blue eyes studying her. "But I don't think you're in any condition to drive. Besides, Stokes Corner is two hours away and the motel probably is filled by now. Let me get you a couple of blankets so you can sleep on the couch." Anticipating her shyness, he added, "My wife will be home soon if you need to borrow anything."

She accepted his invitation out of sheer exhaustion. She was quite sure he wasn't married—as lovely as the cabin was, it lacked a woman's presence—but she was equally sure she was safe in his care. He brought her fresh linens and carried in her overnight case.

"Are you certain your wife won't mind coming home to find me on her couch?" she asked. His face reddened as he mumbled something about Mrs. Thompson seldom noticing little things like that. He then disappeared up the stairs and into the loft.

As Lillian snuggled into the cavernous pillows of the sofa, doubts about her escape to the mountains resurfaced. Somehow, sleeping in a stranger's cabin with the stranger himself just a few steps away from her hadn't been part of the plan. Maybe she wasn't so independent after all. Maybe she was one of those women who would always need direction from a man. Sleep dulled the new panges of homesickness and eventually claimed her completely. Before giving in to the welcomed unconsciousness, her mind darted back to Michigan. Her last thought was of Roderick . . . and how she planned to call him first thing in the morning.

CHAPTER THREE

The sound of crackling bacon and the smell of rich coffee awakened Lillian from a dreamy sleep. *Oh, Mom Mead!* she thought. What a nice switch from your chicken broth! She opened her eyes and slowly focused on the attractive young man standing over the stove.

"Good morning," he said in a rich baritone voice. "Did you sleep well? I'm afraid the sofa isn't the most comfortable bed. But it's not bad. I've slept there myself on occasion." He paused and flipped the bacon. "The bathing area is off to the side of the loft. Breakfast will be ready in about ten minutes." He gingerly smiled at her.

Lillian stood up and ran a hand nervously over her hair, remembering that she had spent the night in a cabin with a stranger. She picked up her overnight case and started for the stairs, anxious to be dressed and more presentable.

"It smells great!" she said. "And I find I'm suddenly famished. I didn't eat much yesterday. There was only hamsalad available at the diner last night."

"Well, there's plenty to eat here. After breakfast we'll drive over to the lakeside cabin and see if it meets your requirements. Like I said last night, there's one facing the woods, if you'd like to change your mind."

"No, I think I'd like the one on the water best," she replied. "What seas, what shores, what gray rocks and what islands, what water lapping the bow—"

"Huh?" he said, looking at her with a baffled expression. "Are you still asleep?"

Lillian chuckled. "No, I'm quoting T. S. Eliot. I'm rather fond of poetry." She was halfway up the stairs and quickly climbed the remaining few.

When she was alone, she began to remember all the events of

recent days. She thought again of Roderick and wondered how far it was to the nearest phone. Madge was right, she noticed. There wasn't a telephone in the Thompson cabin.

As she dressed in the little room, she considered her options. First, she would move into the cabin. Then what? She was so used to the busy corporate world she had come from that she knew it would take some adjustment to live her days without constant awareness of the clock. Now she could get up with the sun or whenever she felt like it. There was no pressing demand on her time.

And how would she like rattling around in a cabin by herself? She thought of Rufus. She already missed him. He was a constant presence in her home life. Maybe she could ask Pastor Mead and Bea to send him to her. But how would they get him to Echo Bluff without bringing him? Perhaps Roderick . . .

Dave was setting plates filled with bacon, eggs, and toast on the table as Lillian came down the stairs. He looked up at her and saw an attractive woman with no makeup, neatly combed hair, and loose-fitting clothes.

"Perfect timing. I hope you don't mind your eggs sunny-side-up. It didn't cross my mind to ask before you disappeared behind that door."

"That's fine with me. I never criticize the cook when someone takes me in and feeds me. That wouldn't be polite, would it?"

They sat together. Lillian followed suit when Dave bowed his head and offered a short blessing for the meal. He looked up, and they smiled.

"How do you like your coffee? Black or with cream?"

"Black, thank you. Tell me, how long have you lived here?" Lillian pulled out her napkin from under the fork and scooted up to the table.

"This is my second year as ranger. And it's my first job since graduation from college two-and-a-half years ago. I took some time off to look for a job. I'm lucky I found this one, I guess. I have friends who haven't been so fortunate. The market isn't big enough for all the fishing and wildlife majors these days. What about you? What brings you to Echo Bluff?"

Lillian had been looking at Dave Thompson until he asked that question. She had admired his blond hair and tanned skin. He looked as if he belonged in the outdoors, as if he could wrestle a bear if necessary. His arms were strong and his shoulders were broad.

"Actually," Lillian stammered, not wanting to lie and not wanting to tell him everything, "I...I...needed to get away from home for a while. My father died not too long ago and my mother has been gone for quite some time. And if the truth be known, Madge—you know, Madge from the diner—brought me to Echo Bluff. She suggested that you might have an available cabin on short notice, since it's the off-season. And I'm feeling quite lucky that you do." Lillian helped herself to another piece of toast and reached for the strawberry jam. "This is delicious. How far is it to the cabin you mentioned? I can't wait to see it."

"It's within a mile of here, directly behind my cabin. I have to live near the edge of the grounds to stay accessible, I'm told. But this cabin is larger than most of the others. And it's more livable for year-round weather. The one I'm going to show you isn't quite this lofty." He glanced at her to see if she caught the pun.

Lillian looked at him quizzically. Then she said, "Hey, since you cooked, the least I can do is offer to clean up. I don't mind, really. I owe you for your kind hospitality."

"You won't hear me protesting. I've got some things to do outside that will only take a few minutes. Then we can be off for the Parks, er...Parker cabin." Dave looked embarrassed at his mistake, but Lillian pretended to ignore it. She didn't want to bring that issue up again—the fact that she had tried to pass off a name that wasn't her real one. She didn't want to explain her situation to him. He already knew more about her than she wanted him to know. Here she was trying to run away from the last six months and all that had happened to her, and the first day out her past had surfaced all over again! Let Dave Thompson think what he might. She didn't have anything to hide, but she wasn't ready to reveal her past with all its recent rejections to a stranger either. She had more pride than that.

She carried the dishes to the sink, located a bottle of detergent, turned on the water, and buried her hands in the warm, soapy suds. The slickness of the water soothed her troubled thoughts. It was like a bubble bath. And even the greasy skillet didn't preclude the welcomeness of the comfortable sense of domesticity she felt in the silence of the cabin after Dave had gone outside.

She began to hum without thinking about what she was humming. There was a little window over the sink, and she watched as Dave split several logs, stacked them, and walked back toward the cabin.

It didn't take long to clean the table and put the dishes in the drainer. She wiped her hands on the dishtowel and turned around as Dave walked into the cabin. He moved toward the fireplace and dropped the wood into the box on the hearth. It clattered into place to await the next fire.

"I'm almost ready," Lillian volunteered. "I just need to fold the bedding you loaned me and pick up my things. I'm sure you're anxious to get to work. I hate to keep you from your duties."

"Most of my work can wait," he said. "I don't have strict hours, so you're not keeping me from anything really important. I wouldn't let you," he said, and smiled. "I don't want to lose my job; I enjoy it too much. You'll find that Echo Bluff is very solitary and peaceful."

Solitary and peaceful, Lillian thought. *That's what Roderick and the Meads said I needed. Well, I guess I've found it. Echo Bluff it is.*

Within minutes Dave and Lillian were driving separately to the little cabin that Lillian hoped to call home during the weeks ahead. As they pulled up to the door, Lillian tried not to feel disappointment after seeing Dave's homey cabin. This one was smaller, and definitely less lofty, as he had put it. In fact, there wasn't a loft at all! The entire cabin was on one level, with two small bedrooms and, thank goodness, indoor plumbing. The people who had vacated it recently left it relatively clean. She looked around and immediately felt she could improve its appearance with a few flowers and plants from the woods. Her books would make it more personal too.

"Not bad, is it? Sort of a cute little place, I've always thought. And the fireplace is nicer than the one in the cabin facing the woods." Dave looked at her. "What do you think?"

"I think I'll need to buy some things to start housekeeping," she said. "I didn't bring sheets or eating utensils or anything like that. I guess I didn't think I'd be needing them."

"Most everything is furnished," Dave said. "There are pots and pans. And dishes are in the cupboard, although they aren't the most elegant plates in the world." He walked over to a cupboard and showed her a melamine plate with blue flowers on one side of it. He opened a drawer and took out a fork, turning it to the side and eyeing the bent tines. "Like I said, it's not the most elegant, but it will do if you're not too fussy. And you're welcome to borrow some supplies from me until you go into town."

Lillian watched him as he surveyed the fork. He was so serious at that moment. She wanted to laugh not only at the fork, but at the irony of it all. Her life had gone from a gun and a Bible to a plastic plate and a crooked fork. What an adventurous person she had become! And what could possibly happen next? Her life seemed so topsy-turvy and out of her control. Well, maybe a few weeks in this little cabin would do the trick.

Dave's voice interrupted her thoughts.

"What?" she asked.

"I said I usually go into Compton Gap once a week. You can come with me if you like. I'll show you where I buy groceries and introduce you to the owner so you'll get fair prices. Old Ed has been known to add a little extra to the bill when he thinks someone is passing through town. The old devil."

"Thanks, but you really shouldn't feel you need to do all this for me. You've been more than kind."

"I don't mind. I'm going anyway. It's no trouble to take you along. And I'd enjoy the company." This last he added after a slight hesitation, looking away as he said it.

Why, he's shy, thought Lillian. *Are there any shy men left in the world?* Lillian smiled at Dave and nodded when he returned her gaze. He smiled back.

● ● ●

After Dave had gone, Lillian selected her bedroom and unpacked her meager belongings. She walked to the window and looked out. This bedroom was lakeside—it was why she chose it. She could see the foamy water splashing on the shore, and she was anxious to explore it.

But first things first.

She walked back to the bed and picked up her books and the Bible that lay there. She carried them into the other room and laid them on the table. Pausing, she again touched the worn Bible and opened it to the marker.

Our light affliction. . .is but for a moment. . . . Lillian hesitated, remembering the last time she had read the passage. But then she began to read on: *worketh for us a far more exceeding and eternal weight of glory.*

She found comfort in the words.

Gee, wouldn't it be great if something would start working for me, she thought. *It hasn't seemed to be happening lately.* Lillian closed the Bible and laid it on the table. At that moment she decided to read a chapter or parts of one each night before going to sleep. Perhaps she could find some answers for herself. It certainly was a good place to look. It hadn't been since junior high camping days that she'd gotten deeply involved in reading the Bible. There was never time, it seemed. So many reading materials had taken the Bible's place when she had started going to college. Even Pastor Mead, who said he loved her like a daughter, chastised her for letting daily devotions slide from her routine. But it had seemed so easy after her mother died. Her mother, warm and loving Sarah Parker, had been the one in their family who had insisted on prayer at mealtimes and daily devotions. After she died that agonizing death, it hadn't been easy to stick to the patterns of life which the Parker family found to be so much a part of Sarah. It only intensified the pain of their loss.

Lillian picked up the key to the cabin door from the counter where Dave had left it. She experimented with the lock for a few moments to make sure she could get back into the cabin once she had locked the door. Then she walked out, locked it, and continued on the narrow, worn pathway to the edge of the water. Looking out, she could see fishing boats in the distance. A fleeting thought of suicide flashed across her mind and vanished with the breeze. Instead, a sense of calm and midday laziness came over her as she watched the water with the sun shining on it.

She stooped and picked up a funny, crooked stick and grabbed it with both her hands. She stretched the stick far above her head and then brought it down behind her back, not letting go of the ends. She brought it back in front of her and let go of one end with a mighty swing, heaving the twig far out into the water. As she watched it sink, she felt as if she had just thrown all her troubles to the bottom of the lake.

Dear God, she prayed. *Wouldn't it be wonderful if solving life's problems were that easy? But You know that it's not. In all Your infinite wisdom, You know we learn from our trials and grow when overcoming the challenges of life.*

She walked on along the water's edge, inhaling the fresh air with its woodsy fragrance and paying no attention to how far she had gone. She was immersed in her thoughts and aware that she was alone. Yet she wasn't uncomfortable with that feeling, because she didn't really feel alone. For the first time in a long time, Lillian was conscious of a divine Presence with her. She heard the birds singing and in the distance the whir of an outboard motor as a boat skimmed across the lake. She came upon a large rock and sat there for a few moments. She thought about how glad she was she hadn't jumped from the East Gate Bridge— that instead of her body, the gun had been hurled into the river. She felt a sense of being guided to this destination. And she felt stronger than she had felt in a long, long time. For once she felt she knew what it meant to feel like a Parker.

As she sat there, Lillian became aware that pangs of hunger were intruding upon her thoughts, and she realized she had no food in her cabin. She considered asking Dave Thompson for those supplies he had offered, but she decided she didn't want to impose further upon his kindness. Maybe he was just being nice and didn't really mean it when he said he didn't mind the company. Enough is enough, she decided; I'll try to stay out of his way.

Then she remembered Mom Mead's chicken broth. She still had the thermos. All she had to do was heat it on the little stove in one of the small pots she had seen. There was also the ham salad sandwich in the refrigerator.

Lillian got up and made her way back along the water's shoreline to where she could see her cabin. She let herself in and found the thermos where she had left it. In no time at all the soup was steaming-hot. As she ate it, she wanted to laugh at her enjoyment of the taste of it. *Mom Mead,* she thought, *your broth has never tasted so good!*

• • •

That afternoon Lillian rearranged the furniture in the little cabin for something to do and to add her personal touch. She explored the nearby woods and collected twigs and branches for her fireplace. She found some wildflowers in soft but cheery colors to brighten the lodge. There were wild daisies, dandelions, and Queen Anne's lace. The rooms were taking on a decidedly warmer tone by the time a knock at the door interrupted her decorating efforts. She was relieved to find that it was Dave Thompson. She smiled at him in delighted surprise and he cast a sheepish grin in return.

"I thought you might like to join me for dinner, since I know you don't have any food of your own yet," he said. "I have some trout we can cook. I'm a good cook when it comes to fish. My fish don't come out fishy, though, honest," he added.

Lillian laughed. She *was* glad to see him and to hear his voice again, even though it had been only a few hours since they parted company.

"I'm honored you would invite me," she said. "And I'm grateful. Fresh trout sounds wonderful. I already know you're a good cook don't I? If you can flip a mean piece of bacon, then surely I can trust you with trout."

He grinned and seemed to enjoy her comments.

"Well...I...I thought you might like to go for a walk before dinner," he suggested. "I could give you a tour of the woods on the way to my cabin. Then if you need anything, you'll know how to get there on foot. After dinner I'll walk you back so you won't have to go alone. What do you say?"

"I say it's a great idea. I'd love to walk in the woods. But I hate to walk too far alone because it frightens me a little. I'm not sure what to expect in this area. Are there any bears or wolves around here?"

Dave laughed. "Not many," he replied more seriously, but with a twinkle in his eye. "I'll promise to protect you if we run across any on the way."

Lillian wasn't sure whether he was joking or serious. She didn't know any more about vicious animals in this part of the country than she did before she had asked him. She shivered at the thought of being approached by a bear. And suddenly she didn't feel so strong.

"I'll get my sweater," she said. "It might be cool on the walk back."

Dave locked the door for her and they started off in a new direction from the one Lillian had taken earlier in the day. They walked apart and in some places went single file because the path was narrow.

As he had said he would, Dave talked as they walked along the trail. He described the trees in the Smoky Mountain area: hemlock, silver bells, black cherry, buckeye, yellow birch, and pine. When he saw one he could identify—and he could identify most of them—he pointed it out and told Lillian its name. She listened, occasionally asking questions. She began to feel she was receiving a lecture when he went from trees to the vegetation found on the slopes of lower altitudes of the Smokies. Flowering dogwood, redbud and serviceberry, the mountain laurel, white-blossomed rhododendron and azaleas grew in thickets, he explained. The rhododendron and azaleas frequently could be seen along the roadside when driving through Tennessee in cities like Chattanooga, he said.

When he started to talk about wildlife, he caught himself and stopped.

"I hope I'm not boring you, Lillian," he said, looking at her. "It's just that I get carried away when I get a chance to talk about what I know best."

Lillian looked at him and realized he hadn't been reserved at all during the time he had been sharing information about the woods. He had almost forgotten she was there.

"Hey, look!" he said, excitedly. "Have you ever seen a jack-in-the-pulpit?" He stopped over a slender plant. Lillian came close to him and bent to see what he was pointing out to her. It was a small plant. The back side of it was higher than the front, and what appeared to be a miniature figure was centered against the background of the slightly curling leaf.

"Oh, look! It does resemble a little person in a pulpit. Isn't that unique?" she asked, and cast a sideways glance at Dave. "Would it grow outside my cabin? I'd like to dig it up and replant it."

He told her she could try; it wouldn't hurt if she dug it up. But he suggested getting something to work with—a spoon or a gardening tool.

"I guess it will have to be a spoon," she said. "Maybe we could dig it up on the way back after dinner—that is, if it isn't too dark and you'll loan me a spoon."

"Sure." Dave got up and put his hand under Lillian's arm,

helping her to stand. "But I'm getting hungrier by the minute. So let's move on."

They walked in silence until Lillian began to speak.

"Seasons of mists and mellow fruitfulness, close bosom-friend of the maturing sun; conspiring with him how to load and bless with fruit the vines that round the thatched leaves run....," she said softly. That was all she could remember, so she stopped.

"More poetry, I gather?" Dave asked.

"Yes—John Keats. 'To Autumn,' I believe. It seems appropriate here. I'm reminded of Rousseau's philosophy of nature and all the poets who wrote about the beauty of the wilderness. So many of them used natural images in their work. I suppose it has something to do with being in the woods," she said and smiled.

"It's nice you feel that way," he said. "I'm not much for poetry although I don't mind it. All the poetry I once had to memorize I've forgotten—except for one poem that reminds me of my mother: 'She Walks in Beauty.' Do you know it?"

"Oh, it's my favorite of all poems!" Lillian said, delighted. "She walks in beauty, like the night of cloudness climes and starry skies; and all that's best of dark and bright meet in her aspect and her eyes...."

"It's a lovely one, isn't it?" he asked. "It sounds so nice when you speak the lines." Dave looked at Lillian and met her gaze. For the briefest moment he looked into her green eyes and saw tenderness there. And then the moment was gone. They looked away from each other. Dave stepped into the clearing behind his cabin.

"Here we are. See, it isn't far, like I told you. If we'd looked for it earlier, we could have seen the loft of the cabin between the trees. And before you know it, there will be smoke coming from the chimney and trout frying in a skillet—we'll create the perfect picture of hearth and home."

Lillian suddenly realized she liked Dave Thompson. As his giant strides quickly put distance between them, Lillian had time to think. And her thoughts compared Roderick and Dave. Roderick—businesslike, cold, and uncaring...at least in the past few days, when she felt she had needed his warm arms around her and his tender lips against her hair. Where was he when she most needed his supportive words and the sense of security that only he could provide for her? He was looking out the

window, that's where he was. He had told her he had spoken
in her behalf at the board meeting, and she was sure he had.
Wasn't she? Surely Roderick wouldn't turn against her in public.
He would lose the respect of those who knew they were engaged.
And practically everyone in Detroit knew of their engagement.

Lillian looked down at her hands and saw the huge diamond
on her finger. She was no longer sure of its meaning, she was
so filled with confusion and doubts. If Roderick had found it so
easy to postpone their engagement for a whole year, perhaps he
really meant to postpone it for a lifetime. Lillian sighed as she
reached the cabin door. She thought of the kind, shy man on the
inside who had been so good to her without asking anything of
her in return. She hesitated, and just before following Dave inside
she removed the ring and put it into the pocket of her trousers.
Perhaps she wouldn't call Roderick after all. He might do well
to have some time to think about her, too—*if* he would think
about her. She began to doubt everything about her past, except
that she seemed to have found another world. And there seemed
to be a shining sun in this one—a shining sun that hadn't been
there when she was sitting in her father's office cleaning out his
desk, or when Roderick had walked in with his news, or certainly
when she was contemplating jumping from the East Gate Bridge.
Now she was glad she hadn't jumped. For the second time that
day, she was glad she had found another way for herself.

*Thank You, God, for leading me out of that moment of dark-
ness,* she prayed.

Lillian stepped into the cabin to see Dave bent in front of the
fireplace starting the fire.

"Hey, you're way ahead of me," she protested. "What do you
want me to do? A salad? Potatoes? Put me to work."

"Okay, okay," he said, laughing. "Set the table, slave. And toss
a salad with whatever you can find in the kitchen. But stick with
what's in the refrigerator, okay? I'll take care of the fish. I have
a mean Thompson batter recipe my mother passed along to me.
It turns plain old trout into plain old battered trout. And it's one
of my favorites."

They began to work and before long were again seated at the
little table in Dave's kitchen area.

"You were right about the trout," Lillian said. "It's delicious.

I can't wait to get some supplies so I can fix a meal and repay you. I'm an expert at souffles."

"I've never had one, so it should prove interesting." he said. "I'm going into town tomorrow and plan on leaving at seven, if you care to ride along. I could pick you up at your cabin. I'll swing by with the pickup. It's not as fancy as a Corvette, but it's more practical for these parts of the country." He paused to look at her.

He hadn't meant to sound as though he was harshly critical of her car, she realized. Still, it must have seemed a bit paradoxical to him that she was driving such an expensive automobile yet was wearing such ill-fitting and drab clothes. Lillian discovered, to her amazement, that she was personally amused by the mystery she must be creating.

They talked of routine things over coffee. Dave talked of his family—three brothers and a sister (all married) plus eight nephews and nieces. The two of them compared experiences from college days. Since Lillian wanted to avoid talking about her past, she asked lots of questions, putting Dave at ease.

"I knew from the time I was a Boy Scout in seventh grade that I wanted to be a ranger," Dave told her. "I was raised in inner-city Memphis and never saw a real forest until a camping trip during the seventh grade. We caught fish in a freshwater stream and fried them over an open fire. I never knew anything could be so delicious. The whole weekend was an experience in freedom."

"And now?" coaxed Lillian.

"Still the same," said Dave. "I'm a private ranger for all the Compton land around here. Hundreds of acres. Old Phil Compton, the owner, wants it left raw and primitive. I see to it that the tourists have fun, but that they don't change things. Mr. Compton's rule is that visitors should leave nothing but footprints and take nothing but pictures. I like that."

Lillian smiled in agreement.

"But doesn't the loneliness get to you after a while?" she asked.

Dave shook his head. "No. During the summer we have hundreds of tourists passing through here. And in the off-season I cut firewood, map out new scenic trails, and make repairs on the cabins. There's plenty to keep me busy."

He paused a moment and gazed out the window. His eyes

seemed to focus on the panorama, yet on nothing in particular.

"Besides," he added slowly, "the solitude you get is wonderful. You get up here alone, among these huge old gray-and-blue mountains, and you feel close to your Maker. The natural beauty of the mountains seems to stir your emotions and increase your faith. You'll see. I can't explain it, but I can promise you that you'll feel it too after you've been here awhile."

"I'm already beginning to," she said, "through your eyes. You really seem content. I'm glad for you. Now, how about some more coffee?"

"Not for me, thanks. But let me give you a hand with the dishes."

Lillian winked. "You silver-tongued rascal; you talked me into it."

She washed the dishes and Dave dried them and put them away. When they finished, Lillian felt she should get back to her own cabin, even though it was so cozy here.

He led the way through the darkened woods, guided by the moonlight and his own knowledge of the pathway. While he was sure of his footing, Lillian was not. When she stumbled, he helped her up and asked if she was hurt. Then he took her hand without asking if she minded. He again led the way, but this time he moved more slowly, so she could keep up with him without stumbling.

They didn't stop and didn't remember their earlier intention of bringing a spoon to dig up the jack-in-the-pulpit. Only the sounds of their footsteps and an occasional hoot of an owl penetrated the stillness of the night.

When they reached Lillian's cabin, she asked Dave to wait until she made sure everything inside was normal. She hadn't forgotten their earlier discussion of bears and wolves.

Once the lights were on, Dave began to say good night.

"Don't forget, 7 o'clock," he said. Then he hesitated. "I . . . I . . . I guess I'd better go. Thanks for joining me for dinner. I . . . I liked having you. You can sure toss a mean salad."

"I can't believe you're thanking me!" Lillian exclaimed. "I'm the one who should be thanking you for saving me from starvation. And it's you who has the mean toss. The trout was delicious, Dave. Thank you."

He grinned at her. Still, he didn't leave.

"Well, I guess I'd better go," he repeated.

"If I hear any bears, I'll scream," she said. "Will you hear me and come running?"

Dave nodded. "Sure, if you see any and if I hear you scream...."

"Seven o'clock?"

"Seven o'clock. Good night."

"Good night, Dave. Thanks again."

He waved his hand casually and disappeared into the darkness. Lillian waited for a moment and closed the door. She locked it and checked to see that it wouldn't open easily. She turned and contemplated her first night alone in her new home. She walked to the table, picked up the Bible and went into her bedroom. An hour later she turned out the lights and fell into a deep sleep.

● ● ●

Lillian awoke with a start, fearing she would be late for work. The sun glared in her window and dared her to get up and face another day. She remembered Dave and the trip into town, and got out of bed more quickly than she might have otherwise. She searched through the clothing and found a fresh blouse to wear with her jeans. Bea's jeans, she reminded herself. She really had to call home today. It was about time she felt like Lillian Parker again in her own clothes.

When the horn from Dave's pickup honked outside her door, she was ready to leave. He reached across the seat and opened the door for her. Putting the truck into gear, they bounced along the dusty roads on the way into town.

It was everything Lillian had expected. There were two blocks of little stores: a drugstore, a grocery, a tavern, and a church. Old Ed's grocery was by far the largest business. The drugstore offered a soda fountain and many of the necessities Lillian felt she would need—toothpaste, several bars of soap, and a few cosmetics (just because she was so used to wearing them).

At the grocery store, Lillian quickly selected such basic items as flour, sugar, milk, cheese, eggs, shortening, and coffee. She more carefully bought some of the foods she enjoyed but didn't really need. Her budget crossed her mind, and she eliminated many prepared dishes she might have bought in a grocery store in Detroit.

Maybe I'll lose a few pounds, she thought. *It wouldn't hurt. And I have to think about banking my check, too. It won't be long before I'll be needing cash.*

She finished shopping before Dave had completed his errands at the post office and the bank, so she went back to the drugstore, where she had noticed a pay telephone. She put in her call and waited while the operator connected her with her party in Detroit.

While she waited, thoughts of Roderick flashed across her mind. She could see his impeccable suits and the gray flecks that sprinkled his hair at the temples. She remembered his mouth, and in her imagination saw it develop into that odd twist. It was as if she had seen it only minutes ago.

Lillian heard the receiver being picked up on the other end of the line. She waited to hear the familiar voice and was suddenly glad it wasn't going to be Roderick Davis.

"Hello?"

"Hi, it's me...Lillian. How are things in Detroit?"

"Lillian, where are you?" Mom Mead asked. "We've been so anxious to hear from you. Rufus misses you terribly. Pastor Mead and I have been praying for you, you know. How are you, Lillian?"

"I'm fine, just fine, Mom," she said. Lillian's eyes misted at the loving concern that shined through the words that Bea Mead spoke. "I've found a cabin and a new friend and everything is just fine. I'm shopping for a few groceries so I can eat."

"Well, you've certainly created a stir," Bea said. "Roderick has been calling twice a day to ask if we've heard from you. He seems oo anxious to learn of your whereabouts. And a policeman called once to ask if we knew where you'd gone. Of course, we didn't have anything to tell him."

"A policeman?" Lillian was baffled. "What would a policeman want with me? Surely there can't be any reason the authorities would need me. The estate has been liquidated. Everything was taken care of. Besides, Roderick can handle any business matters that come up. Tell him to call Roderick at Michigan

Technologies if he calls again. He can't possibly need me for anything. Did he say what he wanted?"

"No, he wouldn't say," Bea said. "It was most curious."

Lillian didn't have any answers either, but decided not to let it bother her. She mentioned the items she wanted the Meads to send to her, and Mom Mead said that of course they'd pack a box that evening. They'd go to the apartment and locate what they thought might be suitable for tramping in the woods. Lillian gave Bea her new address and said she could send any packages to her in care of the local post office.

"I wish you could send Rufus," Lillian said wistfully. She was hoping Mom Mead would think of some way Lillian could have her honey-colored cocker spaniel with her. "Is it possible, Mom?"

"I don't know, but we'll see what we can do," she said. There was a pause on the other end of the line. "What do you want me to tell Roderick when he calls again? Shall I tell him where to reach you? Is there a message you want me to relay to him?"

Lillian thought about it for a moment, wondering if her fiance had had a change of heart and was anxious for a reconciliation. Maybe she should tell him where she was. He might be worried. In the brief moments as she considered her relationship with Roderick, she turned and watched as Dave Thompson climbed into his pickup for the ride back to the cabins.

"No, don't tell Roderick anything." Lillian instructed. "He wanted to give me time to think and be alone. It was his idea, so he can live with it for the time being. I don't want to talk to him or hear from him yet. This is another world. I want to keep Detroit and Compton Gap separate for a little while longer."

"Good girl, Lillian," Bea said warmly. "We'll send your things as soon as we can. And we'll take good care of Rufus until we can send him to you. He misses you, Lillian. And so do we. God bless you. We love you."

There was a lump in Lillian's throat as she hung up the phone. Tears of homesickness threatened to overflow. She walked away from the telephone and out of the drugstore to where Dave waited for her. She stepped up into the cab of the truck and smiled thinly at the young man behind the wheel.

He looked at her with curiosity, then asked, "Is everything okay?"

"Yes, I hope so," Lillian said. Then with renewed energy and vigor she insisted. "Yes, everything is fine. Just fine."

• • •

Mom Mead phoned her husband to tell him of Lillian's call. As they talked, they discussed going to the apartment early that evening for their young friend's possessions. That way Mom Mead could box them and get them in the mail the next day.

It was while Mom Mead was preparing dinner for her husband that Roderick Davis called to ask if they had heard from Lillian. He again expressed his concern for Lillian's well being and his urgent need to get in touch with his would-be bride.

Mom Mead sympathized with Roderick but said she couldn't help him without Lillian's permission. She and the pastor were concerned about Lillian too, she said. And she confessed she had heard from their mutual friend, but that she had wished to be left alone. So, until Lillian wanted to hear from Roderick, they felt they must respect her wishes. She was fine and safe. That was all she could tell him.

Roderick Davis slammed down the phone and kicked the corner of his desk. He had a right to know where Lillian was, and they had no right not to tell him. Lillian didn't know what was best for her. She had never made any decisions for herself. First her father, then the other members of her family had guided her. Now he was the only person living she could lean on. How could she forget that so quickly? He kicked the desk again and tried to get hold of himself.

He sat down in his desk chair to think. *Contingency plans, contingency plans*, he thought. *What are the options available to me to get at that girl? I have to convince her to come back to Detroit. And I can't do that unless I can talk to her.*

The apartment, of course, he thought. *Apartment 5-F, Riverview Apartments on Crestmount. I'll get someone to watch the apartments. And I've got contacts who will watch the old couple. They won't make a move without my knowing it.*

He picked up the phone and placed his call.

"Mickey? Roderick Davis. Remember that favor you owe me?

I need a payback. There's an old couple I want you to keep an eye on for me for about a week. If they travel anywhere I want to know about it. Got it? Right."

He quickly relayed the Meads' names, descriptions, and address. Feeling smug, he replaced the receiver in its cradle and began to smile. He reached into his pocket and pulled out a comb. As he began combing his hair, dollar signs floated through the air in his imagination.

CHAPTER FOUR

A mirror.

Good heavens, it was an actual mirror!

Scott had not seen any real mirrors in more than three years. They were luxury items that were not to be found in makeshift prisoner-of-war camps throughout Laos. But today Scott was at the Cuban embassy in Ho Chi Minh City in Vietnam. And here they not only had mirrors, but razors and combs and aftershave lotion and clean clothes and new shoes as well. And all for Scott...for some yet-unknown reason.

Slowly, gingerly, he reached forward and removed the small wood-framed mirror from where it was held on the wall. He hesitated before looking into it. What could he expect to see?

Cautiously, he turned the mirror toward his face. He saw, at first, a stranger looking back at him. Then, as seconds passed into minutes, the stranger's features became his own.

Yes, there was still enough of his former appearance for recognition to take place. But it caused an odd sensation. It was as if Scott had planned a reunion with a boyhood chum who was now grown, and the memory of the chum's youthful looks had suddenly been brought into time reality as they stepped forward as a man. It was the same person, yet so different.

His eyes were bagged from sleepless nights. His skin was leathery from too much tropical sun. His face was gaunt due to lack of proper nourishment.

He opened his mouth. His teeth had become uneven and were stained dark yellow. His tongue was brown instead of pink. His gums had small white sores on them. It was repulsive. He sat down on a bench to control a sudden wave of dizziness which swept over him.

How long has he looked like this, he wondered? How long had he been deteriorating this way? Had it really been *that* long?

What year was it by now, he wondered? At least 1982 or 1983. Probably 1983. There was no real way of knowing. He had been captured in 1971 and had spent a long time, perhaps five years, doing manual labor at a work camp in North Vietnam. After that he had been moved to places in Cambodia, then back to Vietnam, then Laos. Yes. . . now that he thought about it, it really had been a long time. A very, very long time.

• • •

The Communists had taken his watch from him as soon as he had been captured. He had been isolated in a completely dark room for weeks. He had been fed at irregular intervals, awakened at random times, and interrogated on and off in no particular sequence or pattern. He had lost all orientation to time, which, of course, was exactly what his captors had expected to happen to him. By the time he was released to join the other workers, his confusion and disorientation had also infused some docility into his nature. He was no longer as sure of himself as he once had been.

Though forbidden to speak with the other P.O.W.'s who were moved in and out of the work camp, over the months Scott had learned to use quick hand signals and other basic gestures in order to ask questions and receive answers.

A casual pull high on his collar where his rank pins had once been attached to his uniform meant "What is your rank?" This would be answered when another prisoner would scratch his cheek with three fingers (for E-3, a private first class) or perhaps all five fingers (for E-5, a sergeant). A tug on the sleeve where unit patches had been sewn meant "What unit are you from?" Two fingers laid against one's underwrist meant medical corps; a hand placed in a hip pocket where a wallet would have fit meant quartermaster; folded hands in a prayer stance meant chaplaincy corps.

Using such codes, Scott had picked up bits of news about the outside world. But it didn't happen often, and when it did each piece of news came as a startling revelation to him. Because of his camp's isolated location, Scott saw new P.O.W.'s only once or twice each year.

He remembered how stunned he had been during the fifth year

of his imprisonment when he had used hand signals to ask a new P.O.W. how the war was going. The other man had clenched his fist ("war"), then had pulled at his shirt where his U.S. Army tag had once been ("U.S.A."), and then turned his thumb down ("lost").

War over; U.S.A. lost! thought Scott in amazement. *Lost? That's impossible!* Who...who was going to come and rescue him?

He looked back dubiously at the stranger. The other man nodded affirmatively. Scott was dumbfounded. How could this be? The only thing that had kept him going from day to day in all this pain and misery was his belief that at any moment the skies would be swarming with choppers filled with "grunts" and "leathernecks" all bent on routing the Commies and freeing Scott and the other G.I.'s. Where were the soldiers? Where were they?

Scott looked at the new P.O.W. He bent over and rubbed his hand across his military boots ("soldiers?"). The stranger stiffened his fingers and brought them together at the fingertips in a tepee formation ("home") and then tugged at the U.S. Army tag space ("U.S.A."). He raised seven fingers, then three fingers.

Back home in America since 1973! thought Scott. *No! No! They wouldn't go back without me...without us!* He shook his head in disbelief, but the other man's sad eyes and forlorn look were genuine. He was telling the truth. It was over. They were gone. Scott and the others around him had been abandoned.

He wanted to ask so much more, but the new man was being led away. He was being taken to the darkened room where his disorientation drills would begin. In a final frantic gesture, the stranger wrinkled his forhead questioningly ("What gives?"), to which Scott responded by pushing his thumbs into his ears and overlaping his fingers across his eyes ("solitary confinement"). When Scott removed his hands and opened his eyes, the stranger was gone.

Three days after his visual conversation with the new prisoner, Scott was dragged from his hut before sunrise and made to kneel in a line with the other P.O.W.'s from the work camp. He almost welcomed the forthcoming bullet in the back of his head. He had been extremely depressed for the past three days. His hopes of being rescued had been dashed. His hopes of once again seeing his father and mother and his sister Lillian had been lost. Why go on?

Scott smiled sinisterly to himself. A new thought crossed his mind. If he had to go, at least he would have the pleasure of knowing he had gone out fighting. When his executioner came near him, he would turn and lunge for him. If he could surprise the man quickly enough, he would be able to wrestle the gun from him and then make a break for the jungle. If, instead, he did not surprise the man, he would at least cause enough disturbance so that his buddies could make a grab for the guard's throat.

Scott picked up a handful of dirt and waited pensively for the sound of the clicking pistol hammer. He strained his ears. He waited. He listened. Sweat beads formed on his lips. His neck muscles grew tight, tense, tauter as each second passed.

Footsteps were heard from behind. They stopped.

"American pigs! You will rissen now," a voice called out.

Scott remained ready to spring. The voice was familiar to him. It was the camp director, Captain Lin Wau, a fat little Chinese Communist who spoke with a British accent over broken English. He probably had been a cook or houseboy in Hong Kong before the war, Scott guessed.

We're rissening. . .er, listening, thought Scott. *Get on with it.*

"Today you go to new camp, many kilometer from here," said the director. He paused for dramatic effect.

"But I ain't had my Continental breakfast yet, Porky," protested one prisoner. "Can you make 'em hold the bus for me?"

The men broke out laughing, including Scott, who dropped the dirt he had been clenching. A sudden sound of a swift kick into a rib cage, followed by a groan, caused the men to stop laughing. The director did not understand American wit, but he knew enough to recognize when he was ridiculed. As usual, his response had been wordless and violent.

"Any man who try to escape will have toes cut off. No ta'k when going through jungle. Man who ta'k go without food."

"No Vietnamese food if we talk?" asked Scott out loud. "That's the reward, Porky. Now, what's the punishment?"

The men all laughed again. Scott grabbed a new handful of dirt and tensed himself. When he heard the guard approach to give him a kick, he would make his move.

The men went on laughing. Scott waited.

He clenced the dirt and continued to expect to be assaulted. But nothing happened.

"Very well," announced the director as the laughter subsided. "You rike riddle joke? Good. I give you joke. Today you make wa'k in bare feet. Take boot off now."

Scott couldn't understand it. Why hadn't his wisecrack earned him a kick? The P.O.W.'s never stopped harrassing the camp director, and, in retaliation, the camp director never stopped punishing the P.O.W.'s. Except this time. No one had come over to kick Scott.

The prisoners were told to lace their boots together and to sling them over their shoulders. Cautiously Scott rose to his feet and did like the others.

"Parker! You come now," called the camp director.

So that's it, thought Scott. *A little private rough stuff and then back to the black hole.*

Two armed guards came near Scott and motioned for him to follow the camp director. The rest of the men were marched away.

"Spit in his eye, Scotty," someone whispered as the men filed by.

"Hang tough, Scott," another voice encouraged.

Scott walked away peacefully.

Although the prisoners were kept in grass lean-to structures and thatched huts, the camp director lived in a two-room wooden building with a metal roof. The roof was covered with a heavy layer of branches, leaves, moss, and dried foliage. Scott knew the covering was not there for camouflage, as the camp director had once said. It was there to deaden the noise the peppering monsoon rain made against the metal.

Porky had obviously joined with the Chi-Coms at the start of the war when a call had gone out that officer ranks could be received for anyone who could speak English well enough to interrogate prisoners. But ol' Porky probably had never envisioned himself as a forgotten P.O.W. commandant in a desolate North Vietnamese outpost. He had been used to better creature comforts. Scott smiled at the thought.

Captain Wau sat at a small desk. The two guards pushed Scott down onto a small folding chair opposite the desk. They stood behind him.

"You here long time, Parker. Maybe you think you go home soon. Not so. I have bad news for you."

Scott offered a mock frown. "Don't tell me you've rented my apartment to someone else, Porky. Well, nothing doin'. I won't stand for it. I'll hold you to your lease."

Captain Wau looked nonplussed. He was used to insolence. Americans were cocky, especially this one. But that would change in a minute. He had some news that would wipe the smile from this arrogant young sergeant's face.

"Always joke, always joke," said the captain. "No wonder American make bad soldier. Never serious."

"You're wrong, Porky, you're wrong," Scott protested. "We take our joking very seriously."

Scott smirked, but the paradoxical humor had been lost on the captain.

"Always mister guy-wise, eh?" said Wau.

"Wise guy! Wise guy!" said Scott emphatically. "How many times must I correct you on that? Why don't you write that one down, Porky, and practice it? I mean, you can't expect to do a good job of interrogating prisoners if you keep making them break out in laughter over your lousy English. What you should—"

"Enough!" snapped the captain.

The two guards made a move to grab Scott, but Wau raised a hand and flagged them back. He said something to them in either Chinese or Vietnamese. Scott didn't understand either language.

"Okay, Porky, since I'm obviously not here to get my bones crushed today, why don't you get on with whatever the routine is going to be?" said Scott. "And, by the way, can we try something new? I get so tired of that one you do where you peel and eat the orange in front of me and offer me a bite in exchange for information about American tanks."

"I wait long time to break you, Parker," the captain responded slowly. "Today I do it. I show you something."

Wau opened his desk drawer and removed a copy of *Stars and Stripes*, the American servicemen's newspaper. He held it against his chest for a moment to keep Scott in suspense as to the front page news. But that was a mistake on the captain's part because it allowed Scott to see the back page. It was dated April 30, 1975, and since the newspaper was not yellowed, torn, smudged, or dirty, Scott surmised it was a legitimate current copy.

April of 1975, thought Scott. *Incredible!* He had been a P.O.W. for four years and four months. He suppressed his amazement and feigned disinterest.

"What do you think of this!" exclaimed Captain Wau, as he whirled the newspaper around. He held it across the desk so that Scott could read the bold headline: SOUTH VIETNAMESE SUR-RENDER TO VIET CONG. Below the headlines were two feature-length articles. Scott noted that one was subtitled PRESIDENT FORD ORDERS U.S. NAVY TO EVACUATE REFUGEES and the other was subtitled COMMUNISTS RANSACK SAIGON.

President Ford? wondered Scott. *What? Henry Ford II has been elected President of the United States? Amazing! But when? The election had to have been in 1972. The only thing that would have kept Nixon from running again would have been his death. President Nixon dead. . .that's phenomenal!*

Scott's thoughts whirled. A thousand questions raced through his mind. When had Henry Ford II become interested in politics? How had President Nixon died? Where was Spiro Agnew during all this? What had happened to South Vietnam's President Thieu?

Why, the whole world was in an upheaval! And here Scott was, held in confinement somewhere in no-man's-land. It was maddening, utterly maddening. Worst of all, he couldn't betray his bewilderment or frustration to Porky. This was no time for weakness. He would have to continue the masquerade of nonchalance and arrogance. . .no matter how difficult.

Scott cleared his throat and turned his scrutiny from the newspaper to Captain Wau. "Good, good," he said. "Right on schedule. How comforting."

Wau lowered the paper. "What you say, Parker?"

"I said that it's comforting to know that things are progressing right on schedule," repeated Scott. "The Calcaterra Plan, I mean. No doubt you know of it by now."

Captain Wau took a piece of paper and a pen from his desk. He eyed Scott cautiously. "You no fool me, Parker. You shocked to learn of fall of Saigon. Admit it!"

"Shocked?" said Scott casually "I'm not the least bit shocked, Porky. It's all part of the Calcaterra Plan."

Wau made notes to himself on the paper. "You bluffing, Parker. You trying to hide the terror in your feeble American heart. Go ahead. Cry! It make you feel better."

Scott looked puzzled. "Cry? My goodness, Porky, why on earth should I cry? You've given me some wonderful news today. The Calcaterra Plan is in full operation and we're winning the war. Very soon you'll be in America working as my gardener."

Wau flinched. This was outrageous. Parker should be emotionally crushed by now, reduced to tears, rolling in agony on the floor. Something was not making sense here. Wau had waited years to do something like this to Parker, and now Parker was acting as though he had the upper hand in the situation. Ridiculous!

"Why all time you say plan, plan, plan?"

"Hmmm?" mused Scott, glancing up from inspecting his fingernails. "What? Oh! The Calcaterra Plan, you mean. Yes, well, I had supposed you knew of it by now. But perhaps not. It's really quite simple, quite logical."

Scott rose slightly and shifted his weight in his chair. It gave him a few seconds to recall the foolishness his buddy Ed Calcaterra had spouted one night about his plan to put an end to the war in Vietnam and turn a profit in the process. It had been uproariously funny at the time and all the guys in the tent had been convulsed with laughter. Calcaterra was a mental hygiene specialist, and working with "kooks" all day made him ever sharper-witted and more outrageous than his patients. Now if Parker could just remember the basics of Calcaterra's joke, he might really put the whammy on old Porky. What was it that Hitler had said about telling a lie big enough for people to believe?

"As you know, Porky, we Americans love a good war, but we make it a habit never to fight on our own soil," said Scott. "It messes the landscape so terribly much, you know. Oh, true, we did experiment with a home-held war from 1860 to 1864, but it never quite caught on as a fad, and most people felt that—"

"You tell plan!" interjected the captain. He slammed his fist on the desk.

Scott looked affronted. "My! How rude, Porky! I was talking."

"And you not call me *Porky*!" He bellowed. "You tell plan *now*!" He nodded defiantly, and the two guards moved forward and stood right next to Scott's shoulders.

"No need to get testy," said Scott. "Very well, here goes. As

I said, we Americans enjoy a good war, as long as it's away from home. That's why we chose to fight here in Vietnam. But after ten years we got tired of this war. The North Vietnamese lack creativity. Goodness knows you Chinese Communists have done all you can to help them, but it's rather hopeless. So, in 1971, General Calcaterra devised a plan for us to leave here."

Captain Wau's pen was scratching rapidly across his note paper.

"Phase One called for a total withdrawal of all American troops by 1973," said Scott.

Captain Wau's pen tore his paper. His head jerked up in shock, How could Parker have known this? Parker had talked to no one from the outside world in more than four years. He had seen no magazines or newspapers, heard no radio broadcasts. The other P.O.W.'s had been here as long as Parker so they knew no more that he did. The transient prisoners who came through the camp were not allowed to come with in speaking distance of the camp regulars.

"Is something wrong?" asked Scott.

Captain Wau shook his head in quick jerks. He couldn't speak. He flipped his hand twice, a sign for Parker to continue.

"The next phase of the plan was to put a new President into office in America so as to confuse you people," said Scott. "We decided to choose Henry Ford II for the job."

Captain Wau's head rose. A sly grin formed on his face.

"Stop, Parker!"

Scott's heart began to beat harder. He had apparently said something wrong and Wau had caught him. Now what?

"You take me for fool, Parker? You try to trick me? Maybe you try to confuse me, eh? Well, I read newspaper, too, Parker. I onto your trick."

Scott sighed. *Shoot! Nice try, though. It would have been fun to pull a good one on old Porky.* Too bad he'd been caught.

"You say President named Henry Ford," said Wau. "You think you can confuse me. But I know too much, Parker. You cannot trick me. President's name is *Gerald* Ford. It is Kissinger who is named Henry. I catch you, Parker. Now you tell truth or I cut out your lying tongue. No more tricks. I too smart for you, Parker."

Scott felt relief flood through him. *Gerald Ford,* he thought. *Of course! The Republican leader in the House. Now that did make sense.* Ford was from Scott's own state of Michigan. He should have thought of him. It was a natural mistake, though. When you live in Detroit and someone says Ford, you think of cars, right? Scott smiled at his mistake.

"Ahh, you smile," noted Captain Wau.

"I...I guess I underestimated you, Porky. Okay, no more tricks."

Wau smiled victoriously.

Scott added, "From now on my explication and consummate summations of sociopolitical stratagems of the American nation will be given with revelatory exposition and simplistic offerings. Fair enough?"

"What that you say, Parker?"

"No more tricks," said Parker.

Wau looked satisfied. "Right, right. Now, you tell plan."

Scott smiled inwardly. This was getting to be fun again.

"Nothing much left to tell. After withdrawing our troops and electing *Gerald* Ford, we said we would let the South Vietnamese play war for a while alone before we returned."

"Return?"

"That's right," Scott confirmed. "Our naval ships will come in large numbers and will float offshore for a few weeks. Ha! The story will be that they will be there to rescue the refugees. That's a good one, eh, Porky?"

Wau looked baffled. He glanced at the newspaper he had cast aside. "Why ships really come?"

Scott paused a moment for dramatic effect. He knew that a moment of silence was Porky's favorite dramatic effect. Then he scooted forward, leaned onto the edge of the desk, and whispered hoarsely, "The ships have the bags of cement."

Captain Wau's puzzlement was obvious.

"Cement? What you mean cement?"

"You heard me, Porky. *Cement.* The Marines are going to storm the shores and reclaim the country. After that, the engineers are going to pave Vietnam. We're going to cement the whole danged country. It'll get rid of the mosquitoes, provide ample runways for our military and commerical planes, and give the citizens some ground to build homes on which won't be washed away when the monsoons hit."

Captain Wau was awestruck. It sounded so ridiculous. It was

so silly. Yet, Parker looked so serious. And one could never, never underestimate the outrageousness of the Americans. After all, they had spent billions on getting to the moon . . . and for what? It had been covered with dust and rocks once they had gotten there. They were maniacs, these Americans, raving maniacs. No, it wasn't out of character for them to plan to lay concrete across Vietnam. In fact, the more Wau thought about it, the more logical it seemed.

"Hey, Porky, how about some grub?"

Wau was yanked from his reverie. He looked at Parker. "What?"

"I said, I want some food," insisted Scott. "I gave you your information. Now, how about giving me some chow?"

The captain said something in Vietnamese to the guards. They pulled Parker to his feet.

"These guards will give you some rice to eat in your hand as you walk to catch up with other prisoners," said Wau. "I will not see you again, Parker. For that I am very happy. You will go to new camp to do new work. But you have given me valuable information today. I am still your master, Parker. My superiors will reward me for this story."

"So, you finally upstaged me, eh?" said Scott. "I suppose it had to happen sooner or later."

Captain Wau beamed.

The guards pushed Scott toward the door. "So long, Porky. I'll send you a postcard once I get settled."

"Always joke, always joke," said Wau, shaking his head. "But today laugh is on you. Here! I give you going-away present." He tossed the copy of *Stars and Stripes* to Scott just before the guards pushed Scott outside.

Scott's heart raced. *News! News!* Could it be true that he'd been given a real newspaper? How incredible it seemed that such common things as a newspaper, a razor, a comb, or a mirror could become so precious to someone who no longer had access to them.

Scott couldn't make up his mind about what thrilled him more, the possession of the newspaper or the knowledge that Porky's head would be on a platter once he filed that cement story with his superiors in Hanoi. What a lark!

Scott and one of the guards stood at the edge of the path leading away from the camp. They waited for the other guard to return with some rice for the three of them. Scott was chuckling to himself. What a crazy day, what a supergreat wonderful crazy day!

He leafed through the newspaper not knowing what to read first. It was all so wonderful.

Suddenly he stopped smiling. He grew somber. His eyes were riveted to the page. He drew the paper closer to him and reread a short item over and over. Tears came into his eyes. His hands started to shake.

Porky quite by accident, would get the last laugh on Scott today... although he would never have the pleasure of knowing about it. For there, on the business page of the newspaper, Scott found a short item which said that Sarah Christina Parker, wife of industrialist J. J. Parker, had died of cancer. It went on to say that Mrs. Parker was survived by her husband and one daughter, Lillian, and that her son, Scott, had been killed in Vietnam in 1971.

Scott dropped the newspaper and stretched his hand out to a nearby tree to control a sudden wave of dizziness which swept over him.

• • •

"Ah-ha, Senor Parker, please do come in and sit down. You look transformed. Do you know that you slept for 19 straight hours? Our beds must agree with you, no? And the shave and haircut have done wonders for you. Will you join me for breakfast? We have coffee, cream, fresh fruit, toast, marmalade, scrambled eggs...please, help yourself."

Scott allowed the young Cuban to touch his arm and lead him to a table. They sat down together.

"What is all this?" Scott asked. "I haven't had a straight answer to anything during the three days I've been here."

The Cuban smiled. His teeth were even, his moustache was dark and well-defined, and his skin was smooth and tawny. He wore a white suit with a solid black tie and matching pocket handkerchief. A red carnation was in his lapel. His watch and two rings were silver, expensive and tasteful. He looked to be in his late twenties. He was muscular, but he moved with poise and blatant self-confidence.

"My name is Guadalupe Bentancourt. I work for the Cuban government here at our embassy in Vietnam on special assignment." He waved for Scott to feel free to eat as he listened. He poured them each a cup of coffee.

"I am an attorney and I know you hate attorneys," said the Cuban. "Furthermore, I am a Communist and I know you also hate Communists. Still, I think we can be of mutual help to each other, Senor Parker, and neither of us will have to compromise his principles."

"Your food is good," said Scott. "But don't expect me to work for the Commies. I won't. How do you know so much about me, anyway?"

Bentancourt reached into his suitcoat and extracted a set of folded papers. He opened them, flipped through them, and read at random.

"Your name is Scott Wallace Parker. You were born on August 14, 1948, in Detroit, Michigan. You graduated from college in May of 1969 and enlisted in the U.S. Army in June of that year. You served in the Armor Corps at Fort Knox, Kentucky, until March, 1970, when you were transferred to Long Binh, South Vietnam. You were promoted to sergeant that December. In January 1971, while on special duty near the DMZ, your firebase was overrun by North Vietnamese Army regulars and you were taken prisoner."

Scott pushed his empty plate away from him. "Thank you, Ralph Edwards," he said. "When do we hear the first mystery voice offstage?"

Bentancourt continued to read. "You were held in a work camp at Fu Lon Chi in North Vietnam for 58 months. During this time you were declared killed-in-action, officially. Your mother died in 1975. I believe you knew that?"

Scott nodded.

"From late 1975 until mid-1978 you were held in an agricultural work zone in Cambodia. You proved to be a troublemaker. Three escape attempts, was it? You were then taken back to Vietnam, this time to a stockade in Bei Min for seven months. In 1979 you were moved to Laos...."

"...Okay, Pancho, so you've got a file on me," interrupted Scott. "Big deal. You didn't fly me from Laos, give me new clothes, and feed me like a king just so that you could impress me with your records system. What gives?"

Bentancourt folded the papers and replaced them in his pocket. "Your reputation for, uh…directness is well-earned, Senor Parker. But, of course, you are right. We do have a reason for bringing you here. And since you prefer, as you Americans say, to 'cut the chatter,' I will be direct, too."

Scott helped himself to another cup of coffee. He filled the cup only halfway and poured cream the rest of the way. "It's your show, Pancho," he said. "Go ahead."

"Your father is dead," Bentancourt said flatly. "Heart attack. My assistant will give you a folder of clippings about it later. You'll want to read them."

Scott instinctively knew the man was telling the truth. They stared at each other a moment, then when Scott did speak, all he said was, "When?"

"About six months ago," said Bentancourt. "I'm sorry."

"My sister?"

"All things considered, she seems to be doing rather well," answered Bentancourt. "Her engagement to a Mr. Roderick Davis was announced last spring, but the marriage never took place."

"Davis? Never heard of him," said Scott.

"You wouldn't like him," cautioned Bentancourt. "He's an attorney."

"Is he a Communist, too?" asked Scott, rising to the taunt.

"Worse," said the Cuban. "He's a Democrat."

Scott grinned. He couldn't help but like Bentancourt's style. "Go ahead, Pancho, I'm listening."

"There's an irony to this next part," said Bentancourt. "Your father was found to have embezzled and mismanaged three million dollars of his company's money. Upon his death, his personal estate was attached. Everything was liquidated—house, cars, furniture, land, investments, even his clothes. The company's lawyers hit like locusts. Rather heartless. But then, I suppose you know all about the company's lawyers. They came between you and your father most of your life, didn't they?"

Scott ignored the question. He sat silently and wondered why he wasn't feeling anything. He was numb. Shouldn't he feel shame over his father's actions? Shouldn't he feel remorse over his father's death? Shouldn't he feel anger over the loss of the family fortune?

But, no, he felt nothing. His years of captivity had made him become stoic, perhaps even fatalistic. He had learned to expect the worst, and he usually received it. After a dozen years of continuous desensitizing, it was a wonder he could even find enjoyment in his new surroundings. He reckoned them to be temporary, too.

"The irony of all this, Senor Parker, is that the death of your father in poverty may be the springboard for a life for you in wealth. Your father established a trust for you more than a decade ago. It's waiting for you. There's more than half a million dollars in it by now. That money, and a reunion with your sister, are carrots I want to dangle in front of you. I can get you back to America, if you will agree to help me with something in return."

"Back. . .to the United States?" stammered Scott.

"That's right," Bentancourt affirmed. "Let me quickly give you the whole picture." The Cuban shifted his chair so that he was facing Scott squarely.

"After you were captured, the North Vietnamese Army sent records about you back to China," said Bentancourt. "Your name was transferred to the propaganda section. Orders came back that you were to be kept alive yet made invisible until needed."

"Needed? You mean they use slave labor in Peking, too?"

"You were being held in reserve for future propaganda purposes. The Chinese Communists and North Vietnamese officials knew that in time South Vietnam would fall. It was a matter of numbers. The Chinese *wanted* to lose people in the war in order to ease their population problem, whereas the Americans wept over every G.I. who was killed. No balance."

Scott shrugged his shoulders. It sounded crass, but was true.

"Still, the Chinese realized that the damage done to all of Vietnam by the war would make it unusable even after the takeover was complete. Bizarre though it may sound, the only plan they could think of to overcome the situation was to convince the Americans to feel 'responsible' for their damage and to have them pay for repairs. It would be an Asian version of the old Marshall Plan which was used in Germany after World War II."

"You're kidding," said Scott. "Even the Calcaterra Plan made more sense than *that*."

"The what?" asked Bentancourt.

"Nothing. Never mind, it's nothing. Go on."

"The Chinese wanted some...how shall we put it?...uh, insurance...yes, some insurance that the plan would work. You were part of that insurance, Senor Parker. If the American government would not buy back its P.O.W.'s with reparation funds, the P.O.W.'s would be put on an auction block and sold outright. Your father probably would have paid a million dollars of secretly channeled funds to have you back, don't you agree?"

"Diabolical," Scott hissed.

"True," agreed Bentancourt, "but also functional and realistic. And it may work yet. You are not the only M.I.A. who has wealthy parents. Other M.I.A.'s will be surfacing soon. Your country's President only laughs when the Vietnamese make requests for reparation funds. So, Plan Two will have to be put into use. You, however, are no longer of much value that way. Your parents are dead and your sister is not wealthy."

"Then why am I being treated so royally all of a sudden?" asked Scott.

"Because the Cuban government needs you," said Bentancourt. "You have been out of touch for a long time and it would take me hours to bring you up-to-date on the relationship between our two countries. However, I will explain one situation. In 1980, our President, Fidel Castro, emptied our country's jails and insane asylums of their inmates. These people were put into boats and pointed toward Florida. It caused your country an incredible headache. But it also caused my country one problem, too."

"I'm ready to believe anything by now," Scott said, shaking his head. "Go on."

"Quite carelessly we allowed one of our Russian advisers to be kidnapped in the confusion of the exodus. Some of our departing Cuban citizens wanted to have a gift for the Americans so that they would be welcomed with open arms. The Russian adviser I spoke of happened to be a colonel."

"Ha—I love it!" Scott said with a guffaw. "How did you explain *that* to your friends in the Kremlin?"

Unruffled, Bentancourt smiled sheepishly at Scott and confessed, "Not very well, I'm afraid. In fact, unless we manage to get the colonel back, our aid from the U.S.S.R. will be...hampered."

"No doubt," mused Scott, still enjoying the story. "No doubt."

"We contacted the American State Department to request the colonel's return," explained Bentancourt. "Instead, a trade offer was tendered. The Americans said they would return Colonel Bupchev, the Russian adviser, to us in exchange for a physically and mentally sound American G.I. who was supposedly killed during the Vietnam War. Your government has been trying to get proof for several years that M.I.A.'s and P.O.W.'s are being kept in Vietnamese prisons."

"So if I come back and tell all I know about who I was with in Laos and 'Nam, the State Department can prove its case. Is that it?"

"Yes. You wind up a propaganda tool one way or the other," said the Cuban. "You may even be asked to tell your story at the United Nations. I'm sure the Americans will know best how to capitalize on you, Senor Parker."

Scott sat in silence for a moment. He replayed the entire conversation in his mind, weighing it from all viewpoints.

"There's one thing in this that doesn't fit though, Pancho," said Scott. "I see what's in it for you Cubans and I see what's in it for the Americans. What I don't see, though, is what's in it for your fellow Commies here in 'Nam and up in Peking. Seems like it's gonna mess up their whole show."

"Very perceptive of you, Senor Parker," said Bentancourt.

"That's why you were 'liberated' at night by Cuban guerilas and smuggled here. And that's also why I need your cooperation—a pledge of silence from you. You see, we don't exactly plan to tell our Asian brothers how you were evacuated. We will be more than content to let the Green Berets or the CIA take the credit. I do hope you won't mind keeping our secret?"

Scott again shook his head. "Now you know why I hate lawyers. You can't trust even the ones you can trust. Anything else you need to tell me for now?"

"Just one thing," said Bentancourt, rising from the table. "Although my formal name is Guadalupe Bentancourt, my closest friends all call me Pancho. I hope you will feel free to do so, too. . .Scott."

Scott grinned. The Cuban had style. Yep, he sure had style.

CHAPTER FIVE

The idea had struck Lillian when she arrived at the Post Office to claim her well-stuffed boxes of clothes. A quick check confirmed that Mom Mead had followed her request to the letter—jeans, Shetland sweaters, oxford cloth shirts, jogging sweats. Then she had added a touch of her own. Buried deep in the mounds of familiar clothing, Lillian discovered a long patchwork hostess skirt, a matching vest, and a white ruffled blouse carefully packed between tissue paper. In spite of her own adherence to a serviceable wardrobe, Bea Mead had an eye for style and had the ability to quickly turn bits of fabric into delightfully whimsical designs.

As usual, Mom, your timing is perfect, thought Lillian as she tossed the boxes into the back of the Corvette and continued to walk down Main Street toward Old Ed's grocery and dry goods store. She owed Dave Thompson a meal or two, and the pretty new outfit prompted an idea of how she might pay the debt with interest. Why not invite him to her cabin for a five-star gourmet dinner, complete with candlelight . . . served, of course, by the lady of the house, resplendent in an elegant new evening ensemble by Beatrice of Detroit? She loved to cook and often had acted as hostess for her father's dinner parties after the death of her mother. Cuisine por deux? *Simple!* she thought.

"Let's see, the menu should be something terribly Continental but hearty," she decided. Somehow Lillian couldn't envision Dave nibbling on Gateau de Foies Blonds or truffles. "A cheese soufflé, beef Wellington, some kind of green vegetable, a salad, rolls, and perhaps a chocolate mousse for dessert. Yes, that would be perfect."

Surprisingly, Old Ed's no-nonsense inventory yielded the necessary ingredients, and within minutes Lillian had packed the sturdy brown bags into the sports car, made a final stop at the drugstore for candles, and was on her way back to Echo Bluff.

"First things first," she said after lining her cupboards with her esoteric purchases. "I'd better make sure the guest of honor can come to his own party."

For fun, she took a sheet of her personalized stationery and scrawled a formal invitation:

> Ms. Lillian Parker requests the honor of your pres-
> ence at a dinner party tonight in her cabin by the lake
> at 6 P.M. Attire is casual and promptness will be
> appreciated. RSVP regrets only.

She slipped the note into its blue matching envelope, personal-ized with her Detroit address, and placed it between the pages of her favorite collection of Keats. She then walked the winding path to Dave's lodge. Once there she pounded on the heavy plank door and awaited the friendly grin of her new friend.

"What can I do for you?" asked the woman who opened the door. She was tall and very beautiful and looked totally out of place in the rustic setting of Dave's kitchen. She was country chic, from her designer jeans to her silk shirt to her high-heeled alligator boots. She had an air of distinct boredom.

"Uh, is Mr. Thompson home?" stammered Lillian.

"Obviously not," replied the woman. "But he better come soon, otherwise I've driven all the way up here for nothing." She eyed Lillian curiously. "I'm Cat Compton. Catherine, really, but every-one calls me Cat."

"Hello, I'm Lillian Parker."

"Lillian Parker . . . Do I know you from somewhere? Your name sounds so familiar."

"Sorry, I don't think so. Are your a relative of Dave's?" Lillian asked, anxious to change the subject.

"Not yet," replied Cat. "But you might say I'm working on it. Look, if you're here to pay your rent or something, I can take it. Sooner or later it finds its way into one of my dad's ledgers any-way." Seeing no glimmer of understanding on Lillian's face, Cat explained, "He's Philip Compton." Again, no understanding. "Phil Compton of Compton Gap. Get it? My folks own most of the town and all of Echo Bluff. Not that that's anything to cheer about."

And does the property include Dave Thompson? Lillian won-dered to herself. Instead, she smiled and held up the book of poetry so Cat could see it. "I really just wanted to leave this for him."

"Keats? I haven't read him since grade school."

Lillian's dislike of Cat Compton was increasing by the minute, yet she was curious about the relationship between Cat and Dave. How had the woman gotten into Dave's cabin unless he had given her a key? Were they dating? Were they in love? What had Cat meant when she said she wasn't Dave's relative *yet*?

"I'd like to wait for Dave, if you don't mind," said Lillian.

"Suit yourself."

Obviously familiar with the kitchen, Cat busied herself with putting away the dishes that had been left to dry in the drainer. Although she occasionally stopped to sip tea from a mug on the counter, she offered Lillian nothing in the way of refreshment.

"It must have been wonderful to grow up in the mountains," ventured Lillian. "The country is beautiful and the people in town seem so warm and friendly."

"A bunch of bumpkins, you mean," retorted Cat. "Daddy sent me away to school in Philadelphia as soon as I was old enough, thank goodness. These last few months would have been endless if it hadn't been for Dave."

"I don't understand."

"I graduated from law school in June, took the state law boards, then came home to wait for the results. It takes three months to get your grades. Daddy said it would be silly for me to move to Nashville since I couldn't open a practice until I have my license. So he convinced me to come back to Compton Gap. Actually, I think he was playing cupid. I wasn't home five minutes before he arranged for Dave to stop by the house to talk business. Can't say I was sorry. Daddy has always had excellent taste."

Lillian could feel her face become very hot. *Good heavens, am I jealous? I don't even know this woman, and I hardly know Dave Thompson.* She watched Cat fold the dishtowel and hang it on a hook inside the utility closet. Try as she might, she could find no flaw in Cat's exotic appearance. Lillian guessed the woman to be in her early twenties, although she had the sophistication of someone older. Her dark chestnut hair was thick and untamed and hung in large ringlets on her shoulders. Gold bangle bracelets and hoop earrings lent an almost gypsy air, although her skin was pale and her eyes were bright blue. She wore much more makeup than Lillian, but it was applied with an expert's touch.

Love is strong as death; jealousy is cruel as the grave. The bit of Scripture bubbled to the top of Lillian's subconscious and caused her to feel a welcome calm. "Look, I'm sorry if I've intruded," she said. "Why don't I just leave Dave this book here on the table. Could you make sure he gets it?" She extended her hand to Cat for a quick squeeze. "It was really nice meeting you, Cat, and I hope you did well on your law test."

"Don't run off," said Cat. "I feel as though I've done all the talking. You haven't told me anything about yourself. Where are you from, anyway?"

"Maybe next time," smiled Lillian. "I'm really not nearly as interesting as you are. Besides, I'm having company for dinner and somehow in the next 3½ hours I've got to clean the cabin, make myself presentable, and try to remember how in the world to fix beef Wellington. I don't suppose you know—"

"Are you kidding? I *hate* to cook," Cat said emphatically.

Lillian took the long way home, stopping frequently to gather dried weeds and late fall greenery. Her makeshift bouquets would have to be arranged in the old crockery she found under the sink, but she was sure the final effect would be pretty, though rustic.

For the first time since she moved into the cabin, she eyed it critically. Little more than a hunting lodge, it had the feeling of a temporary residence. So many tourists had drawn on its hospitality, slept in its beds, eaten from its tables, and cooked on its stove that it looked tired and worn. Maybe it was time for someone to put back a little of what had been depleted over the years. A bright coat of paint in the kitchen, plus new curtains and towels, would do wonders, she thought. Who knows, slipcovers might even rejuvenate the sagging couch. Lillian knew her budget wouldn't allow her to underwrite the decorating project, but she could supervise the effort if Mr. Compton agreed to finance it. *Yes, I'll talk with Dave about that tonight.*

She plumped pillows, pulled the chairs closer to the fireplace, carried in several large logs, and placed bunches of wildflowers in crocks around the room. She set the coffee table with the simple country dishes from the cabinet, then added another bouquet and the candles she had bought in town. Then she turned her attention to dinner.

"You'd think with all the books I brought from Detroit I would have included at least *one* cookbook," she grumbled. The cheese souffle was easy; it had been Roderick's favorite, and Lillian often joked that she could make it with her eyes closed. The chocolate mousse and Beef Wellington posed more of a problem. The meat emerged looking remarkably authentic, but the mousse was reduced to simple chocolate pudding when Lillian discovered she had forgotten to buy enough heavy cream. "I'm no Julia Child," she muttered. "But then, I'm not expecting James Beard for dinner either!"

She washed her hair, blew it dry, and piled it high on top of her head, allowing the loose curls to hang softly around her face. She had been pleasantly oblivious to her appearance since she arrived in Echo Bluff, and now was surprised at the changes that had taken place in the short time since she left Detroit. The autumn sun had streaked her hair, adding bright highlights of platinum blonde. Her face had a healthy, tanned glow and her trim frame seemed firmer for all the plodding she had done through the woods. A touch of lip gloss and a light dusting of silver shadow on her eyelids seemed to be all the color she needed in order to earn a nod of approval from the reflection in the mirror.

The outfit that Mom Mead had sent fit perfectly and made her feel very feminine and pretty. She sprayed each wrist with her favorite cologne and slipped gold hoops through her pierced ears and bangle bracelets on her arms. *Not that I'm trying to look like Cat Compton,* she assured herself. *Not that I could if I wanted to!*

The cabin was beginning to fill with the delicious smell of roasting meat. Lillian checked her watch and noted that Dave was 15 minutes late. Just as well, she decided. *For someone who used to give dinner parties three nights a week, I'm not very well organized.* She stooped to light the fire, then turned and used the same match on the candles. With the lights turned down very low, the cabin took on a warm and inviting atmosphere. The dilapidated sofa looked downright comfortable instead of lilting, the cracks in the dishes were barely visible in the flickering light of the fire, and the numerous arrangements of wildflowers added a decided note of cheerfulness to the room.

Now all we need is the guest of honor, thought Lillian, again consulting her watch. *Half an hour late.* She remembered Cat

Compton's intimation that Dave had spent many hours at the Compton residence since Cat's return to the Gap. *Could they be together tonight?* No, surely Dave would have sent word hours ago if he couldn't come, Lillian decided. Her invitation specifically stated "Regrets only." *But perhaps he didn't see the invitation. . . .* Impossible; she had tucked it inside the poetry book and had positioned it in the middle of the kitchen table where he couldn't miss it.

She was hungry, and although she had planned to start the meal with tomato juice, crackers, and cheese, she was beginning to worry that the dinner would be spoiled if it were allowed to cook much longer. She would dispense with hors d'oeuvres and serve the main course as soon as he arrived, she thought. *Please hurry. I don't think I can cope with another rejection quite yet.* She suddenly realized that Roderick's dismissal of her had left scars far deeper than she originally had thought.

It was nearly 8 P.M. when, in tears, Lillian turned off the stove and watched her prize souffle retreat with a slow gasp to the sides of the dish. Wellington had long since shriveled away from his pastry shell, looking like a charred pig in a blanket. The salad was wilted and the vegetables watery. Only the chocolate pudding was no worse for the delay.

Her appetite gone, she curled up like a ball on the couch and burrowed her face in the throw pillow. Why was she crying? He had never said he would come to dinner. But then, he had never said he wouldn't come, either. Was it her pride that stung so? Or was it the knowledge that somewhere Dave Thompson and Cat Compton were probably sharing a cozy dinner for two by firelight? She could hear the wind pick up in velocity and brush the limbs of the pinetree against the windows. It was raining, she knew, and the weather couldn't have matched her mood more perfectly.

Years had passed since she last cried herself to sleep, but memories of former sorrows came back with the great waves of tears and didn't subside until she fell into an exhausted slumber. When she awoke she felt the same kind of fear she had experienced as a child. The lights were out, the candles had burned themselves into a hardened pool of wax on the table, and the fire was reduced to a ridge of flowing white dust. The cabin was cold, causing her to shiver uncontrollably. In spite of the whipping wind and eerie creaks of the log siding as it expanded against the torrents of rain, she could hear another, more frightening, sound. Someone was beating on her back door.

She quickly assessed the situation. The cabin had no phone, and even if she were within screaming distance of the nearby cottages, they were all vacant except for Dave's. *Dave!* She realized there was the smallest possibility that the person on the other side of the door was Dave Thompson. Or, if it weren't Dave, perhaps she could bolt past the intruder and run to the ranger's cabin before being caught. In either case, she knew she must open the door, because anyone determined to gain access to the lodge could easily do so, with or without her permssion. The locks were rusted and the window frames were spongy with age.

"Oh, God, if I ever needed Your protection, I need it now," she prayed. "Bless me with the strength to accept Your will." She closed her eyes and gave a mighty tug on the swollen latch. Then she prepared to sprint into the blackness of the woods.

"Thank heavens, you're all right," said Dave Thompson.

She collapsed against him and for a moment allowed his wet arms to encircle and hold her. Quickly regaining her composure, she pulled away and hurried into the shelter of the kitchen. Dave stripped off his dripping yellow rain slicker and hung it on a hook at the entry. Without asking her permission, he went into the living room, knelt on the hearth, and began rebuilding the fire to a hot blaze.

"There, that should take the chill off," he said. "Come over here and get warm before you catch pneumonia. I thought even a city girl like you would know enough to put an extra log on the fire when the electricity goes out," he joked.

"How *dare* you talk to me as if I were some silly child!" she replied. Anger flashed in her eyes and held in check the tears that threatened to spill down her cheeks. "I may not be your equal in the Smokey the Bear department, but at least where I come from we have the good manners to respond to an invitation."

"I don't understand . . ."

"Do you have any idea of how much work goes into beef Well . . . Well . . . Wellington?" The tears streamed down her face, and the words were lost in the catches of sporadic sobs.

"Lillian, I don't know what you're talking about." He looked around the cabin in bewilderment, and then noticed the coffee table set with two dinner plates, flowers and candles. "Are you saying I was supposed to come . . . that you expected me for . . ." The color rose in his face as he began to piece together the misunderstanding. Then it was his turn to be angry. "You may think I'm some kind of backward country boy, but at least where I come from it's customary to invite someone to dinner, and not just assume he'll show up at the right time at the right place."

"Are you telling me you didn't get the note in the Keats book? It was right between the pages when I put it on your kitchen table. And I specifically told Cat I was leaving it there for you."

"Where did you meet Cat?"

"In *your* kitchen, doing *your* dishes."

"How did she get in? For that matter, how did *you* get in?" His voice was becoming more stern.

"Cat let me in, of course; and my guess is that she got in by using the key you obviously gave her."

"I never gave her a key," he said earnestly. "But her father owns all this property and, of course, he has a master key. She must have gotten hold of it. Honestly, I don't know what to think of that woman."

"Apparently she thinks a great deal of you. Is it possible she might have taken the book?"

"No, I have the book. In fact, I was reading it when the electricity went off. I started to worry about you and that's why I came over here. I never saw any invitation. Cat probably took it and pitched it."

"I can't say I liked her very much," admitted Lillian. "Still, I can't imagine anybody doing something that dishonest." She paused, then added quietly, "Unless . . . she loves you very much."

They stood, looking at each other, as the anger slowly drained out of each of them. "I'm not sure she loves me at all," said Dave softly. "This is a difficult time for Cat. She doesn't really belong in Compton Gap anymore, but she has to wait here until she knows what her future is. Sometimes I think she's just bored and I'm some kind of diversion for her. When she passes her law board exams she'll move to Nashville and forget that Dave Thompson ever existed."

"And how will Dave Thompson feel about that?" whispered Lillian.

"I'm not sure. Maybe relieved," he stumbled. "She's not like anyone I've ever met before, Lillian. She's beautiful, of course, and very brilliant. I've never thought I was old-fashioned; I've always said that any woman with a good head on her shoulders should use it. But *Cat!* She knows more about her dad's business than he does; she studies the stock market and can talk circles around any banker in this part of Tennessee. She reads *The Wall Street Journal* like other women read fashion magazines and cookbooks."

Lillian felt uncomfortable and was grateful for the lack of electricity. *At least he can't see me blush,* she thought. Cat, for all her underhanded ways, actually was more honest than she was. Lillian hadn't lied to Dave, but she hadn't exactly been truthful with him either. Never had she told him about her position with Michigan Technologies, her background in the business world, or her family. The stockmarket? She could probably recite the listings on the Big Board without batting an eyelash. *The Wall Street Journal?* She was on a first-name basis with several of its top writers.

"Speaking of cookbooks, I don't know about you, but I'm starved," she said changing the subject. "This dinner was supposed to pay you back for all your kindnesses since I've been here. I may end up owing you even more, but are you willing to try a deflated souffle, beef briquets, coagulated peas, and limp lettuce?"

"You bet," he laughed. "How can I help?"

"Keep the fire going; we may want to get rid of this mess in a hurry," she quipped.

She warmed the meat, salvaged the vegetable, heated some rolls, and gave up the salad as a lost cause. Once arranged on the plates, the food looked surprisingly edible and smelled almost as delicious as it had the first time around, some five hours earlier.

"Would you ask the blessing, Dave?"

He reached across the makeshift dining table and clasped her hand. "Lord, thank You for this food and for the loving hands that prepared it. May our past misunderstandings be forgotten, and may we go forward from this table as friends of each other and as Your servants. Amen."

Perhaps it was because she was so hungry, but the dinner tasted delicious. Dave, after three helpings, conceded that it was the best beef Wellington he had ever eaten.

"Also the first I've ever eaten," he joked. "If I admit that everything was perfect, does that mean your debt is settled and you won't feel obligated to ask me to dinner again? Because if that's the case, I'm going to lie and tell you it was awful."

"My ego needs all the stroking it can get. Tell me it was great and you're automatically invited back next week."

"It was great. Stupendous. Mouth-watering. Fantastic. Er, am I invited back?"

"You're on."

She cleared away the dishes and brought in a pot of fresh coffee to drink by the fire. It was past midnight, but her long nap had left her refreshed and looking particularly pretty.

"I like your outfit," said Dave, "although it's not your typical woodsy, around-the-old-campfire attire. A sight for sore eyes, if you pardon the cliche."

"You're pardoned. And I thank you, my wounded pride thanks you, and most especially, Mom Mead thanks you."

"Who?"

"She's my pastor's wife. She made the outfit."

"I don't mean to pry, Lillian, but are you close to your pastor? I mean, are you active in your church?"

"Not as active as I want to be," she admitted. "One of the reasons I came to the mountains was to read, study, and straighten out some problems in my life."

"Looks as if you're studying the right book," said Dave, reaching to the table by the sofa and grasping her father's worn Bible. He began turning the pages gently. "If you're looking for answers, there's no better place to find them. May I read you something that reminds me of you?"

"Oh, yes, I'd like that." She settled next to him on the couch and watched as he hunched close to the candle for light.

Who can find a virtuous woman? For her price is far above rubies.

The heart of her husband doth safely trust in her, so that he shall have no need of spoil.

She will do him good and not evil all the days of her life.

She seeketh wool and flax, and worketh willingly with her hands.

She is like the merchants' ships: she bringeth her food from afar.

She riseth also while it is yet night, and giveth meat to her household, and a portion to her maidens.

She considereth a field, and buyeth it; with the fruit of her hands she planteth a vineyard.

She girdeth her loins with strength, and strengtheneth her arms.

She perceiveth that her merchandise is good; her candle goeth not out by night.

She layeth her hands to the spindle, and her hands hold the distaff.

She stretcheth out her hand to the poor; yea, she reacheth forth her hands to the needy.

She is not afraid of the snow for her household, for all her household are clothed with scarlet.

She maketh herself coverings of tapestry; her clothing is silk and purple.

Her husband is known in the gates, when he sitteth among the elders of the land.

She maketh fine linen and selleth it, and delivereth girdles unto the merchant.

Strength and honor are her clothing, and she shall rejoice in time to come.

She openeth her mouth with wisdom, and in her tongue is the law of kindness.

She looketh well to the ways of her household, and eateth not the bread of idleness.

Her children arise up and call her blessed; her husband also, and he praiseth her.

Many daughters have done virtuously, but thou excellest them all.

Favor is deceitful and beauty is vain, but a woman that feareth the Lord, she shall be praised.

"Proverbs chapter 31, right?" asked Lillian. "It's one of my favorites, too. But why does it remind you of me?"

"Come over by the fire so I can see you better," answered Dave. She rose from the couch and stood next to him on the hearth. The licks of flames cast strange shadows around the room, but bathed their faces in golden light and warmed their chilled bodies. He put both hands on her shoulders and looked down into her eyes for what seemed a very long time.

"I don't know very much about you, Lillian Parks, Parker, or whoever you are. All I know is that you're a lot like the woman in the Scripture; you're very rare and very special. So don't give up. This pain you feel—whatever caused it—will pass, and the hurt, however bad, will heal." His eyes never left hers as he raised one rough hand and gently stroked the smoothness of her cheek. She lifted her face instinctively to his, and he softly brought his mouth down to meet hers.

"You're very beautiful," he whispered.

"Even if I don't read *The Wall Street Journal* or follow the Dow Jones—"

He kissed her quiet, this time leaving her almost breathless.

"I'd better go," he said huskily.

"Yes," she replied.

Silently he put another log on the fire, pulled his rain gear over his plaid flannel shirt, and slipped out the back door and into the darkness. After he had gone, she sank down into the shapeless comfort of the old couch and pondered her uncanny ability to complicate her life. *I came here to find some answers, and all I've done is create new questions.*

"Think of the options," she said to herself dutifully. Pastor Mead always said that in order to solve a problem you must first weigh all the possible solutions and then choose the best. "I could go back to Detroit, find a new job, and try to work out my relationship with Roderick." But she wondered if she would be running back to Michigan or merely running away from the mountains? Sooner or later she must stop and face the dilemmas of her heart.

She was painfully aware that neither of the two men in her life knew her at all. Roderick had been drawn to her money, position, and family. He admired her for her business prowess and her knowledge of the ins and outs of international sales. But what about the other, softer side that she had kept carefully under wraps during their courtship? That was the side that had attracted Dave Thompson. He knew nothing of her education and professional reputation. He thought of her as a confused young woman who liked to withdraw into books of poetry, take solitary walks in the woods, and spend hours puttering in the kitchen. Would he even like the other Lillian Parker? The one who, in many ways, resembled Cat Compton?

She stretched out on the couch and watched the strange shadows dance on the ceiling to the rhythm of the crackling fire. In spite of her confusion, she felt a certain peace. For all its shortcomings, the evening had been a success. She wasn't sure what she felt for Dave Thompson, but she knew she was comfortable in his presence. He made her laugh, although their relationship was far from superficial. He made her think although he admitted he knew nothing about the intricacies of high finance (which she had always connected with intelligence). And he made her feel something she had never experienced in her life. Each time she remembered his kiss she felt a warm excitement that caused all other matters to pale in comparison.

She fell into a dreamy sleep and didn't awaken until the morning sun, coupled with the artificial light from the cabin's lamps, flooded the room. Sometime during the night the electricity had been restored, and she hurried to snap off the unnecessary brightness. She changed into jeans, a dark plaid shirt and yellow pullover sweater, and quickly cleaned the cabin. She jotted down a list of items she needed from town, although her primary purpose of driving into Compton Gap had little to do with replenishing her supply of coffee and candles. She grabbed her corduroy blazer—the late autumn air was beginning to turn crisp—and settled into the Corvette for the winding trek to town.

• • •

Cat Compton clutched a small piece of personalized blue notepaper as she hurried against the wind toward the tiny Andrew Carnegie Library on Main Street. She had called the Detroit operator to get the telephone number of the residence printed on Lillian's stationery. Fortunately, it was listed; but when she called the number she got a recording saying Lillian was not at home but might be reached through her Michigan Technologies' office.

Michigan Technologies? Wasn't that the company involved in some kind of scandal when its president died? Cat struggled to recall the details. *Yes, his name was Parker, and his estate had been liquidated to pay the company's creditors. Parker?* Cat looked at the notepaper: Lillian Parker, Apartment 5-F, Riverview Apartments, Crestmount Drive, Detroit, Michigan. *Surely there had to be some connection.*

"Good morning, Miss Compton, what can we do for you today?" asked the librarian.

"Do you keep back issues of *The Wall Street Journal?*"

"Yes, miss, although we don't have many requests from people to look at them."

Cat rolled her eyes in disgust. "Well, I'm requesting to see the last month's worth." She strutted into the head librarian's office, told him she'd appreciate a cup of coffee, and then waited for the stacks of *Journals* to be placed in front of her.

UPSWING EXPECTED FOR MICHIGAN TECHNOLOGIES. The headline on the right side of page 1 immediately caught her eye. She read the article twice, scribbling notes on the back side of the piece of blue notepaper. "Daughter Lillian Parker . . . company attorney Roderick Davis, fiance of Miss Parker...Scott Parker, missing in action...the late J. J. Parker...."

"Did you find everything you needed, Miss Compton?" asked the librarian. As a response, Cat piled the crumpled newspapers on the periodicals desk, topped the heap with her half-empty cup of coffee, turned and hurried out the door. "You're welcome, Miss Compton," muttered the librarian.

Cat's destination was Old Ed's grocery and dry goods store, which boasted the only telephone booth in town. This call couldn't wait until she drove back to her parent's house, she decided. Besides, she didn't want to be overheard by her mother or father. They wouldn't approve, she knew. The phone booth was occupied when she arrived at the cluttered general store, so she tapped impatiently on the glass door to let the caller know she was waiting. Lillian whirled around at the noise, just as the operator connected her with Bea Mead in Detroit. For a moment Lillian said nothing, but stared through the glass panel at Cat Compton, who was staring back in similar surprise.

"Hello? Hello?" said Mom Mead.

"I'm sorry, Mom, it's me, Lillian." She secured the door and lowered her voice. She knew Cat was unscrupulous enough to eavesdrop if she could. "Is Rufus all right? Yes, yes, I miss him too; but it's you and Pastor Mead that I really need. I'm more confused than I was when I left Detroit. Mom, is there any chance at all that you might come here to the mountains? I have plenty of room in my cabin and.... Yes? Oh, I was hoping you'd say that!"

They talked for a few minutes while Cat paced back and forth in front of the booth. When Lillian emerged, she smiled sweetly at Cat. "Thank you for giving Dave the poetry book and the invitation. We had a lovely dinner."

Cat looked down at her boots, embarrassed. Lillian slipped past her, and Cat sought the welcome refuge of the phone booth. The bit of blue notepaper was produced from her pocket, and the digits of the phone number scrawled on the back of the paper were quickly dialed.

"Hello, I'd like to speak with Roderick Davis." Pause. "No, I do *not* want to talk with Mr. Stattman," she hissed. "If Mr. Davis is interested in the whereabouts of Lillian Parker, he better extract himself from his meeting and take my call.

"Hello, Mr. Davis. Short meeting? My name is Catherine Compton, and I have some information I believe you've been trying to acquire."

They talked for several minutes, each trying to elicit as many facts from the other as possible. "Is there any chance that you might come here to the mountains?" Cat asked Roderick. "Yes? I was hoping you'd say that...."

She exited the phone booth and brushed past Lillian, who was carrying coffee and candles toward the cash register. Their eyes locked for a moment in a chilly standoff. Then they exchanged brief smiles, each confident that the business transacted on the telephone would eventually solve the problems created by the other.

CHAPTER SIX

Scott Parker had not seen Guadalupe Bentancourt for five days because, without informing Scott, Bentancourt had flown back to Cuba to check on the prisoner-exchange arrangements. However, Scott had been too occupied to worry much about it. "Pancho" had drawn up a strict regimen for Scott; and Bentancourt's assistants in Ho Chi Minh City were seeing to it that it was followed to the letter.

Scott was allowed to sleep until 9 A.M. each morning. He then was given a high-protein and high-vitamin-C breakfast. At 10 A.M. he was required to shave and shower and then submit to a half-hour back and leg massage.

Each day from 10:30 until noon he was treated by a medical specialist. On the first two days he was attended by a dentist, who fixed several cavities and then cleaned his teeth and treated his gums. The next day he was given an eye examination and hearing test. The fourth day he had to give blood samples and throat cultures and undergo a complete physical examination. On the fifth day he was given an EKG, ten X-rays, and a series of tests to judge his reflexes and agility.

Lunch was served from noon until 1 P.M. each day. It consisted of fresh fruit, whole milk, natural grain breads, and fish or poultry. From 1 P.M. until 2 P.M. Scott was asked to rest. He could either take a nap or sit and read current newspapers and magazines. His requests to be given a radio and television and to be allowed to take a walk in Ho Chi Minh City were all denied.

At 2 P.M. each day he was visited in his room by such people as tailors (who took his measurements), manicurists (who treated his hands and fingernails), barbers (who cut and styled his hair), or staff journalists (who took a series of before-and-after photographs of him).

The hour or so before his 5 P.M. dinner was spent reviewing

files, which were given to him at the rate of two folders per day. One file contained a large stack of clippings about his father's death and the subsequent scandal related to the embezzlement. Some of the magazine articles showed pictures of Lillian.

She had changed greatly—become a woman—since Scott had last seen her 12 years ago. Seeing photos of his now-grown sister made Scott ache to find her, to hug her closely and protect her, to spend endless days talking privately to her about their parents and all the lost years. He wanted to ask about his mother's death, about his father's problems, about Lillian's plans for the future. *In time, in time,* he consoled himself.

The other files contained highlight news summaries of events which had taken place from 1972 through 1982. Scott was overwhelmed by all that had occurred during his captivity. The deaths of LBJ, Hubert Humphrey, Elvis Presley, Steve McQueen, Dave Garroway, Lowell Thomas, Susan Hayward, and Nelson Rockefeller all surprised him. And the news that John Wayne was also dead made Scott feel as though his "era" had ridden off into the sunset during his absence.

He could not understand the complicated file marked "Watergate," but he surmised that it was the cause of the resignation of President Nixon. Other words and catchphrases, such as OPEC, acid rock, PAC-MAN, the muppets, E.T., space shuttle, Opryland U.S.A., EPCOT, VISA card, and SST were like foreign vocabularies to him. It was impossible to catch up on news when you couldn't even catch up on the English language.

Two files did intrigue him greatly, however: the file on the 1976 American Bicentennial and the file on the Iranian hostage crisis. Reading the first seemed to give him an infusion of patriotism, in that it was filled with photos of such things as the Liberty Bell, Old Ironsides, the Alamo, Sutter's Creek, and Cape Canaveral. (*Cape Canaveral?* thought Scott. *They've changed the name back again?*) Reading the second file made him realize that his fellow Americans *did* care about people like himself who were held as prisoners by foreign nations.

Scott pondered this. He saw pictures of towns decorated with yellow ribbons and local churches holding candlelight vigils. He read of the aborted rescue mission. He studied reports of elementary school children who had sent thousands of handmade Christmas cards to the hostages.

It all made Scott feel so lonely, so sad. Oh, how he had missed America for so long! How he had missed *his* people. How he wished he had had someone negotiating for *his* release all these years. How he wished he had had children sending *him* cards. How he wished he had had people decorating towns for *him* and lighting candles and offering prayers for *him*.

"Prayers?" he suddenly said aloud. "What do I mean about prayers?" I quit believing in prayers years ago. What kind of God would put me through what I've experienced and then still expect to be prayed to?

"I don't believe in God! I don't believe in God! I . . .I . . .don't . . . I . . . ."

He leaned slowly forward on his bed. He couldn't help himself; he began to shake. He tried to resist. His eyes misted and then one tear escaped. It was followed by others. Soon he was breaking down, yielding; he began to cry with great sobs.

It was the first time he had cried in the 11 years of his captivity. But now he cried with unbridled emotion, unchecked feeling, unrestrained sentiment. He choked and sobbed. He moaned and whined. He beat his fists against his legs. His chest heaved and fell, his lips quivered, his body felt limp. And the tears, large and wet and salty, continued to flow. Years and years of anguish, fear, and bitterness were being cleansed from him and he had no way to stop it.

It wasn't a nervous breakdown or a mental collapse. It was simply nature's way of purging the emotions and washing the conscience. The fact was, Scott *did* believe in God, always had believed in God. His mother's strong Christian stance had put him under conviction early in life, and upon reading of his mother's death that day in the jungle he had suddenly been captivated by an idea. . . an idea that God was going to reward his mother for her faithfulness by softening her son's heart, saving his soul, and then using him in some incredible way for a great mission.

The idea was spontaneous, and Scott fought it. He refused to believe it had any validity. It was a reflex reaction to the shock of his mother's death—nothing more. Even more logical, he rationalized that it was probably delirium, brought on by malnutrition or sunstroke.

But the idea remained with Scott. He couldn't shake it, even in his dreams. And to think of his mother was to recall the passages she had read to him from the Scriptures or to remember the Bible stories she had told him before bed.

But what could two years of combat and ten years as a P.O.W. do to prepare you for a God-ordained mission in life? *Absolutely nothing*, Scott insisted to himself, *unless we start the Crusades again. I must be crazy.*

Yet he knew he wasn't.

• • •

Bentancourt surveyed the woman once more. She looked *disciplined*. That wasn't a word one usually associated with attractive young women, but it was the only word which aptly fit Juanita Martinez.

Yes, she was *disciplined*. Her weight was exactly right. Her hair was all in order. Her posture remained rigid whether she sat down or stood up. Her gaze was direct. Her words were few in number and spoken with telegraph conciseness. Even her clothes were disciplined—form-fitted, unwrinkled, and orderly.

"Have you ever killed a man?" asked Bentancourt, looking down at the girl's personnel file.

"Not yet," she answered flatly.

Without showing it, Bentancourt smiled to himself. Clever answer. It made his next question unnecessary.

• • •

Alma Hammond was a stickler for details. She felt that her latest assignment had too many loose ends. That annoyed her...no, it angered her. She liked procedures to be followed and routines to be adhered to. That's the way she had been trained at home all her life and that's why she had gone to law school and then joined the Central Intelligence Agency. She liked systems. She liked specific procedures. She liked routines. And when these systems, procedures, and routines were disrupted, she grew very impatient.

Alma knocked twice on the director's door and then entered. The director was a progressive-minded, alert, and organized man—just the sort the Agency needed. He adhered to one "old-fashioned" notion, however. He still believed that ladies should be treated as ladies. And that's why he stood when Alma entered his office. After she took a chair, he too sat down.

"You've heard from the Cubans again?" asked the director.

"Yes, sir," said Alma. "This morning our agent at Guantanamo was visited by Bentancourt again. He's ready for the trade. But I'm afraid I'm not."

The director was not taken aback by Alma's remark. He knew she would not be satisfied no matter what the first trade-arrangement offers were. She was like a computer. If you put a detailed new program into a computer and it played out perfectly the first time, you knew you must have left out some details. It was never that easy. Alma was the same way. If you gave her a complicated assignment and she okayed it right away, you knew you had not given her all the details. But the director believed in computers. And he also believed in Alma.

"What's the rundown?"

Alma opened a folder and extracted some notes.

"We finished our interrogation of Colonel Bupchev long ago, and so we're ready for the trade," she said. "And Bentancourt has agreed to make the swap in Guantanamo, as we suggested. He's also agreed to allow an examination of the P.O.W. by our physicians."

"Good, good, good," said the director, nodding.

"There are hangups, however," added Alma. "Thus far, we still have not been given a picture of John Griffiths, the P.O.W. We also requested a tape-recorded message in advance from Griffiths, but that hasn't come through either."

"Your assumptions?" asked the director.

"We're being led in the wrong direction."

"Details?"

Alma scooted back in her chair, crossed her legs, and rested her chin on her hands. "I've been trying to figure out what I would do if I were in Bentancourt's shoes," she said.

"Standard procedure," noted the director, mostly to himself.

"And I've decided that if I were Bentancourt I'd find myself in a real dilemma. I'd need to reclaim Colonel Bupchev in order to please the *Russian* Communists. The only way to do that would be to give the Americans a P.O.W. But that would anger the *Chinese* Communists."

"So?"

"So I'd need to figure out a way to please all three principals. And there's only one way I could do it."

The director leaned slightly forward. "Go on."

"First, I'd get a P.O.W. of little consequence, some routine dog-face who had little more than propaganda value to the Americans. Then I'd spend some time getting some weight back on him—wouldn't want the Western world to think he'd been mistreated, you know."

The director said nothing—just nodded thoughtfully.

"Then I'd tell the Americans I was going to give them someone special . . ."

"Like Lieutenant Commander John Griffiths, a naval intelligence officer missing for the past six years?" interjected the director.

"Precisely," said Alma. "But I wouldn't provide any visual or audio proof that Griffiths was still alive. At the time of the trade, I'd announce that Griffiths could not be obtained, but a replacement had been secured. I'd then produce the lowly G.I. The Americans would, of course, be too softhearted to send him back. They'd protest, but they'd make the trade anyway. In the end, I'd have the Russian colonel back, the Americans would have no one of real value on their hands as far as military intelligence was concerned, and the Chinese would still have Commander Griffiths in their jails."

The director stood up, walked over to a side cabinet, and took a coffeepot from its warmer plate. He filled two styrofoam cups. He left his black but added one teaspoon of nondairy creamer to Alma's.

"I like your line of thinking," said the director. "But one thing occurs to me."

"Sir?"

The director set Alma's cup on a table beside her. Having coffee with the director was the agency's equivalent to well-done-thou-good-and-faithful servant. Alma almost blushed. She'd had oral compliments and an occasional praise memo from the director, but this was her first cup of coffee with him.

"If this Bentancourt is so clever—and I'm sure you've done a full study of him—wouldn't it still stick in his craw that he couldn't figure out a way to get Colonel Bupchev back without giving us a P.O.W. to show off to the world? Bentancourt, after all, is a loyal Communist. His first allegiance is to Cuba, that's true; but he nevertheless wouldn't want to hamper Communist efforts in Asia. Do you follow me?"

Alma nodded. It made sense. "You're thinking he'd order an assassination of the P.O.W. after the exchange?"

"Yes, I believe he would," said the director. He finished the last of his coffee, crushed the cup, and threw it away. "Now, tell me. If you were back in Bentancourt's shoes again, how would you trade away a healthy man yet make sure he would never live long enough to tell the world his story?"

Alma thought a moment.

"Time capsule poison?" she speculated. "No, no. He knows we won't make the exchange until after our doctors have completed the blood tests and X-rays on the P.O.W. Poison's out."

"Bullets and bombs are out too," said the director. "We'll have the P.O.W. too well-protected. But what about suicidal hypnosis?"

"Possible," said Alma, "but I don't think it's very likely, sir. Brainwashing a man thoroughly enough to convince him to commit suicide on command takes a long time. The Cubans haven't had that kind of time. We've been holding Bupchev since the end of 1980, but we only tendered the P.O.W. trade offer five weeks ago. Besides, any P.O.W. who has resisted insanity for five or ten years is going to be a hard guy to sell any subconscious hooey to."

The director returned to his chair. After a moment, he nodded concurrence. "All right, then *what*? What's left?"

"I don't know, sir. But you're right about Bentancourt. He's too clever to overlook any details."

"How large are you people in Cuban Section these days?" asked the director. "How many agents are you running in Cuba?"

"Twenty-two routine informers, five couriers, and two of our own 'company people' on full-time assignment, sir."

"Put your people down there to work on this. See if they can come up with anything. Bentancourt will try something, you can be sure of that. Let's see if we can tip his hand."

"I'll get on it right away, sir. It won't be easy for our people, though. Cuban security has been greatly improved since the Russians moved in. We lost an agent there just four months ago. The reports simply stopped coming in one day."

"I remember that, yes. Do the best you can though, Miss

Hammond. The President himself called me on this yesterday. I assured him it would all come off like clockwork. I'd like to be able to have breakfast with him in a week or so and have him tell me how pleased he was with our work."

"Yes, sir, I understand."

Alma rose quickly to leave and was gone before the director also had a chance to rise.

She closed the door behind her and paused a moment to rest against the hallway wall. As she did, something occurred to her: She hadn't managed to get one sip of the coffee the director had poured for her.

● ● ●

Until the CIA's midnight message arrived, Guadalupe Bentancourt had been very self-assured and happy. It had been a wonderful plan, but somehow the Americans had guessed his strategy, or at least part of it.

He reread the last paragraph of the message:

> We will bring Col. Bupchev *and* another Russian prisoner, Alexi Sokolnikov, with us to the exchange. Sokolnikov is a former Soviet courier whom we arrested in 1978. If you give us Lt. Commander Griffiths, per our agreement, we will give you Col. Bupchev. If you give us anyone else, we will give you Sokolnikov.

Bentancourt crumpled the communique. He snapped his intercom button.

"Have Juanita Martinez come in."

The private office's door opened. Juanita Martinez entered. She stood before Bentancourt's desk.

"We leave for Ho Chi Minh City at dawn. You've studied the file on Parker?"

She nodded.

"And?"

"I can handle him."

"You're sure?"

"I'm sure."

Bentancourt picked up the crumpled piece of paper. He squeezed it once more with anger, then slammed it into the wastebasket.

"I want nothing to go wrong," he said sternly. "Nothing! You understand?"

"I understand."

"You are to win Parker's confidence, make him fall in love with you, and find out all he knows. He must insist on taking you back to America with him. And that's when you will kill him. You're clear on that?"

Again all she said was, "I understand."

• • •

"Who?"

"Parker, sir," repeated Alma Hammond, who had been working all night and looked it. "Sergeant Scott Parker. The Pentagon is sending over his Army 201 personnel file now. Bentancourt sent a response this morning to our message of last night. He's offering Sergeant Parker."

The director offered a half-grin. "So you were right, Miss Hammond. Bentancourt *is* sending us a common dogface. Did his message say anything else?"

"Yes, sir," said Alma, a slight smile forming on her lips. "His regrets, of course, about the 'misplacement' of Commander Griffiths. . . ."

". . . naturally, naturally. . . ."

". . . and the announcement that Sergeant Parker wishes to bring back his fiancee."

"His *what?*" asked the director, partially amused, partially awe-struck.

"His fiancee, sir. According to Bentancourt, Sergeant Parker has fallen madly in love with the woman who was assigned as his Spanish interpreter and assistant. They want to be married here in the States, he says."

"Incredible!" barked the director, who was secretly wondering what it would be like to encounter a warm and love-offering woman after being a P.O.W. for ten years. Under those conditions, Parker might very well think he *was* in love. "Bentancourt really expects us to go for that?"

"Yes, sir," said Alma, still smiling. "In fact, he says that since we are getting Parker *and* the woman, they are worth the trade for Colonel Bupchev."

"Oh no they're not!" boomed the director. "I know what Bentancourt is up to. It's the last phase of his plan. Forget it!"

"Quite the contrary," said Alma. "Although Bentancourt doesn't know it, we'll be getting the better of this trade."

"Heh? Why? Who's Parker to us?"

"It's Parker's fiancee, sir," continued Alma. "Bentancourt says Parker's fiancee is Juanita Martinez."

The director's forehead wrinkled in a frown of thought. "Martinez? Martinez? Who's...wait a minute! You don't mean...?"

Alma smiled triumphantly. "Yes, sir. Juanita Martinez is Parker's supposed fiancee. And now we know why our 'lost agent' hasn't risked reporting to us for the past four months. She obviously must have been promoted to the office of the Ambassador at Large. Apparently she reports directly to Bentancourt, the Ambassador's under secretary. There's no telling how much information about Russo-Cuban relations she's been able to gather for us since getting that assignment. Now all we have to do is get her out."

The director leaned back in his swivel chair, let out a loud guffaw, and then slapped his knee.

"Ha! This is remarkable!" he roared. "We need to get an agent out of Cuba, and Bentancourt wants to hand her to us on a silver platter. Splendid! Simply splendid!" His laughter was genuine. "By the way, who was it who recruited Juanita Martinez?"

Alma stood up, walked casually over to the warmer plate, and poured herself a cup of the director's coffee.

"I did," she said.

• • •

It was a commercial flight, but Guadalupe Bentancourt and his aide, Juanita Martinez, were flying in the first-class section. Outside, the stars were bright over the Pacific Ocean.

"You'll meet Parker in the morning and will start spending every waking moment with him. I suggest you get some sleep on the flight. I've got some reading I want to catch up on."

The girl nodded, turned her head toward the window, leaned back, and closed her eyes.

Bentancourt watched Juanita. She was very pretty, in a peasant sort of way, he surmised. Perhaps after this assignment, once Parker was dead and Juanita was back in Cuba, he could get to know her in a more personal way. He smiled at the speculation.

Before turning off the overhead light, he reached over to Juanita's purse. He checked the metal clip which attached the purse to the carrying strap.

Good. All was well.

The secret listening device was still in place, still looking like an ordinary metal clip.

This was a little extra last-minute idea of his own which he hadn't told Juanita about. After all, one couldn't be too careful—even with one's associates.

CHAPTER SEVEN

Lillian was giddy with excitement over the arrival of the Meads and Rufus. She looked forward to hearing their voices in person again and feeling the warm security of their presence. And she knew that Rufus would love romping through the woods with her, chasing birds in a new kind of freedom unlike any he had known in the city. She could almost hear him barking at the squirrels he would tree and the rabbits he would find racing along the paths and in the underbrush throughout the woods. She could imagine herself throwing sticks down the shoreline, and this time they would come back to her in the mouth of a wonderful little dog.

To help pass the time until she would meet her special guests in front of Old Ed's grocery, Lillian immersed herself in activity. *I can't wait for them to meet Dave,* she thought. In anticipation of their visit, she shopped for groceries one morning and applied a fresh coat of beige paint to her kitchen walls that afternoon. She had remembered her promise to ask Dave about paint for her cabin rooms and had been delighted to learn he had some paint and supplies left over from a previous cleanup job. She didn't have much of a choice of colors (beige, cream, or tan) but there was decidedly enough for her simple needs. Now, as she painted, the fresh aroma filled her cabin.

Since their late-night dinner three days ago, Lillian had spent two more evenings with Dave. She didn't know what happened to Cat Compton, and she was relieved when she went into town or to Dave's cabin and hadn't run into her again.

I'm not avoiding her, Lillian thought. *There are just other people I'd rather encounter on the streets, at cabin doors, and in my life.*

She began to sing the chorus of one of her favorite hymns. She had sung it in Sunday school as a child and during summer sessions of vacation Bible school. It had a light and catchy melody and the words were familiar to her.

> All things bright and beautiful,
> All creatures great and small,
> All things wise and wonderful—
> The Lord God made them all.

She dipped her brush—Dave's brush—into the bucket of paint and began to sing the first verse:

> Each little flower that opens,
> Each little bird that sings—
> He made their glowing colors,
> He made their tiny wings.

Lillian's voice was rich and warm with a happiness that came from deep within her heart. When she failed to remember the words to the other verses, she repeated the chorus. When she tired of singing the chorus, she switched to humming the melody. This was the way Dave Thompson found her when he knocked twice and walked into the cabin. She was seated on the floor, painting and humming in time to the flowing strokes of her brush.

"I could hear you singing almost all the way to my cabin," he said, teasing her. "You've made some progress in the painting, I see. That's quite a masterpiece. A definite improvement over the last coat of paint."

"Hi. It is at that, isn't it? And how do you like my genius in creating facial features?" Lillian asked as she took the brush and made three dots in the wet paint for eyes and a nose and a big swish for a smile. She looked up at him and grinned before she covered the simplistic picture with smooth up-and-down strokes.

"I like the smile, especially," he said. "Is the paint on your nose part of your creativity too? It's most becoming."

"Be nice," Lillian said, pretending to look disgruntled. "You're a guest in my house. Which brings me to the question of why you're here to criticize my work. Don't you have more important things to do?"

"Yes and no. I've been thinking about your friends the Meads.

I thought maybe they could use a little help with luggage or whatever. I make a great bellboy, and I don't require tipping. Would you like me to go with you when you meet them?"

"I'd love it, and they will too! They're supposed to arrive tomorrow night at about 6 o'clock. We're meeting at Old Ed's because I thought that would be easier than trying to give them directions to my cabin."

Lillian told him more about the Meads and how close she was to them, especially since her father had died. She described Pastor Mead as one of those men in life who served not only his church and his God, but also the community. She mentioned that the Meads were nearing retirement age but weren't the type of people who end up sitting in rocking chairs on the front porch watching the world go by. They were healthy and active, warm and loving people, she insisted.

"Yes, I think I'd like to meet these friends of yours," Dave replied, looking at her with thoughtful eyes. "I'll come here and you can drive. They'll know they're in the right place when they see your red car."

Time passed slowly after Dave's visit. Lillian finished her painting, cleaned the brush, aired the cabin, and prepared a breakfast casserole and a pot of spaghetti sauce so she would be ahead with some of the cooking and would be able to spend more time with her company and less time in the kitchen. That evening she read her Bible and went to bed early. The next day she rose early and busied herself with little tasks and duties until Dave arrived at 4 o'clock that afternoon. As they walked to the car together, Lillian offered Dave the keys.

"Drive for me, won't you, Dave?" she asked. "I'm not in the mood." Dave's eyes showed his delight as he took the keys from her and they switched directions and walked to opposite sides of the car.

He handled the car expertly on the winding road into town, and Lillian tried to still her excitement by laying her head against the back of the seat. She had a peaceful view, watching the treetops pass over her head against the backdrop of the clear blue sky.

Suddenly Dave slammed on the brakes.

"Look, Lillian!" he said excitedly. "It's a deer! Isn't it pretty? Not many of them left around here. They're disappearing because of the hunters. I don't see one as often as I'd like to. Last fall a driver killed a doe along this road. It was the saddest thing."

Lillian watched as the flash of white tail vanished into the brush on the opposite side of the road. "It really was beautiful. I've never seen deer this close before."

"I don't think I could ever shoot one," said Dave. "I love wildlife too much."

"It would be a shame to see such glorious animals perish, wouldn't it? I know I hate to see animals suffer. Their eyes are so appealing. Rufus hurt his paw once, and those sad little eyes made me ache for him. I'm such a mush about that dog."

"You didn't tell me you have a dog."

"Didn't I? Wait till you meet Rufus. He's the most vivacious dog in the whole world. I'm so anxious to see him again." Lillian turned and put her hand on Dave's arm. "He's a cocker spaniel and is well-behaved, if I say so myself. Did I really forget to mention Rufus?"

"You've forgotten to mention a lot of things, Lillian," Dave said softly. "But I can be patient. Maybe someday you'll feel better about telling me more about yourself." He took Lillian's hand and held it gingerly in his own while he maneuvered the car easily with his other hand. She looked away, staring at the road ahead of them, but leaving her hand in his.

"I can't yet, Dave. I came to sort out my feelings about myself and my life. I have to do that in my own time."

Dave nodded, not wanting to press the point. He didn't want to persist with the obvious question: Who is this mysterious woman? Why was she so troubled? And why had she taken off her diamond ring? Who was she running from?

They were nearing the first buildings of Compton Gap. Dave parked the car near Ed's grocery, and they got out and went to the drugstore to wait at the soda fountain. They sipped Cherry Cokes and munched on crackers and cheese from little packages.

When Lillian saw the Meads arrive across the street and get out of their car, she was off her stool in a flash, out the door and running across the street before Dave even realized she was gone. He left money on the counter and casually followed her.

The reunion took place in the middle of the deserted street. Lillian hugged and kissed Mom Mead first, then the Pastor. Everyone talked at once.

"Did you have a hard time finding this place? Have you been waiting long? Where is Rufus? Did you bring more clothes for me? Are you hungry? Tired? You made good time—you're early!"

The answers came as quickly as the questions. "No, no, in the car, yes, no. . . ." They all started laughing at once.

"It's so good to see you again!" Lillian managed to say when there was a break in the laughter. "Mom, look at Rufus! He's so excited about seeing me!" The dog was jumping against the car window, barking wildly at all of them. Lillian went to the door and let him out, stooping to wrap her arms around him. He licked her face and she buried her nose into his warm neck.

It was then that Lillian remembered she had left Dave sitting at the counter. She turned to see him standing there, slightly removed from the group, looking shy and intrusive. Lillian got up and went to him. She took his arm and drew him into the group, making introductions and praying silently that they would all like each other. She needn't have been concerned. "Dave Thompson, meet Bea and Charles Mead."

"Do you like chicken broth, young man?" Mom Mead asked after they had been properly introduced. "I brought four gallons along for Lillian. She grew up with my chicken broth. I wouldn't want her to be without it."

Pastor Mead looked at Lillian and winked. Lillian couldn't help but laugh.

"How sweet of you, Mom. I should have known I could count on you to come with some of your famous recipe. But *four* gallons? Will it keep from spoiling?"

"Only if we get it into refrigeration pretty soon. Where is this cabin of yours? Even Rufus is tired from being cooped up in that car all day." The puppy was studying Dave, who had stooped to pet him and scratch an ear with his hand.

Lillian was about to answer Bea when her eye was distracted by a green Jaguar speeding into town. Cat Compton stopped on the other side of the street, got out, and walked over to the group. She smiled as she approached them.

"Dave, I've been looking everywhere for you. I was beginning to think you were out on patrol without your communication receiver."

Lillian glanced at Mom Mead and saw her look at Cat's boots, designer jeans, and monogrammed shirt. A scarf, knotted at her throat, matched her hair and contrasted with the bright yellow blouse.

She's gorgeous, Lillian thought. She looked at Dave and noticed his admiration as he watched Cat walk toward them. *She gets more attractive every time I see her.*

Lillian could feel Pastor Mead's eyes on her as Dave introduced his friend. He sensed Lillian's discomfort and thoughtfully moved next to her and put his arm around her waist. It was as if he was offering strength to fortify her. She accepted it, even leaned against him. She was glad the Meads were with her—not only at this moment, but for several days to come.

Lillian loved this man who was a combination father and grandfather to her. She smiled at him, leaned toward his cheek, and planted a kiss there. She whispered in his ear, "Why so much soup?" He responded with an equally intimate whisper, "I could never say no to a good heart. It's easier to eat soup."

Lillian smiled broadly and turned her attention to Cat, who was talking to Dave. Lillian overheard plans for a Saturday night dinner at the Compton home. The purpose was business, Cat said, before turning her attention to Lillian.

"You can come too, Lillian, provided you bring your own date. Dave's mine that night unless you've laid an official claim to him. You haven't, have you?" She looked at Lillian in an aggressive and defiant manner, ignoring the fact that Dave was showing obvious discomfort.

"Don't be silly, Cat," Lillian said, protesting. "I hardly know Dave. He offered to help, that's all." She paused, remembering her manners. "Thanks for the invitation. I'll let you know. As you can see, I may be occupied with my guests."

"They're included too. You'll come, won't you?" Cat waited for an answer from the Meads, who looked bewildered and uncomfortable. "See you at seven?"

She returned her gaze to Dave. "And I'll see *you* at six," she said intimately. "Okay?"

Dave nodded. "Tell your father thanks for the invitation. And ask whether I need to bring any records for our meeting, will you? He might want to go over the south range renovation expenditures. I don't want to be caught unprepared."

"That's okay. I'll take care of all the preparations. You can be sure everything is under full control."

Cat turned and walked away. Her strides were sensual, yet almost manly in the way they exuded confidence and self-awareness. When she reached the car, she turned and looked back at the group, all still watching from their cluster on the road. She got into the Jaguar and sped off, just as the Meads, Dave, and Lillian were getting into their cars for the trip up the mountain.

Dave led the way in the red Corvette and the Meads followed.

There was silence until Lillian spoke softly. "I can't believe she did that."

Dave shifted from first to second as they drove out of the town's limits.

"I'm sorry, Lillian," he said, surprising her. "Cat is a competitor, and she doesn't like losing an argument or the upper hand in any situation. She'll probably be a heck of a lawyer for that very reason. She won't give up a fight. And she seems to have staked a claim on me." He paused. "I have to go to her father's under the circumstances. He's my boss."

"You don't have to explain anything to me. I meant what I said back there. You've been a good friend to me. But you don't owe me anything, much less an explanation of your behavior. I wouldn't think of asking you not to see her or anyone else in the world. I have no right to do that."

Dave didn't answer at first.

"Do you think I've been seeing so much of you because I've been kind? Really, Lillian? Do you think that's the only reason?"

She looked away from him and turned her head toward the passing trees and brush moving swiftly past the window. She sighed deeply.

"Dave, you're not the only man in my life. You must have seen the ring I wore when I first came to Echo Bluff. You must sense the problems that are complicating my life and the decisions I have to face."

"Sure, I noticed the ring. The glare was blinding. But I also noticed when you took it off. What was I supposed to think? I'll tell you what I did think. I thought we could enjoy each other's company and be friends for at least as long as you're going to be here. And beyond that, who knows?"

"That's fine with me. I'm grateful for all you've done for me. Please don't think I'm not. But . . . but . . . "

"Hey, it's okay. We can leave it at that." Dave abruptly changed the subject and shared his impressions of the Meads and Rufus. They were all she promised, he said, and they obviously would be good company for her at the lake.

Does that mean you won't be company for me anymore? Lillian wondered as they pulled into the parking space in front of her cabin. *Does this conversation mean I won't be seeing you now that the Meads have arrived? And that you'll feel free to see more of Cat Compton?* Lillian looked at Dave's profile and realized that if this man were to go out of her life, she would miss him. She would miss his strength, his kindness, and even his shyness. A lump formed in her throat and refused to be swallowed.

A friend loves at all times, Lillian thought, remembering the Scripture from Proverbs just as Dave parked the car and turned off the ignition. *Am I to lose this friend? Dear God*, she prayed silently, *don't let me regain the company of two of my dearest friends only to find I'm losing this new one. Every true friend is precious to me. I have no family. . . no father, no mother, no brother, and certainly no children. Help me work to keep my friends.*

Lillian heard the car door opposite her open and close. Dave walked around to help her out of the car. She stepped out and touched his sleeve.

"Dave, thanks for going with me," she said. "I hope I'll see you again soon. Maybe you'll come to dinner and share an evening with the four of us before the Meads return to Detroit."

"I'd like that. It sounds like I'll be eating well in the near future," he joked. Lillian didn't laugh.

Pastor and Mom Mead walked up to them.

"Yes, do come," Bea said, having overheard Lillian. "I'll fix you some of my home cooking. You look like you need to put on a few pounds." Dave smiled his thanks, offered his help if they should need it, and then he left.

Lillian showed the Meads to their room and basked in the compliments about her "quaint little cabin on the lake near the woods." Mom Mead said she loved the new kitchen curtains and could tell it was a freshly painted room. Pastor Mead told her he was glad to see her Bible on the table in the living room. He would have been disappointed if she had put it away since she left Detroit.

"So, how long can you stay?" Lillian asked after the spaghetti supper was finished and they were seated in the living room with mugs of steaming coffee. "Tell me your plans so we can make plans of our own. I have lots of new discoveries to share with you."

Lillian was sitting on the sagging couch with Rufus' head in her lap. He already seemed to be at home is this new environment.

"Well, we've got two weeks to spend with you and complete our business," Mom Mead responded.

"Business? What business?" Lillian asked.

"I expected you to ask that," she said, smiling. "You know we're only six months away from retirement, and a new pastor has been hired to replace Charles here. We have mixed feelings. We're ready for a new assignment from the Lord, but we'll miss the work we've known for so many years."

"The church has been sponsoring a project in Appalachia for many years, and we thought we'd like to see what it's like," Pastor Mead continued. "There are so many needy people in that part of the country and the church can do so much good."

"We intend to see if it's something that might provide us with a chance to be active and helpful," added Mom Mead.

"See, Lillian? You aren't the only one searching these days. We're all looking for answers in our own way," said Pastor Mead, adopting his counselor role. "Seek and ye shall find. Well, I guess that's what we intend to do."

Lillian didn't say anything.

"Tell us, Lillian," continued Pastor Mead, "have you been listening to Andrae Crouch lately? And how about the Gaithers? Did you study those motivational messages I sent with you? And what are you reading in the Bible?"

She laughed and tried to answer his questions frankly. This was especially difficult when they asked how she felt about Dave Thompson. She hedged, not knowing the answer because she hadn't clearly analyzed her feelings. She found herself repeating much of the conversation she and Dave had had that afternoon. But she suddenly seemed rather absentminded. The comment about moving to Appalachia had caught her off-guard. This wasn't her night, it appeared. First she seemed to be losing Dave, and now she might also be losing the Meads.

They talked well past midnight. The Meads were still sleeping the next morning when Dave Thompson rapped on the cabin door. Lillian greeted him in whispers but with a grin. She obviously had been wrong in her fears of losing his friendship, she decided. Wasn't he here just hours after leaving her at the door the evening before? Yet he looked so serious.

"Phil Compton radioed me a few minutes ago about getting a message to you."

"But I've never met him."

"Yes, but everyone in town knows we have a radio hookup between the Compton house and this receiver," he explained, patting the portable walkie-talkie on his hip. "Otherwise we'd be completely cut off in case of an emergency. Whenever folks need to reach me or one of the cabin guests, they get hold of Phil."

"Emergency? Is something wrong at home?" Lillian asked, suddenly feeling frightened. Just as suddenly, however, she remembered she had no serious ties with Detroit any longer. Her parents and brother were dead, her relationship with Roderick was foundering, and the only people she really cared for deeply—the Meads—were sleeping soundly down the hall.

"I don't know what it's all about and neither does Phil. He just said that someone telephoned him with a message that you're supposed to call this number right away. He said the caller wouldn't leave a name, but that it sounded urgent."

Roderick? Is it possible he's located me? Lillian reached out for the piece of paper on which Dave had scrawled the telephone number. She glanced at the seven digits and realized with relief that they were neither Roderick's office nor his apartment number.

"It's a local call," offered Dave. "That's the Compton Gap exchange."

She was curious and slightly apprehensive. Why was a simple phone call so wrapped in mystery? She thanked Dave and declined his offer to drive her to Ed's grocery. She knew he had neglected his regular duties the previous afternoon in order to help her welcome the Meads. She didn't want to impose on his friendship again. After all, she was trying desperately to be independent, although she found his support so very comforting.

She scribbled a note to the Meads explaining she had an errand to run in town and inviting them to enjoy the coffee in the pot and the pastry in the refrigerator. "Pardon the store-bought goodies, Mom. Tomorrow's will be better, I promise."

Ed's store was deserted when she arrived. Before slipping into the privacy of the phone booth, Lillian waved at the sleepy-eyed shopkeeper reading yesterday's headlines in *The Nashville Banner.*

"Pine Acres Motel," answered the voice on the other end of the line. Lillian recognized the motel as the one that Madge, the waitress, had mentioned to her the first night she drove into Compton Gap. She paused, uncertain as to whom to ask for.

"Er, hello, this is Lillian Parker. I received a message that someone at this number was trying to reach me. I'm sorry, I don't know..."

"Yes, Miss Parker, I'll connect you with that room."

"*What room?* As Lillian's confusion mounted, so did her apprehension. She was sorry now that she hadn't accepted Dave's offer to accompany her to town.

"Miss Parker, are you alone?" asked a woman's voice.

"Yes. Yes, I am. Why?"

"It's imperative that I speak to you as soon as possible. How quickly can you come to the Pine Acres Motel?"

Lillian began to bristle at the woman's demanding tone. "I have no intention of going anywhere until you tell me who you are and what this is all about. Are you a friend of Catherine Compton?"

"I've never heard of her."

Lillian was relieved, yet more curious than ever. "Give me one good reason why I should drive to some unknown motel to meet someone who won't even identify herself. Are you a bill collector? My father's estate was—"

The woman lowered her voice and said, "It's about your brother Scott."

"Scott?" Lillian gasped, suddenly losing her bravado and feeling very vulnerable. "Scotty's dead...."

"Look, there's a truck stop down the road. If you won't come here to the motel, will you meet me there? It's public; you'll be safe."

Lillian hesitated, but she knew what her answer had to be. "I'll be there in a few minutes."

Although she wasted little time in driving to the truck stop, when she entered the door, she found Alma Hammond already settled into the back corner booth sipping her extra-light coffee. Madge seemed genuinely happy to see Lillian and offered her a stool at the counter so they might visit.

"Over here, Lillian," said Alma, smiling and waving from the corner. "Gosh, it's good to see you again. When the boss told me I was coming to Nashville on business I said, okay, on the condition that I'll have enough time to stop by and have a cup of coffee with Lill. Hey, you look great, kiddo!"

Lillian felt herself being drawn into some kind of drama without the benefit of knowing the script. Bewildered, she walked back to Alma's table.

"Could we have some more coffee, Madge?" asked Alma. "And do you have any pie in your back room?"

Madge nodded and disappeared through swinging kitchen doors. Having succeeded in getting Madge out of hearing range, Alma dropped her friendly demeanor and began speaking in terse whispers.

"Miss Parker, I'm sorry if all this seems very confusing to you. It's essential that no one should suspect who I am or what I'm doing here."

"Well?" challenged Lillian. "Just who *are* you and what *are* you doing here? And what's this nonsense about my brother being alive?"

Alma pulled a card from her handbag and held it for Lillian to see. Alma's photo and the letters "CIA" were the most prominent features. Lillian was genuinely caught unawares.

"It isn't nonsense, Miss Parker. Your brother is alive. With your help and a lot of luck, we may even be able to bring him home soon."

"But how can....? We were told...."

Lillian's face paled and her eyes began to fill with tears.

"Stop it!" ordered Alma Hammond. "The waitress will be back in a minute and we can't let her think we're discussing anything other than old times. Do you understand?"

"Please, could we go someplace where we can talk in private?" begged Lillian, trying to hold her emotions in check.

"Precisely why I wanted you to come to the motel," replied Alma.

Madge returned to the dining room with a tray of coffee and

two slices of banana cream pie. Lillian buried her face into an open napkin and feigned a sudden fit of coughing. She wiped her eyes and regained her composure.

"Madge, how did you know this was our favorite kind? Remember how we always ordered this at the little coffee shop across from the office?" Alma asked Lillian. "I never figured out how you kept so trim and I had to exist on cottage cheese for a week after we splurged on those wild desserts. Those were the days, right?"

Lillian dutifully swallowed some pie and nodded her head as Alma chattered on like a schoolgirl who had just been reunited with her best friend. After what seemed to be endless minutes, the bill was paid and they left. As a parting bit of play-acting, Alma extracted a promise from Lillian to be taken for a drive in her sports car. The smile on Madge's face as she waved them off convinced Alma and Lillian they had succeeded in raising no suspicions.

"Please tell me about Scott," said Lillian as they sped out of town and into the sloping countryside of rural Tennessee. "Where is he?"

"All I can tell you now is that he's alive, but he's in danger. With your help we'll have him home very soon. That's why I'm here."

"I'll do anything, of course."

"First, you must understand that for the time being no one can know that your brother is alive or that I've come to see you. Is that perfectly clear?"

"Yes. Just tell me what it is you want me to do."

Lillian parked the car in a shady grove of trees and watched Alma open her purse and take out a small cassette tape recorder. Alma quickly checked its batteries, and, satisfied it was operational, explained her mission.

"I want you to record a message to Scott. You should first urge him to obey all instructions that he will receive from a contact named Juanita. And, in order for him to do as you ask, you must convince him that you are truly his sister and you have only his best interests at heart."

"A message?" said Lillian. "What's going on? Can't I just go to Scotty and talk to him? You're moving too fast. I'm confused by all this."

"We *have* to move fast. Your brother has been a P.O.W. in Vietnam and now we have a chance to exchange him for someone we are holding. I'm not authorized to tell you anything else. *Please*. Just help us."

Alma handed the recorder to Lillian and pressed the button to activate the tape mechanism. Lillian sat quietly with tears spilling softly from her eyes down her cheeks. She took a deep breath to compose herself and then began to talk into the tiny machine.

"Scotty? This is *me*, Scotty. They're afraid you won't recognize my voice after all this time, but I know you will. If. . .if I sound a little. . .uh. . .blubbery. . .it's because I still can't believe the news you're alive. I want to stop crying. . .but it's hard!. . ."

Alma rolled her hands one over the other as a signal for Lillian to get on with the real message.

"There's someone named Juanita you have to work with, Scotty. I don't know the details, but I know who she's working for. And it's okay, Scotty. So, just do whatever—"

Alma reached over and pushed the "pause" button.

"We still need some verification," she told Lillian.

Lillian turned away a moment in thought. Suddenly her expression changed. She released the "pause" button and began to speak into the recorder again.

"Scotty, they say I have to tell you something that will prove I'm your sister. . .something only the two of us know about. I can only think of one thing right now. Remember when I was just four and Mom was helping us memorize Psalm 23? Back then we lived in Greenbriar Estates and our neighbor was Mrs. O'Mertsey, the Irish cook. Well, I misunderstood the psalm, and instead of 'surely goodness and mercy shall follow me,' I always said, 'Surely good Mrs. O'Mertsey will follow me all the days of my life.' It used to make you and Mom break up laughing. Oh, Scotty, do whatever they ask you to do. Just come home to me. I miss you!"

Lillian began to sob. Alma reached over, snapped off the recorder, and put it back into her purse.

"You may take me back to my car now," she said.

CHAPTER EIGHT

Juanita Martinez knew it had been one of the riskiest things she had ever done in her career as an intelligence agent. But then, with absolutely no other choice open to her, she had felt forced to give it a try.

And, as far as she now knew, it had paid off.

Four months earlier, Juanita had been reassigned to the office of the Ambassador-at-Large for the Cuban government. It had happened quickly. One day while working at her regular job as a translator responsible for monitoring U.S. Coast Guard broadcasts, she had been told to report to the office of Guadalupe Bentancourt, the ambassador's chief of staff.

Upon arriving, she had been shown to an apartment in the Consulate Building. To her surprise, all of her clothes and belongings had been moved to this new location.

"You've been promoted," Bentancourt later explained. "My previous assistant proved inadequate. He's now a cook's helper at a country hospital. I'm...well...rather intolerant of failure. Please remember that. You'll be given a six-month trial at this job. If you succeed, you'll stay here permanently, with all privileges. If you prove inadequate...."

There had been no chance to get word back to the CIA of her new status. Part of her indoctrination required that she spend all of her spare time studying the various aspects of her new job. She was directed to eat, sleep, and work right at the Consulate Building.

Juanita knew that Bentancourt would be watching her every move. She didn't dare try anything in the way of outside communication. She could only hope that someone back in the CIA's Cuban Section would assume that she had "gone to ground" for a good reason. Knowing Alma Hammond as she did, Juanita felt confident she would not be written off as either a traitor or a casualty for at least a few months.

And then the Scott Parker case had developed and Bentancourt had suddenly needed Juanita for a special assignment. And Bentancourt had convinced his superior, the ambassador, to waive Juanita's last two months of probation so that she could be pressed immediately into full-time service.

She had been given a detailed briefing on Parker and then told her assignment. She was to fly to Vietnam with Bentancourt and become Parker's "helper" during the final few days before the prisoner exchange. She was to play on Parker's masculinity, encourage his affection, engender his trust. In the end, she would profess her undying love and devotion for Parker and beg him to take her to America with him.

Parker, being a typical sentimental American male, would feel an instinctive urge to help the poor young girl. He would either marry her or at very least insist that she be allowed to go back to the U.S. with him. Bentancourt, of course, would protest, but then would act as though Parker had the upper hand over him. Juanita would be allowed to go back to America with Parker. She then would arrange for Parker to have an automobile accident or to swallow a mislabeled drug or to bump his head and drown in the bathtub. Juanita would then charter a fishing boat to take her off the coast of Florida, where she would rendezvous with Cuban agents who would bring her home.

In the end, Bentancourt would have Colonel Bupchev and Juanita Martinez both back in Cuba and the Americans would be foiled in their attempts to use Scott Parker for anticommunist propaganda. Such a plan was sure to secure the Ambassador-at-Large position for Bentancourt when the current ambassador retired in two years.

The success of the whole operation rested heavily on the shoulders of Juanita Martinez. And it was only Juanita who knew how terribly, terribly flawed Bentancourt's plan was. Yet, if she could convince Bentancourt that his plan was workable, she would have a chance to save Parker *and* also enable herself to return to America with all the information she had stored in her head about Cuban surveillance operations and Cuban global networks.

It was Bentancourt's analysis of the American male that made his plan doomed to failure. It was both naive and stereotyped. Contrary to Communist propaganda and European-made films, American men *did* think of things besides sex and capitalism—particularly men whose morals and principles *were mentally still back in the last decade.*

Scott Parker's mind was fixed on 1970. He had never heard of such recent developments as "palimony" lawsuits or "trial marriages" or "wife-swapping parties." According to his file, Parker had not been a "free love" advocate or a hippie or a draft card burner back during the 1960's either. Juanita knew that the very idea of a man like Scott Parker meeting and falling in love with a stranger in three or four days was ridiculous.

Scott Parker, Juanita could sense, would be the kind of man who would wait as long as it took to find a genuine woman for himself. And once he found her, he would spend the rest of his life discovering something new and wonderful about her each day. His "lady's" kinship with her true femininity would make her something majestic in his eyes.

Day after day, year after year, he would become more and more aware of what real femininity was. He would never lose his amazement of it, his respect for it, or his need to be near it. And his strong desire to protect this magnificent femininity would in turn develop his genuine masculinity. The more he became aware of the unique gifts of his wife, the more he would become aware of what his corresponding relationship should be. Through this, his role would become clear and his identify and direction obvious.

It was a shame, thought Juanita, that only someone like herself, with a cross-cultural heritage, could see through the mislabelings of American men like Scott Parker. Juanita's American heritage helped her see through the myths which the Latinos like Bentancourt held about American men; Juanita's Latin heritage helped her find a sensitivity in American men that American women were blind to.

And this led to a bitter irony in her current situation. She was being asked by Bentancourt to pretend to be in love with Scott Parker, while in her own heart she knew she would never be so cruel or so false to so noble a man. Instead, she would be direct and honest with Parker and would do all she could to protect him and allow him to return home safely.

And that was how the bitter irony figured in, for Scott Parker was exactly the kind of man whom Juanita could truly have given her love and devotion to.

• • •

The director of the CIA was torn between feelings of rage and anxiety. He had not been this angry or this nervous in ages, and he didn't know which emotion to yield to first.

"She did *what*!" the Director asked demandingly of Alma Hammond.

Alma flinched. Instinctively she moved to the side of the director's office farthest from his coffeepot.

"She . . . well, sir . . . she mailed me a letter," said Alma. "To my home address."

"She *mailed* you a *letter*!"

The director raised his arms and then let them fall and slap against his sides.

"If she was going to be that nonchalant, why didn't she just put through an overseas call to you here at the office? What's with you people!"

"It's not like you think, sir," Alma tried to explain.

The director wasn't listening. He continued his tirade.

"Do you know what position George Bush held before he became Vice President of the United States, Miss Hammond?"

Alma lowered her eyes. "Yes, sir. He was director of the CIA."

"That's right. This job is supposed to be a perfect springboard to a position in the Cabinet or a chance at the White House itself, Miss Hammond. That assumes, of course, that the person in this seat doesn't put the country in peril in the meantime."

Alma nodded, but said nothing.

"So let me ask you this," continued the director. "How is it going to be when the President calls me this afternoon and asks me how the M.I.A. retrieval operation is going? What am I supposed to say, Miss Hammond? Do I say, 'Just fine, sir. In fact, our agent in the field happened to drop us a letter two days ago from Columbia. She's fine, the weather's beautiful, and the operation seems to be progressing nicely'? How do you think the President is going to accept *that* report, Miss Hammond?"

Alma steeled herself, lifted her head, and took two steps toward the director's desk. She stopped, stared seriously at her boss, and then spoke evenly.

"I readily concede, sir, that sending intelligence material by common mail is a violation of every basic rule in espionage," said Alma. "But I'm also sure that the riskiness of such a procedure weighed far heavier on Juanita's mind than on ours. Had this letter been intercepted, *we* would have lost our mission. Juanita, however, would have lost her *life*."

The director was silent a moment.

"The spy business is filled with risks, sir. This current risk just happens to be one of the biggest ones we've experienced in a long time. But under the circumstances, I believe we should be proud of Juanita for taking this daring gamble rather than be upset at her."

Alma moved sideways and sat down. The director followed suit.

The director pulled a slow hand over his face and paused to pinch his eyes at the bridge of his nose. His facial muscles tensed, then slowly relaxed. He sighed.

"All right, Miss Hammond," he said resolutely, "let's quit worrying about the breakdown in procedure and get back to the business at hand. Give me a quick summation and then leave your written report with me, will you? We can argue next month about procedures. For now, let's try to get Parker home."

Alma flipped open the folder she was carrying, scanned the top sheet, and then quickly briefed her superior.

"As you know, sir, Bentancourt has taken Juanita with him back to Vietnam to meet Scott Parker," she began. "To avoid attention, they flew by commercial airlines under false names. They first flew from Cuba to Colombia and then changed airlines there. During that flight, Juanita excused herself to go to the ladies' room. She got the attention of the stewardess, gave her this letter, and asked her to mail it for her. Passengers are always asking special favors of flight attendants, so apparently the stewardess later mailed the letter without ever giving it a second thought."

"Incredible," the director grumbled under his breath.

"According to the letter, Juanita is being watched very closely by Bentancourt. She's been living and working right in the embassy and has had no chance to get a message to us."

The director slightly raised one of his hands. "Can we do away with the melodrama, Miss Hammond? I'm sure your report is filled with specifics. For now just the bottom line, please."

"Yes, sir," said Alma. "It comes down to this: Our earlier assessment of the trumped-up love affair between Parker and Juanita was indeed a plan devised by Bentancourt as a way of eliminating Parker after the trade."

"The credit for that is yours," conceded the director.

Alma shrugged off the compliment and proceeded quickly.

"Juanita, however, is hoping to convince Parker to play out the charade. She'll need help from us, though. She wants a tape recording to be made of Parker's sister telling him that Juanita is on our side. I took the liberty of procuring that tape yesterday."

"You've met Parker's sister?"

"Yes, sir," said Alma. "Her cancelled checks and credit card purchases helped me locate her. She left Detroit for a short vacation in the Smoky Mountains. She has a cabin in a rural town in Tennessee. Compton Gap, actually."

The director frowned. "What about the woman?"

"We'll have no problem from her, I assure you. She's promised her silence and her cooperation. She made a good tape. She's intelligent and dependable. Besides, in her own way she has as much at stake in this as we do."

The director nodded agreement. "You did right. Good work. Now, about Juanita . . . . ?"

Alma continued, "She included a schedule of the return flight that she and Bentancourt and Parker will be taking back to Cuba. We are to have the tape on board that flight, hidden at the bottom of the tissue dispenser in the forward rest room."

"They're bringing Parker back on a commercial flight?" interrupted the director, showing amazement.

"Yes, sir. He'll be mildly sedated, and Bentancourt will have four plainclothes guards from his staff also on board the flight in case any trouble should arise. Bentancourt is afraid that a military flight might be intercepted somewhere over the Pacific."

The director grimaced. "Daring, but clever," he admitted. "You've got to give the devil his due."

Alma stood and placed the report on the director's desk. More as a vow than as a remark, she responded, "*No, I don't*, sir. This is one time Senor Bentancourt is going to have his plans foiled. I intend to see to that personally."

• • •

If Juanita had been wary of the watchful eyes of Guadalupe Bentancourt before leaving Cuba, that wariness had now been increased to near paranoia. She now had proof that her every move was being monitored.

The proof had come to her with stunning casualness. While making the transoceanic flight with Bentancourt, their plane had been forced to make an unscheduled stop in French Polynesia to check a warning light which had started to flash on the pilot's panel. The plane touched down in Tahiti so that the panel could be serviced.

All passengers were asked to leave the plane and wait in the airport lobby. Naturally, Bentancourt was right at Juanita's side the whole time. They drank coffee and read magazines, but talked very little.

When it was time to board the plane and resume the flight, Bentancourt grabbed their totebags and hurriedly led the way. As is routine at all airports, the passengers were made to walk through a scanning field. Bentancourt threw their bags on the conveyor belt for the X-ray machine and then walked through the upright scanner. No bells or alarms went off.

Juanita then put her purse on the conveyor belt and waited for her turn to walk through the upright scanner. Out of boredom, she glanced at the X-ray machine's picture of her purse. What she saw made her heart skip a beat, then race madly.

There on the strap of her purse, showing beneath a plastic-covered clasp, was a small metal transmitter with two exposed wires attached to it. Juanita's purse had been "bugged."

She was stunned by this discovery. Instantly she looked at Bentancourt. He was not looking back at her, but was instead lifting their totebags from the conveyor belt.

The bored X-ray machine operator, who only looked for guns and explosives anyway, did not seem to notice the small transmitter. Juanita calmed herself and tried to show no sign of emotion. She proceeded through the upright scanner and followed Bentancourt back aboard the airplane.

She was still nervous when they returned to their seats.

Bentancourt suddenly turned to her and said, "I know what happened back there."

Juanita's stomach knotted. A lump formed in her throat. She couldn't speak.

Bentancourt pointed toward the front of the airplane. "A light," he said. "I overheard a stewardess say some kind of light was flashing on the control panel. It's fixed now, though."

Juanita offered a weak smile. Her heart was still pounding hard. "Hmmm," was all she could say.

Bentancourt picked up another magazine. "Sometimes I think we have too many gadgets for our own good," he said, turning to glance at the pages.

Unconsciously Juanita looked at her purse on the floor.

"I agree," she said softly. "Too many gadgets."

• • •

Alma Hammond lived in a modestly furnished but spacious apartment in Virginia. It was usually late when she arrived home, and tonight was no exception. She felt tired and knew she needed sleep, but she also knew that her mind was too crowded with thoughts of the M.I.A. operation to allow her to relax. Tonight she was faced with an awesome problem.

She went to the kitchen and made herself a cup of spice tea. She took it into the living room and sat down. After a moment she got up, pulled open the drapes, and turned off the lights. It was time to think, and darkness offset by moonlight made for a better "thinking atmosphere."

Alma kicked off her shoes and propped her feet on a footrest. She took a full swallow of the warm tea and then set the cup aside. She folded her hands and closed her eyes.

She sat alone in the quietude for a few minutes, then said aloud, "Mene, mene, tekel, upharsin."

She wasn't sure why she suddenly felt the urge to utter these four cryptic words aloud, but she *did* know why she had thought of them.

Back during her days of training to become an intelligence agent, she had been required to take a six-month course on code-breaking. On the first day of class, her instructor, Lieutenant

Colonel Woods, had given her one of the most valuable lessons of her life.

Woods stood at the head of the class that first day and said, "Mene, mene, tekel, upharsin."

When no one is class responded, Woods wrote the four words on the blackboard.

"This, ladies and gentlemen, is the handwriting on the wall," he announced. "And I'm speaking literally, not figuratively. What you see here is the oldest known secret code ever developed. It had all the basic elements of any secret code: It was developed by someone who knew its meaning; it was used to convey an important message; and it was easily understood by the agent who knew how to break it."

Then, to everyone's surprise, Woods took a Bible out of his briefcase and read the fifth chapter of the book of Daniel aloud to the class. It told the baffling story of how the hand of God appeared before King Belshazzar and literally wrote the words *mene, mene, tekel, upharsin* on an internal wall of the king's palace. None of the king's advisers, astrologers, or statesmen could interpret the four words.

Belshazzar offered great rewards for anyone who could decipher the bizarre writings. Finally, at his wife's suggestion, the king sent for the captive Jewish prince Daniel. He offered Daniel great rewards if he could interpret the strange message.

Daniel declined the rewards and instead spent several minutes lecturing the king about his backslidden and blasphemous life. He pointed out to the king his numerous sins and evil ways and reminded him that his predecessor, Nebuchadnezzar, had led a similar life and had wound up both poor and insane.

Finally Daniel broke the code. He told the king that the message was that God had watched him, judged him, and sentenced him. Belshazzar was to die and have his kingdom forfeited to his enemies, the Medes and Persians. And, shortly thereafter, that's exactly what happened.

"The king was not observant," emphasized Lieutenant Colonel Woods. "If he had sat down and logically assimilated all that he was aware of, he could have cracked the code himself. The history of Nebuchadnezzar's life and its outcome should have been an obvious parallel to Belshazzar's own life. The mystical dream of Nebuchadnezzar which proved to be a warning from

God should have been an obvious parallel to the mysterious writing on Belshazzar's wall.

"If Belshazzar had just taken the time to *think* intensely about his situation and to *analyze* his circumstances, he could have cracked the code himself. Let this be a lesson to you. Whenever you are faced with a great problem, remember to assimilate all that you know about the situation, then take time to carefully analyze and think through the problem. There is always an answer. You just need to work hard at discovering it."

Alma repeated that phrase to herself now: *There is always an answer.*

She reached again for her tea and took a sip. It had gone cold.

"Yes, always an answer to every problem," she softly said to herself. "But what happens when the answer is a wretched, distasteful, sickening alternative?"

She knew the answer to that. *You do it anyway.* At least, that would be what her superiors would say to her. *But even this time?*

Her problem tonight was a big one, yet its answer was simple. In its very simplicity, however, it was wretched. *What a merry-go-round!* thought Alma.

It had struck her earlier that afternoon that in the excitement of trying to get Scott Parker home, they had let emotion give way to logic. True, it would be wonderful to be able to free Parker and bring him home safely, and no one would deny that the U.S. would gain global public support for its M.I.A. efforts if Parker told his story.

Nevertheless, of far greater importance was the fact that Juanita Martinez had become an aide to the staff director of the Ambassador-at-Large of Cuba. Now *that* truly *was* something to get excited about. The hoopla over Parker would be lost and forgotten after a few weeks, but the information on Cuban and Russian strategies which Juanita could have access to would prove to be useful for years.

No, thought Alma, *we can't be blinded by emotion or the glory of short-run returns. Juanita will have to return to Cuba. . . and Parker, as expected, will have to die.*

She picked up the telephone and dialed the agency.

"Hello, this is Hammond of Cuban Section. Please schedule me for an 8 A.M. appointment with the director. Priority One, please. Thank you."

• • •

The flight landed in Tan San Nhut airport, three miles southwest of Ho Chi Minh City. The "airport" was actually nothing more than a series of renovated hangars which had been built by the U.S. Army Corps of Engineers in 1964 and had been left behind in 1973.

The landing strip consisted of wide, strong, and well-supported runways of concrete poured over steel-mesh support frames. They had been built to withstand the pressures of heavy U.S. bombers carrying full payloads. But time, weather, and an occasional crash landing had pocked and scarred the great runways so that, strong though they were, they were now in need of some patching, sealing, and leveling. Twice after touching down, the pilot had to swerve sharply to avoid ramming a tire into a pothole.

"I felt safer in the air than I do on the ground," Juanita said to Bentancourt as the plane lurched widely to one side to avoid a rut.

Bentancourt offered a sardonic grin. "Welcome to Vietnam," he said through clenched teeth.

Within minutes the plane rolled to a stop. Juanita breathed a sigh of relief. She turned to say something to Bentancourt, but his face was turned away from her. He was staring fixedly through the opposite window at something visible outside the plane.

"Something's wrong," Bentancourt said in low tones. "Stick close to me. We're going to be the first ones off."

He left his seat and Juanita followed as quickly as she could.

Bentancourt raced down the portable stairwell. He was met by a group of six men, all of Spanish origin. Juanita recognized one to be the Cuban Ambassador to Vietnam. She assumed that the others were either his aides or some special men whom Bentancourt had brought with him on his earlier visits. Everyone seemed to be trying to talk at once. Juanita approached the group with hesitancy. Bentancourt noticed her and waved her toward a nearby open-topped jeep. In a moment Bentancourt joined her. They sat in the back.

A driver got into the front and drove them away at breakneck speed.

"What is it? What's happened?" Juanita asked Bentancourt.

"It's Parker," he answered, leaning closer to her ear. The jeep was in need of a new muffler and its motor needed a tune-up. The front and back noises from the jeep made conversation difficult.

"Has he escaped?" Juanita asked.

"No. It's worse. He's fallen ill. The doctors think his digestive system may not have been ready for all the foods we pushed at him. He has stomach cramps and a fever, and he's complaining of severe headaches. He needs to get to a hospital."

Unconsciously Juanita bit her lip. Although it was a hot and muggy tropical day, her hands suddenly felt very cold. *Why couldn't anything ever go according to plan?*, she wondered in frustration.

"And there's more," said Bentancourt. "There's a nationwide manhunt on for Parker. The Chinese aren't sure who helped him escape, but they've figured out that it had to be someone on the inside. They started a dragnet in the north last week. They're working their way south. They'll be here in three days."

"Can they search your embassy?"

Bentancourt gave a look which said more than words could. Obviously they could do whatever they wanted to do in their own country. Diplomatic immunity, apparently, was for the "other guys" to observe.

"What are you going to do?" asked Juanita.

"We'll have to keep to our schedule. Parker has to go back to Cuba with us in two days, whether he's better or not. Have you ever done any nursing?"

Juanita looked puzzled. "Nursing? What? You expect me to take care of Parker?"

"The doctors will take care of Parker," said Bentancourt. "But I want you at his bedside as much as possible. Who knows? This relapse may work in our favor. If he's weak, he'll be less resistant to your advances. Spoon-feed him. Give him his medicine. Fluff his pillow. Make him appreciate having you around."

"But you said he needed to be in a hospital," she said. "What if he goes into a coma or starts to hemorrhage or something?"

"I don't think that's likely. But even so, we'll have to risk it. I'm going to have an ambulance plane wait for us in Sydney, Australia, on our return flight. The doctors and guards can go on it with Parker. You and I will have to continue on the commercial flight in order not to cause any more suspicions than necessary. I'll alert the hospital in Havana to expect Parker."

Juanita shook her head in agreement.

"I'm impressed," she said. "You're a fast thinker."

"When a life is hanging in the balance, one has no choice but to think fast."

Juanita reached over and squeezed Bentancourt's arm. "I'm sure Parker will be all right."

"*Parker?*" said Bentancourt, almost amused. "I was referring to *myself.*"

• • •

The director of the CIA was drumming his fingers on his desk and staring across at Alma. He seemed at a loss for words.

It was Alma who broke the silence. "The President is a pragmatist, sir. He'll understand. I'm sure he will."

"Pragmatist?" questioned the director. "Perhaps he is. But he's also a politician who is trailing in the latest Gallup Poll. Bringing Parker home was a publicity plum he has been counting heavily on. For me to suggest that we . . . that we put Parker on ice . . . well. . . ."

"If I may, sir?" Alma said as she extracted a typed piece of paper from a folder she was holding. "I spent the night wrestling with this problem. I've come up with a procedure which I'd like to suggest for this . . . circumstance."

She extended the paper, but the director waved it away. He stood up, walked to the coffeepot, and poured himself a cup.

"Highlight it for me," he said, nodding at the paper Alma still held.

Alma waited to see if she was going to be offered a cup of coffee too. When no mention was made of it, she cleared her throat and looked down at the page.

"Just a four-step plan, basically speaking, sir," she began. "First, we make the exchange and bring Sergeant Parker and Juanita

Martinez back to the States. Second, we debrief Juanita. Third, we have her get a report back to Bentancourt that she has killed Parker. And fourth, we hide Parker for the next year, nurse him back to health, allow him gradually to reacclimatize himself to America, and give him plenty of time to tell us all he remembers about his captivity. Simultaneously, we send Juanita back to Cuba, allow her to use her successful completion of the Parker assassination to enhance her standing at the embassy, and we direct her to obtain as much secret information as possible."

"Ultimate objective?" pressed the director.

"Twofold," replied Alma. "To have Juanita Martinez spend the next year procuring data about Russo-Cuban activities in our region, and also to give us time to adequately prepare Sergeant Parker for his public statement about his captivity."

"Time schedule, Miss Hammond? Time schedule?"

"Ten months, sir. We'll get Juanita Martinez back to the States in the spring. By then the embassy will be allowing her some limited travel privileges. One day she'll simply go off on courier duty to someplace in Central America and that's the last Bentancourt will ever see of her."

"Hmmm," grunted the director. "And shortly thereafter it'll probably be the last *anyone* will ever see of Senor Bentancourt, unless I miss my guess."

Alma shrugged her shoulders slightly, as though to imply that getting her agent back was the only thing she was concentrating on.

"Once Juanita Martinez is back in Washington, we can present Sergeant Parker to the press," summarized Alma. "He'll be ready for the ordeal by then. It should make a busy summer for our friends at the FBI and the Secret Service, eh?"

The director returned Alma's small smile. "A busy summer?" he mused. "Yes . . . yes, a busy summer indeed. And a busy summer right before a presidential election in the fall, at that."

Alma said nothing. No comment was necessary.

The director walked to his desk and buzzed the intercom.

"Please call the White House, Mrs. Benson. Arrange an appointment for me to see the President, alone, today. Tell his aide it's in regard to Operation Homing Pigeon."

The Director drew in a large lungful of air and released it slowly. His day was starting to look better.

"Yes," he said. "I can see that you're right, Miss Hammond. Parker must die—at least for the time being. Splendid assessment! Now let's get down to planning the specifics of how I should present it to the President."

He walked back toward the coffeepot. "I'm sorry," he said, turning back, "I've forgotten: Do you use sugar or not?"

CHAPTER NINE

Bea Mead pushed the last bite of sausage around her plate with her fork, eyed it with indecision, then sighed loudly to draw attention to the fact that she wasn't going to eat the final morsel.

"Maybe I'm sick," she said hopefully. "Do I look pale? A little flushed?"

"Sorry, Mom, you look absolutely terrific," replied Lillian. "In fact, the Tennessee Chamber of Commerce should recruit you as an advertisement for what mountain air can do for a person. Your friends in Detroit are going to think you discovered the fountain of youth in Compton Gap. We may be overrun with tourists."

"That healthy, huh?"

"That healthy, Mom."

"Still, I could be coming down with something," Bea insisted "Maybe I shouldn't go to the dinner party tonight. I'd hate to pass along a virus to Kitty Compton's guests."

"It's *Cat* Compton, and I don't think you have to worry." Lillian lightly hugged Bea Mead and refilled their cups with coffee. "I know you don't want to go to the Compton's house. Neither do I. But Cat really has us on the spot. She knows very well that we have no other obligations. What I can't understand is why she's so insistent that we attend her little get-together. I'd think she'd rather have Dave to herself."

Lillian hadn't seen Dave Thompson since the morning he had told her she was to call the Pine Acres Motel. She missed him, but realized she might be tempted to recount Alma Hammond's visit and confide the news of her brother's return if Dave asked about the mysterious radio message. Even if she succeeded in following Alma's directive to tell no one, Lillian was certain her preoccupation would be obvious to Dave. It had been difficult enough not to share the information with the Meads; but whenever tempted, she reminded herself that the shock of the news and the fear for Scott's safety might be too much of a burden on the elderly couple. Why should they suffer as she was suffering? If what Alma said was true and Scott was to have his freedom soon, they would have a lifetime to rejoice. If her brother's escape failed, the Meads need never know. They had mourned his death once and should be spared the pain a second time.

"Lillian? A penny for your thoughts—although my guess is they're not worth a nickel if you're brooding about this confounded dinner party," Pastor Mead said, entering the warm kitchen to find his wife and Lillian with chins propped dejectedly on their hands. "Has it occurred to you two girls that we just *might* have an enjoyable time at the Comptons tonight? I, for one, am looking forward to getting to know Dave Thompson better. Seems like a delightful young man."

His gentle scolding had little effect, so he quickly took a different tack. He'd cheer them into a better humor, he decided.

"Beautiful day, isn't it?" He rubbed his hands together as if in anticipation of what the hours ahead might bring. "If I hadn't slept so late I'd suggest a long hike before breakfast." He noticed the dishes carefully stacked in the sink. "But you've already eaten, I see. All right, how about a long hike *after* breakfast? Lillian? Bea? Yes, Rufus, you're included too, of course."

Mom Mead declined, insisting that if she absolutely had to go to the Compton dinner party she needed to wash her hair and press the wrinkles from her church dress. Lillian, too, was tempted to make her excuses, but thought better of it when she saw the enthusiasm on Pastor Mead's kindly face. She couldn't disappoint him, although she very much wanted to retreat to her bedroom, where she could be alone with her thoughts. The strain of knowing that her brother was in danger was wearing on her. If only she could share her burden with someone!

"Button up," fussed Mom Mead. "I wouldn't be surprised if we have a frost this week. Wear your quilted jacket, Lillian. Wait a minute, Charles, I'm going to get your scarf out of the valise."

Lillian and Pastor Mead good-naturedly allowed Bea to wind mufflers around their necks and tuck gloves in their pockets. When they finally emerged from the cabin, Pastor Mead winked at Lillian and both headed for her car. Safely out of viewing distance of the lodge, they stuffed the extra clothing into the trunk, then walked down the slope toward the lake, feeling the warmth of the Indian summer sun on their faces. Rufus led the way, making frequent detours into the brush in pursuit of an occasional rabbit. When they reached the shore, Pastor Mead ambled over to the discarded rowboat, bottom-side-up, that was wedged between two rocks.

"Sit down, Lillian."

She obeyed, although her intuition told her that a serious talk was at hand and that she should avoid it at all costs. She was unsure of her ability to cope with probing questions. It would be so comforting to confess her fears about Scott to this warm and understanding man. She needed his counsel and his care. She wanted to cry into his big linen handkerchief, as she had when her father had died and the business, which had seemed so solid, suddenly had faltered under the assault of creditors and critics.

"I'd like to ask what's wrong, Lillian, but I have a feeling you wouldn't tell me."

"What makes you think something is—"

Pastor Mead lifted his left hand to silence her. "My dear, you've been so preoccupied since the first morning of our visit. Remember? Bea and I got up that day and found a note saying something about an errand you had to run in town. When you finally returned, you had been crying—at least that's what Bea decided from the look of your eyes—and you seemed nervous. Worried, perhaps. Since then it's been as if you've only been half with us most of the time."

"But we've had fun! We've laughed and—"

"Yes, but you've joked *too* much, and laughed *too* loud. I keep wondering what you're trying to cover up with all this jocularity. But I won't press you; after all, you're a Parker."

"What do you mean?"

"I'm reminded of your father, just before he died. I had known for some time that he was deeply troubled, but he never would confide in me. He was carrying a terrible load, Lillian, but he refused to share it. Of course, if he had told me about the financial problems at Michigan Technologies I couldn't have helped him in a business sense, but perhaps I might have been able to help him cope with his fears and disappointments. He kept saying that he was strong, that he was a Parker, that he'd find a way out by himself. I finally gave him the only advice I could, under the circumstances. It's the same advice I'm going to give you right now."

"And what is it?"

"That it's not a sign of weakness to need help, Lillian. In fact, it's a sign of strength to recognize and admit that you can't do everything alone... that you need guidance, support, and love from other people. Even if you can't share your problems with me, there's Someone else always willing to listen. Your father believed that at the end, but he couldn't bring himself to let go and allow the Lord to bear his burden. He was a Parker all right, and he was strong, but without the Lord he wasn't strong enough. Don't make the same mistake he did. In many ways you're stronger than your father was, but you're not strong enough. No one is."

Lillian didn't try to halt the tears filling her eyes, but instead reached out her hand for Pastor Mead's handkerchief. He smiled as he watched her bury her face in the expansive square of fabric.

"They'll never be replaced by Kleenex, will they?"

"What?" asked Lillian through sniffles.

"Ministerial handkerchiefs."

They laughed, and Lillian scooted over toward Pastor Mead, who gave her a bear hug. "Even though you're much younger, your faith is more mature than your father's," said Pastor Mead. "Still, you have to use it every day for it to grow. Learn to trust the Lord with all your troubles; turn your problems—big ones and little ones—over to Him. Talk to Him like a friend, because that's what He is."

"Even when my problem is as silly as not wanting to go to a dinner party?"

"I think it's much more than that," Pastor Mead said seriously.

"Yes. You're right, of course," she replied. "I wish I could tell you about it, but I promised someone I wouldn't discuss it. I have to keep my word."

"I understand, but I hope you didn't promise not to pray about it."

Lillian smiled and squeezed Pastor Mead's hand. "You go back to the cabin," she suggested. "I think I'd like to stay here for a few minutes." He nodded, slipped down from the old boat, and started up the hill.

"Don't forget to stop by and get your muffler and gloves out of the trunk," teased Lillian. "You never know when that frost is going to strike."

When he reached the top of the hill, he glanced down at her as she sat motionless on the boat, her head bent over clasped hands. She looked so small against the broad sweep of sandy shore, the stately pine trees that reached skyward, and the blue-black lake that lapped the rocks. *Yes, she's small. . . even fragile*, he thought, *but she's strong. She's a Parker, isn't she?*

.   •   •   •

Hattie Compton surveyed the long, linen-draped banquet table and shook her head in bewilderment. As usual, she didn't understand. If Cat had only explained to her the purpose of the dinner party, the whole ugly scene might have been avoided. But no, Cat had preferred to share her plans with her father and let him forward instructions to Hattie. Something had been lost in the translation. Phil Compton merely told Hattie that their daughter had invited a few friends for dinner. The guest list included Dave Thompson, a minister and his wife, and some tourist from Detroit. "Haviland china for a forest ranger and a minister?" sputtered Hattie, running her fingers lovingly over the bright surface of a dinner plate. "Ridiculous!" But Cat had staged one of her fiery tantrums and Phil had acquiesced. The fragile porcelain, never used in the ten years since it was delivered to the Compton home, was carefully unwrapped and arranged between place settings of Hattie's cherished sterling silver flatward. "Cat can whine and Phil can roar," pledged Hattie Compton, "But the Waterford crystal stays in the attic. I can be pushed only *so far!*"

Depending upon their importance, Compton dinner guests had always been carefully categorized by Hattie. Social obligations to local residents were fulfilled during the picnic season, when barbecued beef could be served on paper plates and guests could be encouraged to enjoy the grounds rather than the interior of the Compton compound. Out-of-town business associates were accorded more attention and were elevated to Lenox china status by Hattie. Baked ham and sweet potatoes were the cornerstones of this menu, with minted iced tea served from silver-plated pitchers on the back veranda.

But Haviland! Hattie bristled to herself. The delicate dishes had been purchased when the Comptons had taken their grand tour of Europe and had "done" France in a day and a half. The set, service for 20, had been chosen on the basis of price alone. After all, only the best—and the most expensive—would do. It had been stored in the attic, next to the crates of Waterford, which had been acquired during the Comptons' afternoon in Ireland. Both the porcelain and the crystal had been earmarked for that very special dinner party when Compton Gap's first family would entertain the governor of Tennessee (or at least the lieutenant governor, Hattie often qualified). The fact that the invitation, though often extended, had never been accepted didn't discourage her. An election year was approaching, and she assured herself that surely *this* year the campaign trail would wind through the mountains—especially if Buford Hensley decided to run.

"It looks lovely, Mommy," purred Cat, assessing the table from the doorway. "But call the florist and order a larger centerpiece. Roses this time, *not* carnations." Her voice had an authoritative edge to it, but her smile was sugary sweet.

Hattie was amazed at her daughter's good humor. An hour earlier Cat had shrieked orders to replace the Lenox with the Haviland, to polish the good silver, and to add placecards, even though only seven people were invited for dinner. *Why all the fuss?* Hattie wondered.

"We've added another guest," said Cat offhandedly as she moved Hattie's treasured dishes aside to make room for yet another setting. Then she carefully folded the enscribed, tent-like placecards beside the iced tea glasses.

"Mother, you forgot the crystal!" scolded Cat. "I want the *Waterford* crystal, do you understand?"

All of Hattie's cool resolution wilted under Cat's blazing glare. "Yes, Dear."

●   ●   ●

Lillian had tried on three different outfits before deciding to wear the long patchwork skirt that Bea Mead had sent her from Detroit. She had wanted to buy a new dress, partly because Dave Thompson already had seen the patchwork skirt and partly because she needed a boost to her lagging confidence. Wearing something new would have helped, but Compton Gap's selection of women's wear looked as though Dan'l and Davy's wives still were the trendsetters. Besides, Lillian knew that Bea would be pleased to see that her gift had been appreciated.

"Ah, look at my girls," exclaimed Pastor Mead as he walked into the living room dressed in his best black suit and smelling of freshly dabbed after-shave lotion. "I must be in heaven because I'm in the presence of two angels. You're never looked prettier, Bea; and Lillian...you could pass for a princess."

Lillian executed a quick pirouette. "On a scale of one to ten, how do I rank?"

"Hmmmmm," Pastor Mead said thoughtfully. "At least an eleven-and-a-half."

They wrapped themselves in winter coats and hurried out to the car for the trip into town. Even Bea seemed determined to make the best of the evening, although she muttered once that Rufus, left sleeping by the stove had the right idea.

"I still think I may have a slight fever..." she ventured.

"Mom!"

"And I coughed once in the shower...."

Dave Thompson was waiting for them when they drove through the wrought-iron gates and up to the antebellum mansion. He immediately put them at ease by warmly shaking Pastor Mead's hand and stretching his arms lightly around the waists of Lillian and Bea to guide them between the pillars and into the spacious foyer. Lillian stifled a gasp when she noticed the decor, an inharmonious mix of several styles and eras. A French provincial credenza, laden with gold-sprayed remnants of Hattie Compton's ceramic period, jockeyed for space with a brooding Victorian grandfather clock. A Greek statue with arms bobbed at the biceps peeked out from an overgrowth of artificial greenery in the corner. Pastor Mead eyed the figure with dismay.

"He looks like an embarrassed Adam *after* he ate the apple," whispered the pastor to Lillian as they were squired into an equally ornate parlor.

Phil Compton jumped to his feet and greeted each guest with a bone-crushing handshake. Hattie Compton assessed them from the couch and then politely urged them, "Do sit down, please." It wasn't until everyone had settled into chairs and had been offered tomato juice that Cat chose to make her entrance. The impact of her breathtaking appearance was overshadowed only by the presence of her companion. Cat stood poised in the wide archway, her wild beauty enhanced by the emerald green kimono she wore, with her left arm laced loosely through the arm of her escort.

"Roderick!"

Although Lillian breathed the name in a voice barely audible to the group, everyone's eyes turned toward her. She went immediately pale, both hands gripping the juice glass to prevent it from spilling. Pastor Mead hurried to her side, removed the glass from her grasp, and deposited it in one of Hattie's ceramic candy dishes.

"Roderick, what are you doing here?" whispered Lillian.

"Aren't you even going to kiss her hello?" prodded Cat playfully. Roderick sauntered over to Lillian's chair, stretched out both hands, drew her to a standing position, and then kissed her squarely on the lips. She drew back in embarrassment.

"I don't understand," she said. "How did you find me? Why didn't you tell me you were coming?"

"Don't you like our surprise?" pouted Cat with mock disappointment. "Daddy, ring for champagne. This is supposed to be a celebration!" She strode confidently into the room, taking full control of the uncomfortable situation. "Roderick, I don't believe you've met Dave Thompson, Lillian's mountain mentor. Dave, this is Lillian's fiance, Roderick Davis from Detroit." She paused, allowing a trace of irritability to surface. "Daddy, the champagne, *please.*"

She wheeled around, obviously enjoying the chaos she was creating. "Roderick, these are my parents—Mommy, Daddy, say hello to Roderick Davis—and, of course, you know Pastor Miller and his wife."

"Well, I'm not sure about a Pastor *Miller,*" corrected Roderick, "but I certainly know Pastor and Mrs. Mead."

"Oh, I'm terribly sorry," apologized Cat. Bea smiled forgivingly. "That's perfectly all right, Kitty."

The champagne arrived, and Phil Compton popped the cork with great flourish. The Meads, Dave Thompson, and Lillian declined the drink, but obligingly lifted juice glasses for Cat's toast.

"To the reunion of new friends and old lovers." She winked, then sipped the bubbly liquid. Roderick, Hattie, and Phil followed suit.

The maid arrived to announce dinner, and Hattie ceremoniously rose to lead the way into the candlelit dining room. Since the party was divided equally among four men and four women, the guests lined up couple by couple behind their hostess. Rather than join his wife, Phil Compton purposely lagged to the back of the group, sought out Lillian, and gently steered her to one side.

"My dear, I have no idea what my daughter is trying to accomplish by this little drama, but you don't appear to be enjoying the performance. Would you like to use my den to compose yourself? Surely you and your fiance would prefer some privacy," he said.

Lillian was grateful for this concern and was surprised to find that she liked Cat's father. Far from being the overbearing local power broker she had expected, he seemed to be a kind, hospitable gentleman who probably enjoyed trekking through his considerable stretches of woods rather than overseeing the property from a plush suite of offices.

"I think you'd find my den more comfortable," said Phil Compton. Then he lowered his voice: "I didn't let Hattie decorate it."

Lillian was tempted by the promise of solitude, but the thought of being alone with Roderick frightened her. She wasn't ready to revive their relationship. She was as doubtful of his feelings toward her as she was of her feelings for him. She only knew that his presence upset her, and his kiss had repelled her. No, she was quite certain that she didn't want to face him without the presence and support of the Meads.

"Thank you, Mr. . . . er. . . Phil. There will be plenty of time for Roderick and me to talk later. I'm fine now, really. Why don't we join the others?" She gratefully linked her arm through his and allowed him to lead her into the dining room, where the other guests were seated according to Cat's placecard arrangement. She slipped into her designated chair between Roderick and Hattie Compton.

"To be honest, Pastor Mead, we don't usually say grace before dinner," said Phil apologetically. "But if you'd like to lead us. . . ."

Hattie Compton clapped her hands loudly to bring a maid

scurrying from the kitchen. "How many times must I tell you it's *red* wine with venison," she chided. "Now take this back and bring the red." She pierced a large slab of meat with her fork and passed the platter to Pastor Mead, who mumbled a quick "Amen" and accepted it.

"Isn't this romantic?" asked Cat. "I feel just like Cupid. Lillian, tell us about how you and Roderick met. I know you were director of sales at Michigan Technologies when your dad was president; and I know Roderick was your father's chief counsel. But when did business turn to pleasure?"

Dave Thompson stared at Lillian in disbelief. "Lillian, is all this true?"

She nodded her head slowly, but didn't have a chance to explain.

"Of course it's true," declared Cat. "Lillian is quite a celebrity in industrial circles. In fact, she should have succeeded her father at Michigan Technologies, but there was some sort of ugly little scandal. I'm sure your father was innocent, Lillian. What a shame he never was able to clear his name."

Pastor Mead, infuriated by the underhanded attack on his young friend, began to speak in her defense but was stopped when Lillian put one finger to her lips in a plea for silence. Roderick, however, did not feel bound to obey her wish.

"It was love at first sight, if you'll pardon an old cliche," he said. "Lillian always had the ability to walk into a boardroom and absolutely take charge without losing a bit of her femininity. I've seen her sway a ballroom full of stockholders to vote the Parker line. I guess I fell in love with the businesswoman first and then with the woman herself." He leaned toward her, stroked her hand, and gave her an awkward buss on the cheek. She sat motionless, responding neither to his words nor his kiss. The platter of meat was passed to her and she quickly gave it to Hattie without taking her portion. Her appetite was gone, especially when the main course was venison. She remembered the beautiful doe that had darted through the brush the day she and Dave had driven into town.

Dave! Any hope of a close relationship with the ranger seemed gone. He had looked so hurt by the revelation of her past. She glanced across the table and was struck by his strong good looks. Unlike Roderick, with his carefully arranged hair, designer suit, and contrived country appearance, Dave was casual, yet he exuded good taste. His Harris tweed sportcoat, khaki slacks, button-down-collar shirt, and knit tie looked comfortably correct. She suddenly felt great sadness at the realization he would never look at her again with the emotion he had shown the night they shared dinner in her cabin. She had learned a great deal from him in her short visit to the mountains. He had introduced her to a slower, more sensitive lifestyle. Without intending to, he had helped her realize that she had no future with Roderick Davis. For that she would be forever grateful.

"Have you set a date yet, Lillian?" probed Cat. "I hope we're all invited. Dave, won't it be fun to go to their wedding? Of course, it will have to be in Detroit, what with all your business connections. It will probably be the social event of the season! Please, Dave, say we can go."

Dave looked embarrassed, but seemed overwhelmed by Cat's insistence.

"Will it be formal?" pressed Cat. "Dave hates to dress up. He's not like you, Roderick." She made no attempt to hide the admiration she felt for Roderick's dashing, if dandified, appearance. "Why, I'll bet you had that suit custom made, right?"

"I have this marvelous tailor in the garment district," said Roderick, responding to her attention. "I make it a point to get to New York at least four times a year."

Cat and Roderick seemed to shut out the other guests as they continued their superficial conversation about clothes. Lillian endured as much as she could, then rose to make her exit. Pastor Mead took a final bite of mashed potato, blotted his mouth, and prepared to follow her out of the room.

"No, I'll see Lillian home," insisted Roderick. He shook Phil Compton's hand and made a sweeping bow to Hattie, Bea, and Cat. "Lillian and I haven't been alone for some time. You understand, of course?" He winked slyly at Dave Thompson.

Roderick caught up with Lillian as she hurried down the front steps. She didn't try to discourage him when he steered her toward his car, but when he slid in next to her, wrapped his arm around her shoulders and attempted to kiss her, she pulled away.

"Please don't, Roderick."

He glanced up at the brightly lit Compton mansion and interpreted her hesitation as shyness at the possibility of being seen.

"Of course. Let me take you to your cabin where we can talk privately."

They drove in silence, each mentally preparing remarks to be delivered to the other. When they arrived at Lillian's lodge Roderick began to open the car door to escort her inside.

"No," said Lillian. "What I have to say won't take long. I'd like to say it now, and then I want to go into the cabin alone."

"Lill, do we have to say anything tonight? I just want to hold you. . . ."

"*Stop it!*" she said defiantly. "Don't you understand? I don't *want* you to hold me." He looked surprised at her outburst. She calmed herself and continued in a quiet, controlled voice. "Roderick, I left Detroit at your insistence to try to sort out my problems. I haven't found all the answers, of course, but I'm on the right track. I've had a lot of time to think about you. . . about us. . . and now I wonder how we ever thought we had a future together."

He started to object, but she held up her hand to silence him. "We have different priorities, different interests, different goals. Roderick, we have *nothing* in common!"

Her words stung his ego and caused him to retreat in an effort to save face. He gave her a quick hug with the arm still draped across her shoulders. Then he yawned.

"Look, Lill, I'm exhausted, and you are too. Why don't we both get a good night's sleep and postpone this whole thing until tomorrow? We can meet for lunch, okay? I'm staying at the Pine Acres Motel in town. I'll be there for a few days, so let's just relax, get reacquainted, and maybe. . ."

"Roderick, I'm not going to change my mind."

"Shall we say tomorrow around noon?"

"Roderick. . . ."

He turned the key in the ignition. "I'd love to chat, Lill, but I'm *really* tired. Do you mind?"

Lillian jumped out of his car, walked up to the door, and turned and watched as the taillights were swallowed by the blackness of the woods. The confrontation had ended in a stalemate. He had pressed; she had held her ground. But for Lillian that was a victory.

CHAPTER TEN

Not until Roderick turned off the highway and pulled up next to the blinking vacancy sign of the Pine Acres Motel did he realize that he had been telling Lillian the truth. He was tired—exhausted, in fact.

The trip from Detroit had been long, and he had arrived in Compton Gap only minutes before Cat's dinner party. Now, with the evening behind him, he looked forward to a hot shower, a phone call to his answering service, and then *sleep*. The dilemma of Lillian and her new stubbornness would surely keep until tomorrow, he decided. With a little persuasion from him, she'd come around. Didn't she always?

With some irritation he remembered that he had been required to turn in his key at the motel desk. For security reasons, the clerk had confided. Roderick sniffed and wondered if it wasn't a ploy to keep track of guests for gossip's sake. He suspected that the local network of party lines received its best news tips from the elderly proprietors of the town's only haven for out-of-town guests. And from the look of the empty parking lot, he also suspected that he—Roderick Davis—was the day's main attraction.

"Room 8, please," said Roderick, after raising the clerk from a sound sleep with several raps on the old-fashioned desk bell.

"Your name, sir?" inquired the elderly gentleman, consulting his ledger.

"Come on, pops, I'm probably your only boarder. Roderick Davis, remember?"

"Ah, yes. Here you are," the man said as he located the lone name on the page of the guest register. "You're in room 8."

"Just give me the key." Roderick was becoming angry.

"Here you are, sir. Did you have a nice time at the Comptons' party?"

"How did you know I was with the Comptons?" Roderick retorted in an accusing tone.

"Miss Cat called a few minutes ago to see if you had gotten back from the cabins yet," replied the clerk.

"You know Cat?"

"Everyone knows Cat."

"And Phil Compton?"

"He owns this motel."

Roderick's manner softened as his curiosity increased. "Phil seems like quite a guy. Just how much property does he own, anyway?"

"Couldn't say," said the old man, scratching his head. "Don't know. Not even sure if Phil knows."

Roderick was losing his patience again. "Good night, Mr.—"

"Heckert. Lyle Heckert, here." He stretched out his hand but Roderick already had turned and was out the door.

When he arrived in his room, Roderick wasted little time in calling his office partner, Paul Stattman.

"Counselor, old boy," was the cheery greeting from Detroit. "What can I do for you? Besides get you back to the city, that is. Say, it's almost midnight! Haven't they rolled up the sidewalks and switched off the switchboard by now?"

"Cut it out, Paul. I want you to do a favor for me. I need you to run a financial check on Phil Compton of Compton Gap. And do it fast. I'm curious as the devil to find out what's behind this guy."

"Slow down, Roderick. You lost me. What's going on down there? Who's Phil Compton?"

"Compton is the father of the woman who called me about Lillian. He's the owner of half a town and has a nice private spread, too. I'd just like to know more about him, that's all."

"Hey, Roderick. This is Paul, remember? I know you, don't forget."

"Okay, so I won't forget. But get on it right away. And get the information to me as soon as possible. Call me here at the Pine Acres Motel or, if you can't reach me, send it by overnight express. Got it?"

"Sure, counselor. You'll have the info by tomorrow."

They said abrupt goodbyes. Roderick replaced the phone in the cradle and started stripping for a quick shower. He hissed under his breath when he discovered that the water was lukewarm, a fact which made the shower that much briefer. He toweled himself dry, pulled on pajamas, and crawled into bed with *The Wall Street Journal* and several professional magazines he had brought with him. All the time his mind was racing over the day's events, Cat Compton, Lillian, and Cat's father. He mentally explored alternatives to one plan and another and played "what if" exercises in relation to what Paul's information might be. He was deep in thought when he heard a loud knock on the door.

Doesn't anyone ever go to bed around here? he grumbled to himself. He halfway expected to see Lyle Heckert and a tray of warm milk at the threshhold. Instead, it was Dave Thompson. The two men faced each other with a direct stare that showed only too evidently that neither man appreciated the other.

"I'd like to talk to you," said Dave, clearing his throat.

"Sure. Happy to oblige you, but I'm not exactly dressed for a business meeting or a social call."

"That's not important. What I have to say won't take long." There was an uncomfortable silence while Dave hesitated and Roderick waited.

"I want you to know exactly how I feel about you. I think you're after something from Lillian, and I don't mean just her affection. Your interest in her is obviously shallow and callous. I don't like it and I don't like you. This area will be better off when you've gone back to the city where you belong."

"What makes you think I care how you feel about me?" Roderick said smoothly. "And who are you to say what my relationship with Lillian is supposed to be? I've known her longer and *more intimately* than you have in the short time she's been here. Don't you think Lillian should determine how things stand between us?"

"Only if she chooses to. But I'm not sure she's chosen anything for herself lately. And I don't want to see her manipulated into a situation where she'll be unhappy for the rest of her life with someone like you. She deserves better and I intend to see that she gets it."

"Oh you do, do you?"

"Yes, I do," he said. "Look, Roderick. I know you don't love Lillian. Anybody with two eyes in his head could tell that. So why don't you leave her alone?"

"I think you'd better leave," Roderick said calmly. "I don't need to stand here and listen to this."

"Fine, I'm going. But I want to tell you one more thing before I leave." Dave pointed his finger at Roderick. "You try to hurt Lillian and you'll answer to me. Leave her alone. She doesn't need you."

Roderick backed away from the door and closed it.

• • •

Guadalupe Bentancourt ate a hurried breakfast before going to the military post on the day Scott Parker was to be traded for Colonel Bupchev. The ambassador's chief of staff was anxious for everything to go well and, as far as he knew, it would. All the groundwork had been laid for a smooth exchange. He had planned it carefully.

The swap was to take place in Guantanamo, on American soil in Cuba, and the Russian colonel was more than ready to be swapped, Bentancourt was sure. *Those stupid Americans*, he thought, smiling. *They swallowed my idea about getting both Parker and Martinez as a fair trade for the colonel.* Bentancourt was glad that Alexi Sokolnikov, the former Soviet courier, was out of the picture.

Bentancourt walked out into the hot sun and climbed into a waiting military car for the drive to the military base. This morning the city was alive with activity surrounding the agricultural trading of sugarcane and coffee. He had hoped there would be time for some small purchases of the city's fine chocolate and fresh fruits, but suspected there wouldn't be.

When he was once again on foot, he strode past the guards and entered the building where the trade was to take place. He walked down a long narrow hall and flashed his identification card before joining others in a formal and sparsely furnished room. At one side, Juanita was supporting Scott, still very weak as he slumped in a hardbacked chair. He leaned against her shoulder and Bentancourt restrained himself from smiling.

The room was filled with army personnel in uniform and intelligence officers in plain clothes. Alma Hammond was there, as well as Scott Parker's boot camp training officer for identification. Scott had already been examined by doctors, who had declared him to be in need of immediate medical attention. But it was determined that he was well enough to make the lengthy flight, provided emergency equipment was on board.

"Sir, are you ready to make the trade?" an official asked, walking up to Bentancourt. "All personnel are here and awaiting your arrival."

"Yes, let's get going. Right on schedule. I'm sure we all have other duties to attend to," Bentancourt responded briskly.

"Yes, sir."

All those persons present in the room who were not already standing were instructed to rise. The interpreters repeated the rules of the exchange and looked to Bentancourt and his American counterpart for a nod. The signal would give Colonel Bupchev, Scott, and Juanita the go-ahead for that walk across the imaginary line dividing the representatives of the two countries. Once across, each would be under the second country's jurisdiction.

The air was tense. Alma looked at Scott and then at Juanita. She caught Juanita's eye, then looked away before their gaze could be construed as familiar. Moments passed slowly while all action seemed at a standstill. When Bentancourt was just about to give the final nod, an attache rushed into the room carrying a telegram.

"What?" Bentancourt asked, startled by the interruption. He accepted the message and opened it, skimming the contents.

"The trade has been delayed," he announced in Spanish only. "There is a question as to the identity of Colonel Bupchev. A positive identification must be made before we can release Scott Parker and his fiancee."

The Cuban interpreter translated Bentancourt's words into English, along with his instructions that everyone return to his seat.

Alma looked at the man dressed in civilian clothes next to her. She said to him under her breath, "Is it a trick?" The director of the CIA answered with a negative nod that was perceptible only to Alma.

Minutes passed. Then a half hour. It was 45 minutes before a special communique arrived with permission to again proceed with the trade.

Alma breathed a sigh of relief and watched as Scott Parker,

leaning on Juanita Martinez, and Colonel Bupchev crossed the line. It was a crucial point in reaching their respective homes. And even so, she knew that it would be days before they could consider themselves free citizens again. There would be army debriefings and CIA debriefings before Scott Parker could think about seeing his sister again. And somewhere in that process it was hoped he could regain his health.

Each governmental entourage left by a side door going in opposite directions. Juanita and Scott were led away with Alma close by. The Central Intelligence men flanked the trio. They were followed by armed soldiers who backed out of the room, ready for action.

More government personnel were waiting outside the chambers. They led the way to a limousine. When all the doors were closed and the passengers inside, the limo sped away. The director of the CIA followed in the car behind.

It was Juanita who broke the silence with softly spoken greetings to Alma. Their eyes met in a friendly, yet worried, camaraderie as they considered Scott's state of exhaustion.

"We're not safe yet, unfortunately," said Alma. "I would guess that interruption was a stall tactic, but I'm not sure why. I don't suppose you'd like to make me feel better by telling me Bentancourt is a trustworthy and honorable man?"

"I wish I could, but unfortunately he's been known to bug his most trusted people," she said. "He planted a small device on my purse when we flew out of Cuba. No, I don't trust him. I think he'd do anything to achieve his personal goals. Not to mention his country's."

"Well, stay alert. It's not far to the plane and then we'll get out of the country. It's a long ride home, but we'll have plenty of protection and company."

Alma looked around to check the director's car and the military escort. The sight was an impressive one. A convoy of several cars followed them, and motorcycles with armed military police kept pace with the motorcade.

When they reached the airport, Scott was placed on a stretcher before being boarded on the plane. Juanita stayed at his side. She made sure the blanket covering his body was secure. Alma sat up front with the director of the CIA. In less time than it had taken for the earlier delay, they were airborne. With each foot of altitude, Alma felt that much safer. Each silver cloud that passed by her window meant they were that much further from Guadalupe Bentancourt and his government.

During the long flight, Alma relieved Juanita as nurse so the tired undercover agent could eat a meal and sit in a cushioned seat for a few moments before resuming her station at Scott's side. It was Alma who was sitting next to Scott when he regained consciousness and started calling out in delirium. It was Alma who took his hand and held it in her own.

"Hi, Scott. My name is Alma Hammond. Juanita will be right back, I promise you," she said, consoling him. "We're flying over the Atlantic Ocean just off the coast of Virginia. It won't be long now."

"Virginia? In the United States? You mean it's true? I'm really almost home?"

Scott's voice was barely more than a whisper. Juanita walked up behind Alma and gazed down at their patient. She could tell his eyes were having trouble focusing on her.

"Can I get you something to eat, Scott?" she asked. "Some tomato soup?"

"Yes, I'm hungry, I think. But not tomato. I'd rather have some chicken broth or even beef. I like it better." When Juanita had gone to get the broth, Alma tried to tell Scott what was in store for him in the days ahead.

"You'll be hospitalized at Walter Reed, where they'll help you regain some weight. You'll be tested physically and mentally and probably put on a high-vitamin and protein diet, or whatever they do to help restore normality to someone who's been deprived of adequate nutrition for ten years.

"I'm sure you won't be there too long before you'll undergo a battery of questions from both Army Intelligence and the CIA," she said, smiling. "But you'll be stronger by then. I don't suppose you're looking forward to that, but we'll try to be kind in our probing. At least I will, if I'm in on it."

"I think I'll stay sick a while longer...to delay the interrogation," Scott quipped faintly. "I've been interrogated enough already to last a lifetime. Old Porky saw to that."

"Old Porky? Who's that?" she asked.

"No one you'd ever want to meet, I assure you," he said with a weak smile.

Juanita and Alma helped Scott eat. He was even weaker than Alma had suspected, and it was necessary to spoon-feed him the broth. When there was nothing more she could do, Alma left Juanita to her task. Five minutes later, Juanita came forward.

"He's asleep?" asked Alma.

Juanita shook her head just slightly. "No. He's listening to his sister's tape again. That's probably the fiftieth time. He prefers to be alone when he plays it. Want to hear a long story about that tape?"

Alma smiled. "I'm not going anywhere," she said.

• • •

It was late at night when they transferred Scott to an ambulance that would deliver him to Walter Reed. They were all exhausted, both emotionally and physically, from the tension of the day's events and the lengthy flight from Cuba. There had been only naps aboard the plane, and those had been taken in uncomfortable positions. The loud drone of the roaring engines had made the short interludes of sleep fitful.

Both Juanita and Scott were admitted to the hospital for the night. Physical examinations were scheduled for the morning, and Juanita wanted to be nearby in case Scott needed a familiar face to tell him where he was and how he got there.

However, it wasn't until early afternoon of the next day that Juanita saw Scott again. He was weak, but he had had the benefit of catnaps every few hours. The tests were moving slowly, he said. The doctors wanted to give him a chance to rest before major medical evaluations were made.

Their afternoons and evenings together soon fell into a pattern. Hours not spent under the careful scrutiny of a delegation of doctors were enjoyed in long conversations about their families and their childhoods.

One day a young nurse's aide walked into the room with a cart of books.

"Scott, don't you want something to read?" Juanita suggested. "Look at the selection. Surely there's something that might interest you. Oh, here's one of my favorites."

"Jack London? I can't stand his work. Oh, well, give it to me.

The Son of the Wolf and Other Stories, eh?" he said as he held out his hand and accepted the volume.

He handed the book to Juanita.

"Won't you read it to me? My eyes get tired easily. Besides, I like the sound of your voice." He smiled at her, then looked up at the ceiling and folded his hands over his body.

Juanita laughed, opened the book and skimmed the contents until she found a short story. She read until Scott fell asleep. Setting the book down, she tiptoed out of the room.

That evening Alma took a message from Juanita to be delivered by courier to the telegraph office. It was addressed to Guadalupe Bentancourt and read:

DEEPLY SORROWED STOP BABY DIED A CRIB DEATH STOP CAN'T STAY HERE STOP COMING HOME POST ARRANGEMENTS STOP JM

Juanita knew Bentancourt would assume she had turned off the oxygen to Scott's tent and he had died at the hospital. It was exactly what Bentancourt was supposed to think. It was the final step of the plan.

The next morning Alma returned to Walter Reed Hospital to find Juanita having breakfast with Scott in his room. She delivered the news that Juanita's message had been sent and all had gone according to their arrangements.

"So I'm dead as far as Bentancourt is concerned, eh?" Scott asked. "That's a shame. I'm sure he'll be sorry to hear that. We were rather fond of each other. I'd hate to make him cry on my behalf."

"I wouldn't worry too much about that, Scott," replied Juanita. "We both know him well enough to know he couldn't be sorry about anyone's death....unless it was his own."

"Can't say I blame him on that score. I'd hate to part present company, too," he said. "I'm just starting to feel alive again."

Juanita picked up a clean water glass and poured orange juice from a pitcher on Scott's tray. She offered it to Alma and picked up her own.

"I'd like to propose a toast to Scott's homecoming," she said. "And to our victory over the infamous Guadalupe Bentancourt."

"Mission accomplished," chimed in Alma.

"Hear, hear!" cheered Scott. They laughed and clinked glasses first with one and then with the other. As Alma started to leave, Scott handed Juanita the book of Jack London stories.

"Juanita, dear and tender nurse, read to me," he said in jest. "I'm beginning to like this writer."

• • •

Guadalupe Bentancourt had received the telegram and understood its meaning immediately. He read it over several times at his office, then destroyed it by lighting a match and carefully placing it in a large ashtray. He watched until it disintegrated into soft gray dust.

His mood was brighter and his day went better because of the telegram. He anticipated Juanita's return and hoped for an opportunity to pursue a relationship with her. *Who can know about these things?* he asked himself.

Bentancourt completed his business for the day early, and after eating dinner alone in a neighborhood restaurant he went home to his apartment. It was dark and silent; there were no welcoming noises from pets or people to greet him. But he had long ago become accustomed to being alone. He knew he was destined for political greatness, and he had never met a woman who was worth his time...until now.

The next morning Bentancourt's spirits were still soaring. He fixed a cup of coffee in his little kitchen and wandered into the living room to read the day's paper and think about the work ahead. There was a lot to do now that Colonel Bupchev had been returned to Russia and Scott Parker was dead. As he approached the hardwood table where the paper lay, Bentancourt glanced in the overhead mirror. He grinned at himself: He felt strong and successful. He knew he would soon celebrate a promotion. And if things went according to his plans, he would have a desirable lady in his arms—Juanita Martinez.

Bentancourt lifted his coffee to the level of his cheek and smiled broadly at himself in the mirror.

"Good morning, Guadalupe," he said as he toasted his reflection. "You've done quite well for yourself lately, haven't you? Well, then, it's no time to slacken the schedule. After all, you *are* going to be the next ambassador-at-large of Cuba." He took a sip of the hot coffee.

"You deserve it. No one deserves it more. You've worked hard and you've done your job. The sacrifices have been worth it. And in the end, you will also get the girl." Bentancourt chuckled and went to sit in his chair. He was not worried about being a few minutes late for work. No, not today. It would be slower than the activities of the past few months. Much slower indeed.

• • •

It was late evening and Scott was peacefully listening to Juanita read "The White Silence," another story by Jack London. Her voice flowed over the words. He could feel the vastness of the barren snow-covered terrain. But he didn't feel the solitude of the main character.

Juanita stopped reading when she realized Scott had lost interest in the story. She watched as he stared at the ceiling, and wondered what he was thinking about.

Without turning his head, Scott began talking to her. His voice was tactful. His words were well-chosen.

"Juanita," he began. "I've had lots of time to think lately. Lots of time." He glanced over to her and grinned, then returned his gaze upward. "How would you like to go out to dinner when I get out of here?"

"Oh, Scott. Didn't Alma tell you?" she asked.

He looked at her, puzzled.

"Don't tell me you're married and have four children?" he said, trying to keep things lighthearted.

"No, it's not that... it's just that..."

"You don't want to see me after I get well and am dismissed from the hospital?"

"No, of course not."

"No, of course that's not it, or no, of course not, you don't want to see me?"

"The first one. No, of course that's not it."

"Oh. Then what?"

"I thought Alma told you I'm still in the... Company."

"I know that. What has that got to do with not seeing me?"

"I'm returning to Cuba. Bentancourt still trusts me and I can be even more effective than I was before I left, if I return."

"Bentancourt. You're returning to Bentancourt?"

"No. You know I'm not returning to Bentancourt," she said. "It's my duty to finish the job I started, if I can. And I guess it's good we're having this little talk, because my plane leaves tomorrow afternoon. This will be our last evening together."

Scott didn't say anything. This goodbye was happening much too quickly for him. Neither one of them was ready to say goodbye. And it wasn't helping matters any that Juanita was returning to Cuba to work under the authority of Bentancourt.

"Scott, it's only for a year—that's all," she said lightly.

"A year? I guess that's not so long. After all, I've been gone ten years. One seems like nothing."

Juanita nodded.

"Maybe you'll consider looking me up a year from now. I could leave word with Alma or someone so you could find me."

"I'd like that, Scott," she said as she stood to come stand near the side of his bed. She took his hand from where it lay on the white sheet and held it between both of hers. He looked up at her and smiled.

"Scott, I've grown very fond of you in the short time we've known each other." Juanita caressed his hand tenderly with her fingertips. "It's hard to care about someone and spend a year apart. You should know more than anyone." She paused. "It'll be hard not to be with you when I want to. . . to talk to you. . . or reach out and touch you. And for that I'm sorry."

There was a lump in Scott's throat. He didn't feel like he knew Juanita well, but he knew in his heart that he had had too much taken away from him in the last ten years—his freedom, his parents, his inheritance. Now Juanita Martinez was adding herself to the list. Life was terribly unfair at times.

"Hey, look, Juanita. A few months, a year, that's just about how long I'll be busy answering questions about how they treated me as a P.O.W., what I learned, who I was imprisoned with . . ." he said, and looked away because there were the beginnings of tears in Juanita's eyes. "If we're destined to meet again, we will. And I think we will."

She nodded and wiped a tear. She bent over and kissed him on the cheek. He turned his face to meet hers and they kissed.

"I think you should ask someone else to read the end of that story."

He nodded.

"See you later."

"Goodbye."

They looked at each other again for the briefest moment, then she turned and walked out of Scott's hospital room.

The next day was sunny and warm when Juanita boarded her plane to Miami. She wore a wide-brimmed hat and was perfectly tailored in a navy suit and low-heeled pumps. When she turned and waved goodbye, the woman on the ground waved also.

"I promise," she said out loud. "I promise to send word if I can. He asked me to send word of you, too." Alma Hammond's voice trailed softly with the wind. The meaning and promise of her words were to stay with Scott and Juanita for the entire 12 months ahead of them.

CHAPTER ELEVEN

"Hello?" Roderick fumbled with the telephone receiver as he attempted to prop himself up against two wafer-thin pillows.

"Good morning, Sleepyhead," whispered the husky voice on the other end.

"Who is this?" he grumbled. "Cat?"

"Sorry, I thought you'd be up by now. I waited until 9:30, then my curiosity got the best of me. How did it go last night? Are congrats in order?"

"Er. . . well. . . let's say there's work in progress. I'm going to drive up to the cabin around noon. Lillian was tired last night and so we didn't talk much." He shifted his weight and groaned as another corkscrew bedspring gouged his backside. "No offense, Cat, but this motel of yours is never going to earn Carte Blanche's blessing."

"Awful, isn't it?" said Cat. "Daddy keeps it open just to give the Heckerts a job. They've been with him for years."

Roderick was standing now, stretching with one arm and holding the phone to his ear with the other. "How do I get a cup of coffee in this one-horse town?"

"By meeting me at the diner down the street in about half an hour," replied Cat boldly. "My treat."

Roderick hesitated, not certain whether he wanted to commit himself to Cat's company. Still, he was curious about her, her family, and especially about her father. "Give me an hour and you've got yourself a date. And a Danish."

He shaved, then began sorting through the layers of clothes carefully arranged in his suitcase. He hadn't unpacked, since he had no intention of staying in Compton Gap; however, he had brought enough outfits to carry him through two weeks without fear of duplication. He checked the weather, selected a pair of Calvin Klein jeans and a Ralph Lauren polo shirt, then began peeling stickers and price tags off both.

Once dressed and outside, he hesitated with his hand on the door to his car. Strategy was important at this point. If Lillian called and he wasn't in, she might jump to a right conclusion. He couldn't *afford* that—literally—right now. Still, by meeting Cat he could pump her for more information about Lillian, Dave Thompson...and Cat herself. It never hurt to hedge your bet, he rationalized.

"Leaving now, sir? I'll go and straighten your room while you're gone."

Roderick looked up. Mrs. Heckert was standing down the sidewalk, a toilet bowl brush in one hand and dustrag draped over one shoulder.

"Yes. I thought I'd try to get some breakfast. Can you recommend some place?"

"The local diner," she said, pointing.

Roderick waved. "Thank you. I'll find it. By the way, if I should receive any calls while I'm out, will you tell them where you've sent me? I'll only be away an hour. Say I'll call back."

"Will do," Mrs. Heckert responded, flashed an O-K with her thumb and forefinger, and grinned a toothless grin.

Roderick got into the car and smiled. *I had no idea Cat would be there*, he mentally rehearsed. *The motel manager was the one who directed me to the diner, Lillian. You can ask her yourself.*

He backed out the car and hurried to the diner.

"Wow!" Cat said appreciatively from the small corner table. "After breakfast I'd like to parade you up and down Main Street to show everyone what the well-dressed city slicker wears when he visits the boondocks." She stood up, extended her hand in greeting, then reached over and pulled off a gummed inspection ticket from his collar.

"How long will you be in Compton Gap?" she asked. Then, without waiting for an answer: "You really made an impression on my mother. She insists that you should move out of the motel and into one of our guestrooms. Her opinion of the Pine Acres makes yours look like a Duncan Hines endorsement."

"Thanks, but I don't plan to be around that long."

He studied her as she fingered, with obvious distaste, the slightly greasy menu. She was wearing narrow brown cords, a hooded orange sweater, and a zippered fur jacket. The total effect

was one of understated style and class. She possessed the kind
of panache he had always aspired to—the kind that drew attention not only to herself but also to anyone lucky enough to share
her spotlight.

"Bagel and cream cheese, Madge," she ordered.

Roderick looked surprised. "Sounds good. I'll take the same."
He waited until Madge had disappeared behind the counter. "You
mean they actually serve bagels in Compton Gap?"

"They order them just for me," replied Cat.

"I suppose your father owns—"

"The diner? Actually, it's in Mother's name. For tax purposes."

"Since you Comptons obviously call the shots around here, I
wish you'd put in a good word for me with your Lone Ranger
pal. He'll never make it in public relations."

"Dave?"

"Yeah. He stopped by my room last night to deliver a friendly
threat."

"Dave Thompson?" she repeated in surprise.

"You really ought to keep him chained to his pen. In his silent,
macho manner he told me to 'get lost' and particularly to get out
of Lillian's life. I thought I was going to have to take a swing at
the guy. Lucky for him, he got the message and left. It's none
of my business, Cat, but that guy doesn't seem to be in your
league."

Cat nodded her head thoughtfully. "No wonder you and Mother
get along so well. Those are her sentiments exactly."

They ate their bagels and dawdled over a second cup of coffee.

"What I can't figure out is where you two are going to do your
happily-every-aftering," said Roderick. "You don't strike me as
the type who delights in putting tomatoes in Mason jars or
unwinding at the Grange Hall hoedown. Yet I can't see Dave
Thompson in downtown Nashville, either. So who's going to give
in? Sounds like a no-win situation to me."

"Maybe there's no contest."

"What do you mean?"

"Well," she said quietly, "maybe the same traits that attract
Dave and me to each other are the ones that keep us apart. And
maybe we're smart enough to realize it. Does that make any
sense?" She looked at him directly, waiting for an answer.

"Sure it makes sense," he said, then laughed. "I think. I'm just glad Lill and I don't have that kind of problem. We like the same things, travel in the same circles, and want the same kind of life together. At least we always did. The sooner I can get her back to Detroit, the sooner we can get on with our plans. She seems to have gotten a little offtrack down here. I guess it was a mistake to let her come alone." He looked at his watch and reached for the check simultaneously with Cat. Always the gentleman, he let her sweep it up first. He started to leave a tip, but gallantly retreated when she tucked a dollar bill under her coffee mug.

"Well, is this goodbye?" she asked as he walked her to her car.

"I'm not sure," he replied, eyeing the Jaguar with obvious appreciation. "If so, let's make it temporary. We can keep in touch."

"Remember," she said, leaning just close enough so he could get the full effect of her perfume, "if you're ever in the neighborhood, there's always room at the inn." She smiled broadly. "And I don't mean the Pine Acres Motel."

● ● ●

"Mr. Davis: Paul Stattman from Detroit phoned twice. No message. Call him at his office. Mrs. Heckert." The note was scratched on a slip of pink paper and tacked to the outside of Roderick's motel room. He hurried inside and reached for the phone.

"Hi, Paul. What did you find out?"

"Hey, counselor, back from your nature walk so soon?"

"Cut the comedy, Paul, I'm due at Lillian's in a few minutes. What do you have for me on Compton?"

"Well, you sure know how to pick your friends. The guy's worth a mint. Wait a sec, let me pull his file." Roderick could hear paper being shuffled on the other end. "Here it is, Rod. Let's see...Philip W. Compton, 54, real estate speculator; financier; chief executive officer, Compton Industries, Inc.; owns and operates Compton Stables in Lexington, Kentucky; has property in three other states plus controlling interest in some kind of resort community in the Virgin Islands; sits on the board of one bank, a computer software company, two foundations, and a hospital in Memphis. Want more? I've got another page of info on him and a page-and-a-half on a Harriet L. Compton. Any relation?"

"Yeah. That's Hattie, Cat's mother," said Roderick. "Sounds like the guy's worth big bucks."

"An understatement, counselor. Did I mention politics? Apparently he's got buddies in high places because he's served on a couple of trade commissions in Nashville. Oh, and here it says he's a trustee of a land grant college in—"

"Enough, Paul. That's plenty. I promised Lillian we'd get together around noon, and I'm late already."

"One thing, Rod . . ."

"Sure, what do you want?"

"This Cat Compton. Tell me she weighs 300 pounds, wears corrective shoes, and had an incurable case of acne as a kid."

"Right, Paul. Coke-bottle glasses . . . a lisp . . . the works."

"Thanks, I needed that."

● ● ●

Lillian reached to the back of her top drawer, past the scarf and extra pair of gloves, and drew out a small brown velvet box. She hesitated, took a deep breath, then opened the lid. With surprise she realized that the sight of the ring had little impact on her anymore. If anything, it struck her as garish and cold.

I've changed. I've really changed, she thought. How proud she had been when Roderick had presented it to her during a family ski trip to Aspen. He designed it himself, he told her that night as they sipped warmed cider by the fire. The emeralds surrounding the tear-shaped diamond solitaire were to match her eyes, he said. The inscription promised "Yours, with devotion—Roderick."

She slipped it on her finger one last time and nervously twisted it around and around. It no longer fit her physically or emotionally. Her loss of weight caused it to move too easily, and it looked ostentatious and alien on her hand. She smiled as she decided the ring suited her as poorly as the relationship it represented.

"Lillian? Roderick is here." Mom Mead was standing in the doorway of Lillian's bedroom. "Shall I tell him to come back later? Lillian! You're wearing the ring! Did you two patch things up last night?"

"No, Mom. I'm going to give it back to him. I guess I just don't know how to do it. Endings are hard—even good endings."

Bea Mead smiled understandingly.

"I know this is best for both of us," continued Lillian. "But I keep thinking of all the plans we had, all the hours we shared, and all the people who knew us and liked us as a couple. Will they take sides and divide into separate camps now that it's over?" She sighed and repeated, "Endings are tough, Mom."

"Tell you what—Pastor and I will take Rufus for a long walk on the shore so you and Roderick can have some privacy. Just be honest with him, Dear." She studied Lillian's pale and drawn face for a moment. "You look so thin, Lillian. Has Roderick done this to you? Never mind; don't answer that. I promised Pastor I wouldn't pry."

"Thanks, Mom," Lillian said with a smile as she scrutinized her image in the mirror and stroked a bit of blusher on her cheeks. Roderick had always demanded that she look her best, no matter what the occasion. "Tell him I'll be out in a minute, okay?"

Roderick was seated on the couch when Lillian entered the living room. His eyes went immediately to the brown velvet box in her hand. He realized she was serious about ending their relationship, but he was equally determined to deny her the opportunity. He refused to be cast in the role of rejected suitor. After all, he had initiated their romance and he, not she, would end it.

"Sit down, Lillian," he ordered, indicating which pillow of the sofa she should occupy. When she made no move to obey, he continued. "This is probably the hardest thing I've ever had to do." He walked over to her, put his hands on her shoulders, and stooped to kiss her forehead. "I have something to say that's going to hurt you. In time, you'll forgive me."

She ignored his words, stepped back, and held out her hand with the velvet box in it. "Please take the ring, Roderick. I meant what I said last night. I don't love you, and I don't believe you love me."

When he didn't accept the box, she bent over and put it on the coffee table.

Color came into Roderick's face. He was angry, but above all he was embarrassed. Before he let his feelings surface, however, he reached out, took the box, and tucked it securely into his jacket pocket.

"You're a fool, Lillian. You come down here for a few weeks, start running around with some park ranger who fills your mind with idealism, and you forget all about the real world. You're so *weak*," he hissed, well aware of how to hurt her the most. "You let anyone within three feet of you influence you and change your opinions. To think that I believed you were strong like your father! Well, let me tell you something—J. J. Parker would be ashamed of you right now, just as I am." He glared at her with disgust, turned, and started for the door. Once there, he paused. "I hope you and your country bumpkin ranger will be very happy. You deserve each other."

The door banged behind him, and within seconds Lillian could hear the tires of his car angrily grinding gravel as he sped away. She sank down onto the couch and sat quietly. No tears flowed and no emotion was felt.

What's wrong with me? she wondered to herself. *The man I was supposed to share my life with has just walked out, and I feel nothing! Will the pain come later or does this mean there was never any love between us at all? Even his words didn't hurt. They weren't true. I am strong; and for the first time in my life I feel I can handle being alone.*

The Meads tiptoed quietly into the room, not knowing in what condition they would find Lillian.

"I'm okay," she assured them. Then she smiled, "Look, Mom, no tears."

Bea Mead sat next to her on the sofa and put her arms around her. Pastor Mead nodded his head in admiration. "I'm proud of you, Lillian. And your father would be too, if he were here."

"Not according to Roderick," responded Lillian with a grin.

"What do you mean?" asked Pastor Mead.

"Inside joke. I'll explain later. Right now I'd really like to go lie down for a while. For some reason those few minutes with Roderick left me exhausted."

"Good idea," agreed Pastor Mead. "We'll make sure you aren't disturbed."

"Charles, what about the message?" Bea Mead reminded her husband.

"Message? What message?" asked Lillian.

"I'm sorry. I must be getting forgetful in my old age," joked Pastor Mead. "We met Dave Thompson down by the lake. He was coming this way, but we discouraged him since we knew

Roderick was here. Anyway, he had just received a call on that walkie-talkie box he wears on his belt. Seems you're supposed to call this number." Pastor Mead fumbled in his jacket pockets and finally produced a wrinkled piece of paper with a series of numbers written on it.

Lillian studied the message and took care not to show her concern. *Scott*, she thought. *It has to be news of Scott.*

"Hmmm," she said, nonchalantly. "Maybe I ought to drive into town and find out what this is all about. I need to pick up a few things at the store anyway."

"Can't it wait, Lillian?" asked Bea Mead. "You said yourself how tired you are."

"I know, but maybe it will do me good to get out for a few minutes. Want to go for a ride, Rufus?" She purposely diverted the attention to the dog, who responded by running to the door. If she took Rufus in her small sports car, lack of room would prevent either of the Meads from accompanying her. She couldn't risk their being present when news came of her brother—especially if the news was bad.

"I promise I'll be back in an hour," she assured them, scooping up Rufus and reaching for her sweater. "We can have an early dinner and I'll be in bed by ten. Okay?" Assuming their agreement, she walked out.

She drove slowly until she was safely out of sight. Then she pushed hard on the accelerator. She hadn't recognized the telephone number on the slip of paper, but she was familiar with the 202 area code—Washington, D.C. She remembered another telephone call from Washington several years earlier which had informed her parents that their only son was missing in action and presumed dead. Was she to endure similar news again? And this time alone?

If Scott's attempt to escape had failed, Lillian could share her sorrow with no one. The Meads would not be told, she decided, and neither would Parker family friends in Detroit. What would be the purpose? Accepting the death of her brother a second time would be difficult enough; but coping with condolences, telephone calls, and pity would be too much. Only the Meads could help her bear the grief, but she would spare even them the pain. This would be her personal burden, and she knew it would test her new strength and renewed faith.

"Lord, I believe You are a kind and merciful God. I know You would never allow one of Your children to suffer pain without reason. If my faith is being tested, I pray for the strength to endure the test. If Scott is to be taken away from me a second time, I pray that my belief in You will sustain me."

She quietly whispered the words over and over as she expertly followed the twisting road that led into town. When she arrived in front of Old Ed's store she felt composed and ready for whatever news awaited her. She ordered Rufus to stay in the car, then entered the grocery store and walked back to the tiny enclosed telephone booth.

Her hands were shaking as she fumbled for her telephone credit card.

"Hello?"

Hearing a woman's voice answer so informally on the other end surprised Lillian. She had expected to be greeted by a secretary announcing an office or governmental agency. Had she dialed the wrong number?

"Yes. Hello. My name is Lillian Parker, and I was given this number to—"

"Hello, Lillian. This is Alma Hammond. You remember me, don't you?"

Lillian's pulse quickened and her hands began to shake uncontrollably.

"Yes. Of course. Please...what's happened? I did everything you told me, honest. I haven't said a word about...well, you know...to anyone. Please, tell me what's happened."

"It's good news, Lillian. I'm sitting next to your brother. We're in a room at Walter Reed Hospital. This is a private line, so we can talk freely. We had it installed because Scott's...er...situation is still top secret."

"Walter Reed Hospital? Is Scotty hurt? Is he sick? Please, I've waited so long."

"He's fine. Or at least he will be in time. Your brother has been through a tremendous ordeal, Lillian. His recovery—his total recovery—will take months. I want to talk more about that, but first I'm going to turn the phone over to our patient, who right now is being anything but patient!"

Lillian could hear Alma laugh and then order Scott to calm down before he suffered a relapse.

"Lillian? Are you there? This is Scott."

Tears began spilling down Lillian's cheeks. "Scott, is it really you? It's been so long. I...I...can't believe this is happening."

"Oh, Lillian, you sound so grown-up. I've thought about you every day, but in my mind you've always been that little girl I remember back home. Are you all right? I know you've been through a lot. I heard about Dad just a few weeks ago. I still can't believe it all. I'm sorry I wasn't there to help you."

"It's all right. Everything's all right now," Lillian said through tears. "But you, what about you? All those years...it must have been awful. When can I come to the hospital? We've got so much to talk about. When can I come? I'll leave tonight if they'll let me. Please, Scott, I want to see you right away. Don't let them make me wait."

"No, I'm going to come there. Alma said you've got a place in the mountains, right? I've got to stay out of sight for a while, but that should be a lot easier to do in Tennessee than in Washington. Wait a minute, Lill...."

Lillian could hear him talk with Alma, but the words were muffled and she couldn't follow the conversation. Then Alma was on the line again.

"Lillian, you had company staying with you when I was in Compton Gap. Have they left yet?"

"No, but they're very close friends of our family. Scott remembers them: Pastor Mead and his wife. I'm sure they'd never tell anyone about Scott, if that's what you're afraid of."

"We have to be very careful," cautioned Alma. "It's essential that Scott's whereabouts—his very existence—remain top secret. I don't think we should take a chance on telling anyone. Your friends, the Meads, are probably very trustworthy, but...excuse me, Lillian, Scott wants to say something."

"Lillian? Are you talking about Pastor Mead? Are they there in Tennessee with you?"

"Yes, Scott. They're back at the cabin right now," replied Lillian. "I haven't told them anything about your escape; I was so afraid something might happen to you."

"Gosh, I'd love to see them!" said Scott. "Hang on again, Lill."

More muffled dialogue was exchanged between Scott and Alma. Lillian waited patiently until Alma again picked up the phone.

"If we were to allow Scott to come to your cabin, could you

accommodate him and his...er...escort?" she asked.

"Yes, yes, of course. But I don't understand—who will be with him?" replied Lillian.

"For security purposes, Lillian, for the next year or so Scott will be dogged by one of our agents. We don't feel he's in any serious danger, but we want him to keep a low profile, regain his health, and slowly ease back into a normal lifestyle. We've assigned a man about Scott's age to travel with him. He'll help with the debriefing and make sure Scott's transition back to civilian life is a smooth one."

"Of course," said Lillian. "Send anyone you want. But please let Scott come, Miss Hammond. I'll do anything you ask; just let my brother come here."

There was a pause as Alma Hammond weighed the proposal. Finally she agreed.

"I'll make the arrangements on this end," she said. "You be prepared to welcome two houseguests within a day or two. And you can tell your friends, the Meads. But no one else, understand? And make sure you won't be visited by anyone else for the rest of Scott's stay. Follow me? I'll be in touch with you as soon as I finalize the details of the trip. Now I'll let you say goodbye to your brother."

"Lillian?" said Scott. "I'll be counting the minutes till I can see you. I guess in the meantime I'll keep listening to the tape you sent. I've practically worn it out! Don't go to a lot of trouble now, Lill. I'm not used to a bunch of fussing, you know. Hey! Does Mom Mead still make that awful soup? Tell her to mix up a batch because Scott's coming home!"

Lillian laughed and wiped tears away at the same time.

"Gotta go, Lill," said Scott. "Alma's having fits about me getting too worked up. See you soon. I love you."

" 'Bye, Scotty. I love you, too."

She hurried to the car and hugged Rufus until he squealed. *He's coming home! My brother's coming home!* she thought to herself jubilantly. At the turn of the key the engine roared to life. *There's so much to tell him...where do I start?... so many lost years to remember.* The road was deserted as she retraced the route she had taken only a half hour earlier. *It's a miracle—an unexpected, wonderful gift from God.* The scenery was a blur through her tears of happiness. *What will he look like? How much has he changed?*

When she pulled the car up to the lodge, her tears had dried and her eyes were blazing with excitement. She opened the door and ran inside, Rufus scurrying to keep up with her pace. She stopped short when she saw that the Meads were not alone.

"Perfect timing, Lillian!" said Mom Mead. "Dave stopped by to make sure you received your message, and I invited him to stay for dinner." She paused as she noticed Lillian's flustered expression. "Are you all right, Dear? I hope that telephone call wasn't bad news."

"No. No, not at all," stammered Lillian. "Just the opposite. It's...well...it's wonderful news. But it's...I mean...I'm not supposed to tell anyone except...."

Dave Thompson stood up. "We can have dinner together some other time," he said politely. "I have a feeling tonight isn't a very good idea." He extended his hand to Pastor Mead. "I meant what I said about the offer to take you fishing, sir. They're really biting this time of year."

He reached for his coat, nodded to Bea Mead, and began to walk toward the door.

"No! Please don't go!" said Lillian. Dave stopped and turned toward her. "I know I'm not supposed to do this," she said. "They told me not to tell anyone but the Meads, but...well...I want you to hear too, Dave." She smiled at him, walked over to his side and took his hand. "Please sit down and let me share this with you. I want you to hear my news—my wonderful, glorious, unbelievably good news."

Dave grinned at her and sat beside her on the couch, his hand still in hers.

"Mom? Pastor Mead?" she said with a trace of mystery in her voice. "I think you better sit down for this too."

● ● ●

It was nearly 6 P.M. when the Comptons, who had gathered in their living room to await dinner, were interrupted by the front doorbell.

"Miss Cat," announced the maid with eyes turned dutifully to the floor, "you have a caller."

Cat lazily extracted herself from the chair, walked to the foyer and nearly tripped over a suitcase.

"I just happened to be in the neighborhood," joked Roderick Davis from the center of a pool of matched luggage. "Is there still room at the inn?"

Cat smiled, and without saying a word she reached for his hand to lead him into the living room.

"Mother, guess who's coming to dinner?"

Hattie Compton rose to greet their guest with a syrupy smile, then whispered to the maid at her side.

"The Haviland. Get the Haviland. *And* the Waterford."

CHAPTER TWELVE

Alma had said the boyguard's name would be Kent. When he arrived, Scott asked, "Is that your first or last name?"

The broad-shouldered, muscular young man sidestepped the question with "You just yell 'Kent' anytime, and I'll be there."

He was about 28 years old, Scott guessed. He wasn't chummy, nor did he show signs of wanting to be. Scott was Kent's *assignment*, not his friend.

Scott had never been quite sure of what he really needed to be protected *from*. "Tell me, Alma, how someone can kill a man who's already supposed to be dead?" But whatever danger might arise, Kent seemed capable of handling it.

Alma arrived at Scott's private room at Walter Reed Hospital after he and Kent had had dinner. Scott was told that two suitcases filled with new clothes had been packed for him.

They left by the back entrance of the hospital, but Scott refused to wear the dark sunglasses Alma had brought for him. Nobody—not even Garbo—wore sunglasses at nine at night.

A blue, late-model station wagon was parked behind the hospital. Alma gave Kent the keys.

"I fixed a pallet in the back in case you want to lie down," Alma told Scott. "You'll probably be too excited to actually sleep, but at least you can rest if you like. I'll ride in front with Kent. We'll be there around dawn."

"You called my sister again today?"

"Yes, much to my chagrin," answered Alma. "I told her not to tell anyone about you except that preacher and his wife, remember? Well, she told her boyfriend, too. He's going to be with her when they meet us at the cabin."

"Boyfriend? Who, that Davis fellow Bentancourt told me about?"

Alma shook her head. "No, this one is a forest ranger she met down there a couple of weeks ago. Dave Thompson. Your sister must be a fast mover."

Scott frowned. "That's not funny, Alma."

"Don't get so touchy. I was just kidding. I take it back, okay?"

They got into the car and Kent moved them into the evening traffic. Scott leaned against a backseat door and stretched his legs across the seat. Unconsciously he reached to his shirt pocket and touched the cassette tape there. It had become his talisman, and he had started carrying it with him everywhere he went.

"Tell me again about my sister," he said.

"No," said Alma. "I've described her to you in every detail I can remember. Twenty times is enough. I'm starting to feel like a trained parrot."

"Just once more."

Alma grimaced. "Streaked blonde hair...pretty face...cute clothes...fast car. Now that's it. Close your eyes and rest. You're worse than a kid." She reached over and turned on the radio in a gesture to show she was through talking about Lillian.

"Did you bring my cassette player?" asked Scott.

Alma sighed.

"Let me put this as tactfully as I can, Scott," she said. "Shut up!"

Scott reached behind him and retrieved a pillow. He placed it behind his head. "So, look," he said. "I'm resting, I'm resting. Satisfied?"

They rode for a few minutes without talking.

"Well, how about it?" Scott said at last. "Did you bring my cassette player?"

Alma turned in her seat. "*Yes, I did.* But it's staying up here until you rest awhile. Now keep quiet. If I hear another word out of you, I'm going to swap you back for Bupchev."

Scott grinned. "Nyet, Comrade Hammond," he said. "I yield."

He could hear his name being called to him from a great distance. It was a woman's voice. It was coming nearer, becoming louder.

"Scotty...Scotty...wake up, Scotty...."

Cool, tender hands touched his hot cheeks. His eyes popped open.

Streaked blonde hair...pretty face....

"Lillian?"

She kissed his cheek, wrapped her arms around him, and started to cry.

It was daylight. The car was stopped. Scott blinked twice and tried to sit upright. His sister pulled back and helped him sit up.

"Oh, Scotty, I'm seeing you and touching you and I still can't believe it's really you!"

She kissed him again, and this time he was the one who gave the bear hug.

"Lill," he said, "you're all grown up. I don't even know you."

"Yes, you do," she said, still sobbing. "I'm still me."

"Hey! Is this a private party or can the rest of us join in?"

Pastor Mead stuck his head in the car and reached out a hand.

"Hey, yourself!" answered Scott, grabbing the hand and allowing himself to be helped from the car. He pulled both Meads against him in one hug. "This is incredible. Aw, don't cry, Mom, I'm fine. Yeah, I'm happy, too."

Scott felt a clawing against his leg. He looked down.

"Who's this?"

Lillian pushed her dog away. "Get back, Rufus. Leave Scott alone."

Bea Mead caught the apprehensive expression on the faces of Alma and Kent.

"Inside, inside, everyone," said Mom Mead. "Coffee's already hot and the bacon is sizzling. How many flapjacks, Scott—five or ten?"

Lillian grabbed Scott's arm and hurried him into the cabin. She was like a high school girl whose big brother had come home from college to escort her to the prom.

"Scotty, this is Dave Thompson," said Lillian. "I've been anxious for you two to meet."

Dave came forward and extended his hand. "Welcome home, troop. Glad you made it back to 'the world.' "

Scott's face flashed special recognition. The term "the world" was used universally by Vietnam vets. South Vietnam had been "the 'Nam" and America had been "the world." Even among veterans, there was a greater bond of brotherhood among those who had actually gone to the 'Nam.

"What outfit?" was all Scott said.

"First Cav," answered Dave.

"At Fu Loi?"

"Duc To, 1968," said Dave.

Scott whistled low under his breath. He lowered his head. "I'm sorry," he said.

"A long time ago," said Dave.

"Yeah."

"Breakfast?"

Scott nodded. "Right. I'm starved."

The day was a full one, although no one did anything more than talk, drink coffee, laugh, eat sandwiches, share a few tears, and sip chicken soup. Only the bodyguard chose not to participate. Kent stayed outside most of the time, finding out where paths led and where neighboring cabins were located. Alma stayed inside the cabin, but was primarily a listener. She had cautioned Scott about "saying too much" about his years as a P.O.W., and she intended to stay close enough to monitor his conversation.

After supper, Scott looked tired. Mom Mead saw it and whispered something to her husband.

"Scotty, it's been great being with you today," said Pastor Mead, "But an old codger like myself needs his beauty sleep. I'm going to be bunking over at Dave's with him, but I'll be back each morning. Ready, Dave?"

Dave shook hands once more with Scott. "If you need anything . . . ."

"I know," said Scott. "Thanks. See you guys tomorrow."

Bea kissed her husband on the cheek before he left. She untied her apron and draped it over the sink counter.

"I'm turning in too," she said. "Are we all set now? Lillian will sleep upstairs in the loft with me in the double, Alma will have the cot next to us, and, Scott, that couch folds out into a bed. Alma, are you sure that boy wants to sleep in the back of the station wagon? We've got sleeping bags and—"

"Please, Mrs. Mead, just let Kent do his job," said Alma. "He'll be fine, believe me. This is paradise compared to the last assignment he had. At least this time there aren't any boa constrictors."

Alma led the way upstairs, with Bea hurrying behind her. "Boa constrictors!" she said. "Well, I never! Where do you send these young people, Alma? You just wait a minute. You and I are going to have to—"

Her voice disappeared behind a closing door at the top of the stairs.

Scott turned to Lillian. "Do me a favor, will you, Sis? Pour this soup down the sink."

"With pleasure," she said. She took both of their bowls, tiptoed over to the kitchen area, and emptied them. "I'm getting where I can't look a chicken in the face," she whispered across the room to Scott.

She came back to the couch. "You look bushed. I hope we didn't wear you out today."

"Naw, of course not," said Scott. "It was a fabulous day. I may look a little tired, but believe me, I haven't been this content inside for ages."

"Me too," said Lillian. "I'm so glad you're back, Scotty. After Daddy died, I thought I was all alone. I'm ashamed to say it, but I actually thought about suicide. I was so depressed."

"I've been there," said Scott softly. "But you remember what Mom always used to say about 'the harder the storm, the brighter the rainbow afterward.' Well, she was right. Our storms have been hard, but now our rainbows are looking really bright. And speaking of rainbows, you sure seemed to light up when that Dave was around. I like him, Lill. His hands are rough, his eyes are clear, and his voice is kind. He's a good man, isn't he?"

"He's been good to me," said Lillian. "And good *for* me. We all need someone."

Scott smiled. "Don't I know it. Would it surprise you if I told you I had someone special too?"

"What? Already? You move fast, don't you?"

Scott remembered Alma having said that about Lillian. "It runs in the family, I guess," he said very low.

"Don't tell me it's Miss Hammond. Oh, Scott, I'm not sure I—"

"Alma? No, no," said Scott, chuckling. "It's someone else. I want to tell you all about her. And since Alma says I can't leave this cabin all this week, it looks like we'll have a chance to catch up on all our news. But now I'm afraid you are getting fuzzy around the edges."

He rubbed his eyes and yawned.

"Go brush your teeth," said Lillian. "I'll fix your bed. Rufus likes to sleep by the fireplace, but he won't bother you. We usually get up with the cows around here, especially since Mom

Mead arrived. Pastor will be back in time for some devotionals before breakfast. It gets our day off to a good start. You'll like it. Do you want pancakes again tomorrow? Scotty? Scotty?"

Lillian located a large afghan and put it over her brother. Before going upstairs she knelt beside him and said a silent prayer.

It had been a good day.

CHAPTER THIRTEEN

Scott had had it. Enough was enough.

He refused to be held captive any longer—by anyone. Today he would escape, even if just for a few hours.

He sat up in bed and checked his watch. Not quite 5:30 A.M. Perfect. Everyone else would still be asleep.

He slipped out of bed, pulled on his jeans, sweatshirt, and deck shoes, and eased himself out the back door of the cabin. Alma would have a fit if she knew. But Scott knew he would have fits if he didn't get away from enclosures.

A heavy mist was settled over the nearby pond. Scott grabbed a cane fishing pole which was leaning against the cabin and set off toward the bank.

The air felt damp but comfortably cool. Along the path he stopped twice to turn over rocks so he would have crickets and worms for bait. One time, while walking, he froze in his tracks, thinking he had heard someone following him. But all remained silent, so he went on. Old war-zone habits were hard to break, he assumed.

Once at the water, Scott felt at ease. This would be a good place to relax and think. He always did his most serious thinking early in the morning. Like today. He baited his hook and tossed the line into the water.

"Up kind of early, aren't you, son?" said a voice to Scott's left.

Scott was slightly startled. He peered into the mist.

Pastor Mead slowly walked into view. He was carrying a string with six fresh perch on it. He smiled.

"They're hittin' well this morning," he said, completely ignoring the fact that Scott was not supposed to be outside the cabin.

Scott looked somewhat amazed. "I . . . didn't think anyone else was up and around."

"I got out here right about dawn," explained the pastor.

"Actually, I just came to sit and do some thinking. Never expected to catch anything, but I brought the pole along as window dressing. Wouldn't you know it—when you're not trying to catch anything, that's when they're jumping into your lap."

"You came out here to think?" asked Scott.

"Sure," said the pastor as he set down his catch and started to bait his hook. "Don't you ever like to be alone, just to think?"

"Well, yeah, of course," said Scott, "but I didn't suppose that anyone else would...I mean, I just thought that—"

"Is that why *you* came out here this morning?"

Scott nodded.

"Good," said the pastor. He sat down on a log. "Now we can think out loud. With a little luck, our talking will scare the fish away. Don't tell this to anyone, but I *hate* to clean fish."

Scott smiled. "Shame on you. You can say that, knowing that most of the disciples were fishermen?"

"Frozen fish fillets from the supermarket," said the pastor. "Now that's my speed." He grinned.

The two men fished in silence for a moment.

"I've been thinking a lot about feelings...you know...love, lately," said Scott, suddenly pulling a subject out of nowhere. "I hadn't had any love shown toward me in a long time, and now, well, it's being thrown at me in waves. It's made me examine my feelings about people. But it's confusing. It's kind of hard to understand a person's heart—or even your own heart—at times, isn't it?"

"Men have been trying to do that for centuries," said the pastor. His tone of voice was relaxed and casual, as though he was simply agreeing with Scott and not trying to teach him anything.

"I heard some philosopher on TV when I was in the hospital who said the heart was nothing more than a big muscle," said Scott, "and that to ascribe any emotional role to it was nonsense."

"Um-hmm," mused the pastor, nonchalantly, as he played with his line a little. "They do make pretty valentine cards, though."

Scott smiled at that. Pastor Mead still had his sense of humor. And he wasn't pushy. Scott was starting to feel comfortable with him, just like old times.

"'Course, when I say I'm examining my heart, you know what I mean," added Scott. "Those feelings I carry around with me. I mean, I *know* that everyone has a *real* heart."

"Not the Tin Woodsman," cautioned the pastor.

Scott looked confused. "What?"

"I said 'not the Tin Woodsman,' " repeated the pastor. "You know—the fellow in *The Wizard of Oz*. He had no heart. Made his life miserable."

"Yeah, okay. Ha. You're right," said Scott. "You caught me on that one. All right, then, let's say *most* people have a heart. Fair enough?" Scott was still smiling.

"Well...maybe," said Pastor Mead, "...and maybe not."

He pulled in his line and then cast it out again. More than one fishing contest was now going on.

"Is this another joke?" asked Scott.

The pastor smiled, but shook his head. "No, I guess not. Take me, for instance. Despite the fact that I may not like to clean fish, my heart really is in the country. I've been living in Detroit more than 20 years, but I'm still no city slicker. I grew up in Arkansas. Bea did, too. We still play old-timey gospel records at home, we eat grits for breakfast, and when I work in my garden I wear bib overalls. You can take the boy out of the country, but—"

"I hear what you're saying," said Scott, nodding his head. "You're right, too. Ten years in 'Nam didn't get America out of me. Why should 20 years in the city get the country out of you? One thing, though—I couldn't change *my* situation."

"Me either, really," said Pastor Mead. "The Lord called me to preach. And He worked things out so well for me in Detroit that it was obvious He wanted me there. We made wonderful friends and we had a nice home...I've got no regrets. Still, I've had a secret prayer for the past two years."

"Secret prayer?"

"Yep. I've been asking the Lord do so some checking to see if there's a little country church somewhere that could use an old, feisty preacher. And you know something, Scotty? He found me one."

"You're serious?"

"It makes me so happy when I think about it, I can't even sleep," confided the pastor. "I've only seen it once. It's in the Allegheny Mountains. Appalachia, you know. Bea and I went there for three days last year. It's been on my mind ever since then. It's gorgeous, Scotty. Breathtaking."

"You're going there then? I mean, it's definite?"

"We sure are. I just can't wait to get started. From a *logical* standpoint, I shouldn't be interested in the place at all. The congregation can't pay me, the church has been boarded up for years, and the people are poorer than you can ever imagine."

"Like church mice?" teased Scott.

"I guess I'll soon know," said Pastor Mead. "The old shack that served as a mission church years ago probably has plenty of mice in it. We'll make peace with them, though."

He tugged once on his line to try to scare away a persistent nibbler.

"Yeah, Scotty, from a logical standpoint, there's no reason in the world why I should want to spend my retirement years there. But somehow I know it's what I need to do. So I'm selling our home in Detroit, packing up all we own, and staking everything on this venture. It's a genuine leap of faith. Every man has to take at least one in his life. You don't think I'm a senile old fool, do you?"

Scott's face turned serious, thoughtful. "No. You're not senile. You may be talking to one of the few men in this world who can truly understand your feelings. Believe me, I do. I took my own leap of faith not long ago. And, if it's any comfort to you, it was the best thing I've ever done for myself."

The pastor rested his pole on the Y of a twig he had shoved into the ground. He removed his fisherman's cap and began to inspect it, as though trying to determine which lure to remove and try next. Without looking up, he said casually, "If you don't mind sharing the story, I could use the encouragement."

Scott shrugged his shoulders. "I suppose it has to do with what I was saying before about love. I've been thinking a lot about it because it was a woman's love that helped me make it home."

"Your sister, eh?" said the pastor. "I heard you tell Lillian how much her tape meant to you."

"No," said Scott. "It was the woman who brought the tape to me. Her name was...*is*...Juanita. We're in love. It's the most wonderful, spontaneous, natural, real love I've ever known. For her, too, I'm sure."

"That's good," said the pastor.

"I think it *will* be good, eventually," said Scott. "But it's not good now. She's gone away on another assignment. A dangerous one. I couldn't stand to see her go. But I think there was something in both of us that made us want to prove that what we felt was real love and not just the emotional loyalty two people share after they've come through a traumatic event together."

Pastor Mead cleared his throat. "Maybe I'm prying into matters I have no right to ask about."

"No, please," insisted Scott, "I *want* to tell this to you. And not just because you're a preacher either. I want to tell *you* because you told me about *your* experience. You've made me your friend. That means a lot to me just now."

The pastor was silent. His eyes showed appreciation. He suddenly realized how much he wished he had had a son like Scott. And he also realized something else. But he said nothing about that. Yet.

"Uh...Juanita...?"

"...Martinez," added Scott. "She works for Alma Hammond as an agent in Cuba. The Cubans think she's one of their own. In fact, as far as her boss back there knows, she killed me last week."

Pastor Mead flinched. "She what?"

"Killed me," said Scott. "The Cubans arranged for me to get away from Vietnam so they could trade me for a Ruskie colonel being held by the CIA. Only the Cubans didn't want me to cause any grief for their buddies in the Orient. So they sent Juanita along as my 'escort.' Her job was to get me to fall in love with her and bring her back with me. Then, once we were in the States, she was supposed to do to me what the female black widow spider does to her mate after she's used him."

"And I thought *my* life got complicated at times," said Pastor Mead.

Scott laughed. "Yeah, but the weird part, of course, was that Juanita was really out to help me."

"So you two really did fall in love."

"No...well, yes...I mean, yes, we fell in love, but not when we were pretending to be in love."

The pastor stared blankly at Scott.

"Let me try that again," suggested Scott. "You see, when Juanita arrived in Vietnam, I was sick. The doctors told me it was probably a reaction to the food I was eating, either too much too soon or maybe even a bout with food poisoning. The idiots couldn't recognize a nervous breakdown when they saw it."

"Who? You? But for ten years—"

"For ten years I was cut off from everything," interrupted Scott. "I led a day-to-day existence. I didn't make plans because I assumed I would never be free. I forgot about people, places, holidays, and everything else. I had no mail, no calendars, no books...nothing to make me feel as though I was part of the real world. I became numb. A zombie."

He paused for a moment in his narrative and perked his ears. A bird? A rabbit? Probably nothing. He went on.

"So then this Cuban named Bentancourt started treating me like royalty. He fed me great foods, gave me magazines, put some decent clothes on me. Everything! And that's when it hit me that ten years of my life had been wasted. When I didn't have to worry about food anymore, I had time to worry about not being in America. When I didn't have to worry about rats and bugs and jungle rot and sunstroke, I suddenly had time to worry about my dead parents, my sister . . . ."

"I'm sorry, Scott. I understand," said Pastor Mead. "It must have been incredible agony."

Scott looked away, as though searching for words.

"I felt as though I was in a coma and someone was trying to bring me out of it by spraying me with ice water from a fire hose. I went into shock. I knotted up. I felt nauseated, feverish, dizzy. I thought I was going to die. I actually wanted to die.

"And that's when it seemed as if God spoke to me and said, 'No, not yet.' Maybe that was delirium on my part—I don't know. But I do know that when I opened my eyes for a moment, I saw this pretty girl—Juanita—kneeling next to my bed, praying. And that's when I did it."

Pastor Mead squinted his eyes. "Did it? Did what?"

"Took my leap of faith," said Scott. "I said a short prayer to myself, something like, 'I'm going to trust this girl, Lord, and trust You. If she double-crosses me and I die, I'll be with You. If she helps me get home, I'll know it's Your will.' I was too tired to resist anymore."

"So what happened?"

"I must have started blacking out and regaining consciousness off and on," said Scott, "because every time I opened my eyes and regained consciousness, Juanita was there. But from time to time her clothes would be changed or her hairstyle would be a little different. When I was stronger, she sat by my bed and whispered to me. She told me everything. She said she was an American agent, that Bentancourt planned for me to fall in love with her, that she was eventually supposed to—"

"Didn't she worry that you might talk during your fits of delirium?" asked the pastor, getting caught up in the story.

Scott raised two hands sideways. "Few people were ever around. They had planted a hidden mike, but Juanita knew about it and was able to muffle it at times. Besides, she could always have claimed that anything she said to me was part of her scheme to win my confidence."

"And obviously she *did* win your confidence," said the pastor.

"No, not really," admitted Scott. "The truth was, I just didn't worry about it anymore. I just decided to trust the girl and then to accept whatever the outcome was. I was too mentally and physically exhausted to do anything but turn it over to the Lord. I had used up all my own strength. By then it was going to be His strength or nothing."

"Not a bad decision," said the pastor. "The apostle Paul said that God's strength was made obvious in Paul's weaknesses. When we get so weak that the only One we can turn to is God, we often discover the real source of our strength. We bounce back stronger than ever."

Scott looked at the pastor with an expression of understanding.

"That's what I learned," said Scott. "Yet, even though I was convinced that God was caring for me and working in my life, you still can't imagine how I felt when I got to the hospital in Cuba and Juanita arrived one night with the tape from Lillian. I mean . . . there it was. The proof. It was all true. Juanita *was* an American agent. I *was* going to go home. I tell you, I felt as though my heart was going to burst. I cried and prayed and replayed the tape all night long. Juanita had to pry it from my hands at daybreak when it was time for her to go."

"And now?" asked Pastor Mead.

Scott stood up. He began to pull in his line and to wrap it around the end of his cane pole.

"Now I'm waiting for God to show me my destiny," said Scott. "He has given me a depth of understanding these past ten years that will be useful to me somewhere. I believe that. I truly do. And He reduced me to nothing before I left Vietnam as a kind of final reminder that I can live through anything and rise up from any weakness as long as I lean on Him. So now I'm ready to go where He leads me."

"Any idea where that may be?" ventured the pastor, trying to keep the excitement from his voice. He began to reel in his line.

"Nope. Just someplace where suffering people need encouragement and a couple of willing hands."

The pastor lifted his bobber and line from the water.

"Empty," said Scott. "You didn't catch anything."

"Who knows?" mused Pastor Mead.

"How's that?" asked Scott.

"Oh, nothing," said the pastor. "When we get back up near my car, I want to show you the pictures I made of the Allegheny Mountains last year. Beautiful place, Scotty. Simply breathtaking."

● ● ●

It was Pastor Mead who planned to drop the bombshell. But he waited until after lunch. Full stomachs made for happier people, easier negotiations—sometimes.

They were all seated around the living room coffeetable, sipping fresh coffee.

"You're not an overly religious person, are you Miss Hammond?" asked the pastor.

Alma tried to keep the conversation light. "I believe in God," she said, "and the CIA and in my own abilities. But please don't ask me in what order."

She smiled, but the pastor didn't.

"I need to explain something to you," Pastor Mead began. "Consider it a brief preamble, not a sermon. It has to do with Scott."

Alma looked toward Scott; he nodded his head at Pastor Mead as though to say *he speaks for me.* Lillian leaned forward but, taking a cue from the complacent Bea, she remained silent.

"Scott and I had a chance to be alone and talk this morning," said the pastor. "We went down to the bank to fish."

"You went *out*?" gasped Lillian, forgetting herself.

Scott started to speak, but Alma was first. "Don't worry, he only thought he was alone. Kent, here, was behind him all the way."

Pastor Mead and Scott looked at each other. The pastor seemed amazed, but Scott only shook his head as though admitting he'd sensed something like that all along.

"From the time Scott turned over some rocks to find bait, right up until he and the preacher fed their morning's catch to a couple of stray cats—"

"Charles!" admonished Bea when she heard about the fish.

Pastor Mead shrugged his shoulders and looked very much like little boy who'd been caught with his hand in the cookie jar.

Alma grinned. "You can relax, Preacher. I know all about your scheme. And, believe it or not, I approve. When Kent told me that Scott wanted to go off with you to Appalachia, I instantly realized it would be a perfect place to hide him."

"Appalachia? Scott?" mumbled Lillian. "What's going on around—"

"Scott's decided to come with us to the Alleghenies," said Pastor Mead. "He's going to help us build the new church there and work with the local people. I need him."

"Well, so do I," insisted Lillian, suddenly sounding both selfish and protective.

Scott stood up and came near his sister. He sat on the arm of her chair.

"Let's all calm down," he said. It's my life we're talking about here. Maybe I'd better do the talking, okay?"

Lillian clutched at Scott's hand and refused to release it.

"You can't be serious," she said.

She scanned the faces of everyone around her and suddenly realized the jury was in. The verdict had been rendered and she hadn't even been given a chance to present a closing argument. She looked up at Scott. His smile was benevolent, but unmistakably resolute. He intended to go.

"No, Scotty . . . no . . . ."

"Hey! We said the Allegheny Mountains, not the Aleutian Islands," said Scott. "No one is going to keep us apart, Lill. I've got to settle somewhere, don't I? Shouldn't it be among friends? After all, one of these days you'll want to get back to Detroit, and we both know I can't be seen there."

Lillian caught herself starting to say something about Dave Thompson. She stopped in time, however. What was there to say? Would Dave do anything if she announced her intentions to return to Detroit?

"Besides, there's more to this," continued Scott. "I really *want* to do this. Being here in these mountains has moved my faith in strong ways. I've had enough of jungles forever. I want to stay among the mountains—*any* mountains—for as long as I can."

"From Tarzan to Peter the Goatherd," mused Alma to herself. "Whoopee."

Pastor Mead frowned at Alma. "Let the boy finish," he said.

Scott freed himself from Lillian's grip. He stood up and began to pace slowly. He obviously had something to share, but was hesitant in knowing quite how to get it out.

"I know this is going to sound wild," he said, "but I think I've solved the riddle of what life is all about. It took me ten years in Vietnam and one week in these mountains to figure it out, but it all finally came together for me. It all comes down to this: People can only love when they are free, and you can earn their love by helping to make them free."

"Mene, mene, tekel, upharsin," Alma said to herself, too low for Pastor Mead to hear.

"I used to feel bitter about the fact that God had allowed me to become a prisoner of war," said Scott, still pacing. "I felt He should have protected me more, focused my life in different directions, guided me more directly. Now I realize that when I enlisted in the Army and volunteered for duty in Vietnam, I was exercising a free will which God *had* to give me access to use, even if my choices were not necessarily for my own good."

He continued, "If God had dictated my actions, my decisions and my behavior, I would have been nothing more than a wind-up toy. Instead, I was created for fellowship with Him. For us to have real fellowship, He has to give me freedom. I have to be able to accept or refuse God's love."

Scott moved closer to Lillian and looked directly at her.

"If I sat down at a typewriter and typed out 'I love you,' that wouldn't mean the typewriter loved me, would it? I would have *made* it say that. But if a little child runs up to his daddy and hugs him and says, 'I love you, daddy,' then that's *real* love. The child doesn't have to say that—he just does it because he *wants* to and because he really feels that way. That's freedom. And only with freedom are people able to express real love."

For an instant Lillian thought of the freedom the mountains

had provided her the past few weeks from her own private pressures. And she realized that this freedom had enabled her to have time to know, and fall in love with, Dave Thompson. Suddenly she understood exactly what Scott was talking about. . .and she knew she would have to let him go—let him be free—and that she would have to find her own freedom in some other direction.

"The people Pastor Mead will be working with need freedom," said Scott, still intent on explaining his decision. "I can help them get it. They're poor people, but I can teach them skills. And I can witness to them by sharing my story with them. For the first time in ten years I feel needed. . .truly, truly needed. You can't begrudge me this, Lill."

Lillian looked directly into Scott's eyes. "You're going to be happy, I can see that," she said. "And that makes me happy. Go do whatever you have to. Just expect to see a lot of me."

"Bring your work clothes," said Pastor Mead. "We'll have no loafers in our clan—right, Scotty?"

"Right," he said aloud. Then, privately, he whispered something into his sister's ear. When he finished, she put her arms around his neck and hugged him tightly.

"Me too," she said through tears. "Me too."

• • •

In the predawn hours of the morning of the departure for the Allegheny Mountains everyone was busy. Mom Mead was filling thermos bottles with soup, Kent and Pastor Mead were packing the car, and Alma was packing her suitcase in preparation for her trip back to Washington. Only Rufus lay half-asleep near the hearth.

Scott and Lillian were standing together in the corner of the living room.

"Have you made up your mind about whether to go back to Detroit?"

Lillian shook her head.

"I like Dave, you know that," said Scott. "I hope something works out, if that's what you want. He's a nice guy."

"I'm praying for Juanita, too," whispered Lillian. "I wish I could have met her."

"You will. Next spring."

"You'll take care of yourself, won't you?" asked Lillian.

"Will there be any choice? Kent will be there...and the Meads...and Alma's coming up in a week with her squad of brain-pickers. I'll have so much attention I'll feel like a V.I.P."

"You are," said Lillian, reaching up to button a pocket on Scott's flannel shirt. "To all of us."

Scott gently caught his sister's hand. He reached into the unbuttoned pocket and pulled out a folded business envelope.

"This is for you," he said. "Whether you go back to Detroit or do something else, this will enable you to have the kind of life you want."

Lillian looked puzzled. She accepted the envelope cautiously.

"What is it?" she asked.

"A check," he said, "for 51,000 dollars."

"What!"

"Shhhh," he cautioned, putting a finger to her lips. "I want you to have it. It's my military check for more than ten years back pay. Alma got it for me and I've signed it over to you."

Lillian looked genuinely astonished. "No, Scotty, I couldn't...."

"Please, Lill, don't argue. This isn't even a tenth of the money I'll be coming into next year once I claim my trust. I don't need money. What I'll ever do with more than half-a-million bucks is beyond me. I don't even want to think about it. Let me do this for you...for all the years we missed being together. You said you would be happy as long as you knew I was happy. I feel that same way about you. Please. Take it."

Scott squeezed Lillian's hand around the envelope.

CHAPTER FOURTEEN

Something was wrong. No, not exactly wrong, just different, decided Lillian as she shivered and burrowed deeper into the mounds of quilts that Mom Mead had piled onto the bed as a parting gesture.

They're gone, remembered Lillian. *That's it. That's why it's so quiet and cold. Scott, Mom, and Pastor Mead left...one? two? three hours ago? But it's so dark outside....* She groped for the alarm clock and shook it in disbelief. *Six thirty!*

She had crawled back into bed shortly after Scott, Kent and the Meads had driven away. She had expected to sleep late—till noon, even—but here it was 6:30 and she was wide awake. *I guess the old rise-and-shine habits of Detroit haven't been put to rest after all*, she decided. She had assumed those habits had permanently succumbed to more leisurely rituals, like Pastor Mead's insistence on rekindling the fire at dawn to take the chill off the cabin, and Mom's penchant for braiding long tubes of sugared dough into coffee cake rings that filled the kitchen with wonderful smells. But the Meads were gone, and no one was scurrying around, attending to details so she might sleep comfortably for an extra hour or two.

They're gone, repeated Lillian, trying to turn over under the burden of four quilts, a blanket, and a bedspread, only to find both her legs soundly asleep.

"We're on our own, Rufus," she whispered, reaching toward the floor for the usual cold-nose greeting. "Rufus?"

Somewhere in the dark abyss of her deadened feet she felt a squirming movement. She jerked up to a sitting position and stared in fear toward the end of the bed. Rufus looked back with sheepish eyes.

"Okay, okay, so the floor was too cold for you, huh?" said Lillian. "I guess it's all right just this once." She reached out and he wriggled toward her with his tail rotating like a tiny propeller. Free of their burden, her feet began to tingle to life.

"If we want a fire, we build it ourselves. If we want coffee, it's up to us to make it," she said, stroking Rufus's head. "And right now they both sound pretty good."

Her toes touched the floor and instantly recoiled at the chill. "My gosh, we must have had a f-f-f-frost last night," she chattered. A sweep under the bed with her hand yielded her old fuzzy slippers, which she put on quickly. The flannel-lined khaki pants she had purchased in Compton Gap were located in a bottom drawer of the dresser, and she pulled them over her pajamas. The slacks were several inches too long, so she rolled them up in a manner that was stylish in Detroit. She chuckled at the thought of fashion...it seemed so silly under the circumstances! A red-plaid shirt and a dark blue Shetland sweater completed her sensible outfit and helped calm her shivers.

Fortunately, Pastor Mead had stocked the old copper washbin with kindling wood, and within minutes a fire was crackling in the fireplace. She put a kettle on the stove for instant coffee (there was no sense in brewing a pot just for her), and then sat down at the kitchen table with a pad and pencil in her hand.

So I'm a little depressed, she admitted to herself. *That's understandable, isn't it? After all, my houseful of company has just left en masse and I'm alone...again.*

She shrugged off the temptation to feel sorry for herself and tried to concentrate on the happy aspects of the last few days. Her brother was home. Yes, that was good. *Good? It's wonderful!* she thought, feeling more buoyant. *And Scotty and the Meads are beginning an exciting new adventure in God's service.* That was good too. As for her, well, she finally felt in control of her life. Now it was time to make some decisions. Winter was coming on and she couldn't stay in an unheated vacation cabin forever.

"But what's next?" she asked quietly. "Where do I go from here?"

There were the obvious tasks to attend to: The lodge needed a thorough cleaning; an abbreviated "cooking-for-one" grocery list had to be prepared; she must call Detroit and notify her landlord of her intention to...to *what*? Move? Renew her lease? *Decisions!* She jotted these items on her pad and decided to tackle them one at a time. First on the agenda: housecleaning detail.

A light knock on the door interrupted her doodling and brought a quick smile to her face. *Dave*, she thought. *Who else would come calling at*—she checked her watch—*7:15 in the morning?* She hurried to lift the latch.

"You haven't eaten, right?" he asked abruptly, as soon as she opened the door.

"How'd you know?"

"And you're probably feeling a little down."

"Well, maybe just a—"

"My gosh, Lill, where are your manners?" he scolded. "Aren't you going to invite me it? I'm freezing out here."

"Sorry, C'mon in."

"We've got a gourmet breakfast planned for you, Miss Parker," he said as he set a grocery bag on the counter. "So just sit back and relax."

"*We've* got a gourmet breakfast?" she repeated. "Who's the 'we'?"

"I get by with a lot of help from my friends," he replied, reaching into the brown bag and producing an assortment of boxes and bottles. "Meet the girls: Sara Lee, Aunt Jemima, and Mrs. Butterworth."

Lillian laughed and squeezed Dave's hand appreciatively.

"Thanks for coming over," she said. "The cabin seems so empty with everyone gone. Could I take a raincheck on the breakfast, though? I'm really not hungry, but I'd love some company. Cup of coffee?"

Dave sat down at the table and watched her as she carefully measured coffee into the old percolator.

"What's the list for, Lill?"

"Oh, I decided it was time for me to make some plans. My apartment lease is up soon and I've got to renew it or find someplace else. I feel sort of at loose ends. Detroit doesn't seem like home anymore. Sometimes decisions are easier for me if I list the options."

"And what have you decided?"

"To clean house," she said with a laugh. "That's as far as I got.

Time's running out on me, though. These cabins definitely aren't geared to year-round guests. Rufus and I woke up shivering this morning."

"Yeah, but it's beautiful up here in the winter. Last year the road into Compton Gap was closed for three days because of snow drifts. You should have seen it."

"What did you do all that time?"

"At first, I felt fidgety...I kept thinking of all the things I should be doing but couldn't. But then I decided that maybe God was trying to teach me something. Maybe He wanted me to slow down for a while and reflect on things more important than cleaning up a tract of ground or fixing the roof on one of the cabins. So I stopped fidgeting and kind of paused for three days. I read, I slept, and sometimes I just sat in front of the fire for hours and thought about things I never took time to think about before. By the time the road was cleared I felt good—sort of cleansed, I guess."

"It sounds wonderful," Lillian said thoughtfully. "A year ago the very thought of being snowbound in the Smoky Mountains would have given me chills, not to mention claustrophia. I guess that shows how much I've changed, because today it sounds so inviting."

"Sometimes I forget you're a city girl," said Dave, warming her hands in his. "A working woman."

"Who's currently out of a job," added Lillian.

Dave leaned across the table and kissed her.

"Speaking of jobs, I better get back to mine." He started for the door, then turned toward her. "About that raincheck...."

"What raincheck?"

"Breakfast, remember? You weren't hungry."

"Right. But it was really sweet of you to think of it. Maybe tomorrow...."

"Nope. You don't get off that easily, young lady. How about dinner tonight?"

"Okay. Want to come over and help me deplete a year's supply of chicken soup?"

"Er, I had something a little more special in mind."

"Well, we could do a steak on your grill. It could be our official sendoff to the picnic season. But we better hurry before it snows."

"Now, wait a minute. I asked *you* to dinner, remember? I'm calling the shots here. I'll pick you up at 7:00. I made reservations for 7:30."

"Reservations? Where are we going? You mean this was all planned? How did you know I'd say yes?"

"And wear your best dress," he said, ignoring her barrage of questions. He opened the outside door.

"Hey, wait a minute . . ."

• • •

She was excited. "Reservations," he had said. Where was he taking her? She suddenly realized this would be her first real date with Dave, and she was as excited as a schoolgirl.

"Wear your best dress," he says. He should have said, "Wear your only dress!" She thought of her patchwork outfit, the one she already had worn twice in Dave's company, and she shook her head. *Darn! I wish there was a shopping center, or at least a department store, close by.*

The irony of it all made her smile. Thanks to her brother and the check he had insisted on giving her, money no longer was an immediate concern. She surely wasn't wealthy in the old J. J. Parker tradition, but she was at least *comfortable*, and she certainly could afford to splurge on a special outfit for a special evening. *But no luck . . . unless, of course, I want something from Old Ed's gingham collection.*

She thought for a moment of the days back in Detroit when she used to pamper herself before an important date. First she would schedule an appointment with Renee, her favorite hair stylist, for a wash, set, and manicure. Then she would visit the little boutique across the street from Michigan Technologies to browse through racks of designer originals. Meticulously coiffed salesgirls—wardrobe consultants, they were called—would parade outfit after outfit past her eyes for her approval. The owner knew Lillian's tastes well and usually had some wonderful *piece de resistance* tucked away that was perfect for the occasion, whatever the event might be.

But those days are gone, thank goodness, she thought.

She retrieved the patchwork skirt and ruffled blouse from the back of her bedroom closet and surveyed the damage done at the Comptons' dinner party. A drop of tomato juice here, a smudge of makeup there. She was dabbing cold water on the stains when she heard a car pull onto the gravel under the kitchen window. A few seconds later there was a knock on the door.

"May I come in?" asked Cat, looking almost shyly at Lillian through a crack in the door. Lillian must have appeared uncertain because Cat talked quickly, as if she were afraid the door might slam shut at any second. "I don't blame you if you don't want to see me, but it's important. Please. I'll only stay a minute."

"Of course, Cat, come in." Lillian held the door open, then led the way into the kitchen. "How about some coffee? I just fixed a pot for Dave, but he couldn't stay."

She poured two mugs of steamy black liquid, then sat down next to Cat at the table. She was nervous, and she always rambled when she was nervous.

"I'm on my own now—the Meads left this morning—and I've got enough food to feed the entire state of Tennessee. Mom Mead stocked the 'fridge with all sorts of hearty stuff. Actually, I'm looking forward to getting back to my mainstays—cottage cheese and hamburgers—you know, the simple things. But if you're hungry, I think there's some coffee cake in the—"

"No, thank you, Lillian. Really, I just came by to say I'm...well...I'm sorry about the other night at our house—the dinner party. My dad's still fuming about how I treated you, and he's right. I was pretty awful."

As Cat spoke, she kept her eyes down, as if she couldn't bear to look Lillian squarely in the face. Lillian guessed that Cat hadn't had a great deal of practice offering apologies, and the exercise was new and difficult for her.

"I didn't behave very well myself," said Lillian in an attempt to ease Cat's discomfort. "I didn't even thank your parents for their hospitality. I was so flustered at seeing Roderick I said all the wrong things. But, Cat, I don't regret that night for a minute. I'm grateful to you for forcing the issue."

"What do you mean? I don't understand."

Lillian took a deep breath, wondering how candid she should

be with Cat. She was tired of the cold war they had been waging since that first morning in Dave's cabin. She was tired of playing games.

"I think I've known for a long time that Roderick and I were totally wrong for each other, but I couldn't admit it. I hung on because I needed security...emotional security. And Roderick needed me for a different kind of security... financial security."

Now it was Lillian's turn to look down, avoiding Cat's eyes. Admitting that Roderick had only been interested in her money was painful.

"So you see, forcing us to face each other after we had been separated for a couple of weeks helped us to realize we had no future together," continued Lillian. "You may have stopped us from making a mistake we'd regret the rest of our lives."

"Thanks for saying it that way."

For the first time since they sat down, Cat and Lillian looked at each other. They smiled, as if in truce.

One of Cat's long, graceful fingers circled around and around the rim of the mug in front of her. When she finally spoke, it was in a voice quieter, more thoughtful than usual.

"I've been seeing quite a bit of Roderick since the party. We...we seem to have a lot in common. I don't know if we'll ever be more than good friends, but he's helped me understand how important it is to be on the same wavelength with... someone you care about."

Lillian sensed the emotion in Cat's voice.

"What about Dave?" asked Lillian. "Are you two on the same wavelength?"

Cat sipped her coffee slowly, thinking about the question.

"I wanted to be," she answered. "But, no, we aren't. I guess you might say opposites attract, but they don't make each other very happy."

She rotated the coffee mug between her gloved hands for warmth.

"Dave loves you very much, you know," Cat said simply.

"He's never told me so," replied Lillian.

"Maybe not, but he does."

Embarrassed by the conversation, Lillian carried the mugs to the sink and then began soaping the stains on her patchwork skirt.

"Do you sew all your clothes?" asked Cat, looking at the garment with mild disdain.

"Mom Mead made this," replied Lillian defensively. "It's very special to me."

"Sorry."

"I just wish I had something different to wear tonight. I...I have a date."

"Where are you going?"

"I wish I knew. Dave said he made dinner reservations somewhere and that he'd pick me up at 7:00."

"He's probably taking you to Croft's Inn. It's the nicest restaurant around here. You'll like it."

"I just keep thinking of all the clothes I left back in Detroit. If only I had brought along a few more things. I've already worn this twice when I was with him."

Cat cocked her head and studied Lillian's figure.

"Size eight?" she asked. "Which way to your closet?"

"Huh? Er, down the hall, to the left. Why?"

Lillian scrambled to keep up with Cat, who by this time was striding toward the back bedroom.

"What are you doing?" Lillian asked.

Cat opened the closet door and began examining the contents.

"Hmmm, the preppie look must be big in Detroit. Gosh, Lillian, don't you have anything that doesn't button clear up to your nose?"

Hangers were shifted from one end of the closet to the other as Cat assessed each item. Her comments were restricted to terse appraisals such as "Where did you ever find this?" "Wow, I haven't seen one of these for years." "Like plaids, huh?"

Lillian cringed as judgment was passed on her taste—or lack of taste—in clothes.

"Now, this is more like it!" exclaimed Cat, pulling out a dark blue voile shirt. "How about boots? Do you have any high-heeled brown boots?"

Before Lillian could reply, Cat was on her knees, rummaging through the shoes at the bottom of the closet.

"Here we are; these will be perfect."

Lillian sank down on the bed in bewilderment. "Wait a minute, Cat, are you telling me I'm supposed to wear a blouse and a pair of boots tonight?" she asked. "Aren't you forgetting some minor detail like a skirt?"

"Aha, the missing link," Cat replied with a grin. "No problem. It's hanging in my closet back in town. You're going to look absolutely smashing. I guarantee no one will mistake you for a college coed tonight. Now, when you put on this shirt, leave the top three buttons undone."

"The top *three*?"

"Oh, all right, the top two. And wear a couple of gold chains. Do you have any?"

Lillian nodded dutifully.

"And gold earrings like these." Cat swept her long hair aside to show large pounded gold discs. "In fact, why don't you just wear these?" She unclipped the jewelry and set it on the dresser.

"I can't wear your jewelry," objected Lillian. "And what's this about a missing link in your closet? For one thing, we're not the same size, and for another...."

Cat looked hurt. "Please listen, Lillian. I know we're not friends, but maybe we could be someday. Friends do things like this, don't they? I mean they borrow each other's clothes and help each other get ready for special dates. I remember that from school. Of course, I never...."

Lillian smiled.

"Tell me about this missing link I'm wearing tonight."

"It's a camel-hair wrap skirt with a matching shawl. It's a one-size-fits-all kind of thing, and it's supposed to be long. I bought it in Nashville last week and haven't even taken it out of the box yet. Wear it, Lillian. Please wear it for me."

Cat's voice was almost imploring. For some reason this gesture of friendship was very important to her.

"I'd love to, Cat. Thank you. I promise to be very careful, use three extra napkins, eat only dripless food, and have it back on your doorstep in the morning."

Cat smiled. "Actually, I won't even be here tomorrow," she replied. "Roderick and I are driving to Nashville in about an hour to look at office rentals. I passed the bar exam, so now I'm ready to hang out my shingle."

"Compton and Davis?" asked Lillian.

"Davis and Compton, I hope. Roderick's thinking about it, and I have my fingers crossed."

"You'd make quite a team, professionally and otherwise," said Lillian. "Just be careful, Cat, and be strong. Roderick needs someone strong."

Cat's face flushed with color. "I know you have pretty good reason not to like him, but he's not the same person you knew in Detroit. He has a very sentimental side...a very generous side."

"Roderick?"

For the first time since she arrived, Cat pulled off her black leather gloves.

"Look what he gave me. I know it's just a friendship ring, but maybe someday...."

Lillian knew, even before she glanced down at Cat's hand, exactly what the ring would look like.

"It's beautiful," she said.

"He designed it himself," explained Cat proudly. She gently removed the large, tear-shaped diamond from her finger and handed it to Lillian for closer scrutiny. "He chose emeralds to surround the solitaire because he said I was wearing green the first time he saw me. Funny, I was sure I had on a red pantsuit that day we met at the diner. Rubies would have been nice. Oh, well...look inside; read the inscription."

Lillian repeated the message that originally had been meant for her: 'Yours, with devotion—Roderick' "How...sweet. Roderick always did have a way with words."

She gave back the ring for the second time in two weeks.

"I hope very soon you'll be wearing it on your left hand," said Lillian.

"Me too," whispered Cat. She replaced the ring on her finger and looked at her watch. "Gosh, look at the time. I've got to run. I promised Roderick I'd be ready to leave by noon. Now don't forget to stop by the house for the skirt. I'll leave it with the housekeeper, okay?" She gave Lillian a quick hug and hurried out the door and toward her car.

"Good luck with Dave," called Cat over her shoulder. "Not that you'll need it."

"And the same to you, Cat," responded Lillian. She closed the door and leaned heavily against it. "It'll take far more than luck, I'm afraid."

CHAPTER FIFTEEN

From the outside, Croft's Inn looked only slightly more impos-
ing than the scattering of modest cabins that dotted the steep side
of the mountain. It was a little larger, perhaps, but hardly worthy
of "inn" status, decided Lillian as Dave turned the car off the
highway and began the winding ascent to the restaurant.

She realized that she must have passed the inn dozens of times
on her way to and from Compton Gap. She either had failed to
notice it before or else it had been obscured by the thicket of
bushes and trees on the fringe of its property line. It was October
now, autumn had thinned the foliage, and Croft's Inn suddenly
was stripped of its obscurity. She struggled to find the right word
to compliment the simple cabin-turned-restaurant without
resorting to false superlatives.

"Nice," was all she could think to say.

Dave laughed.

"Okay, okay, so it doesn't have a top floor that swivels or a
maitre d' with an accent. Reserve judgment, Lill, until you see
the view."

They walked arm-in-arm up the path leading to the entrance.
He opened the door to the reception area, then waited to respond
with a smug "I told you so" as she noticed the wall of windows
overlooking the mountains.

"Oh, Dave," she whispered almost under her breath. "It's wonderful."

"I told you so," he responded right on cue. "Of course, if you'd
rather have soup at the cabin...."

She poked him in the ribs.

"You don't need to make reservations this time of year, but I
did anyway," he added. "I wanted to make sure we got the best
table in the house—over by the windows. But if you're afraid of
height, we could always go back to my place and toss a steak

on the grill. You know, sort of a sendoff to the picnic season."

Another poke to the ribs, this time harder.

"Be serious," she said. "Is that our table? The one in the corner?"

He guided her through the maze of tables and chairs and seated her so that she could fully enjoy the spectacular view.

"Maybe this wasn't such a good idea," he joked, sitting across from her. "I can't compete with the Smoky Mountains. Not in October. And certainly not at sunset."

"You have my undivided attention," said Lillian. "But could you move a little to the left? I can't see. Thanks. Just look at those hills. They almost seem to be on fire with all the reds and yellows."

"Lillian!"

"Sorry."

They studied the menu, asked the waitress what the soup of the day was, and when she didn't know ordered it anyway.

"I like your outfit," said Dave.

"Me too," replied Lillian. "It's only on loan, but it's really special. In fact, it means more to me than any dress I've ever owned." She hesitated, then explained, "It belongs to Cat."

He looked up in surprise.

"*Cat?*"

Lillian nodded.

"She came over this morning right after you left. We had a long talk, and we sort of got to know each other. I think someday we might be friends. Even good friends."

Dave shook his head, almost in bewilderment. "What did you find to talk about?"

"You."

"Me? What did Cat say about me?"

Lillian hesitated, wondering if she dared to repeat Cat's words.

"Cat said that you. . .love me."

There was silence, and Lillian interpreted it to mean that she had been too bold. She knew she couldn't retract what had been said, but at least she could apologize.

"Look, I'm sorry. I shouldn't have—"

"She's a very smart girl. . .Cat," he said.

The waitress interrupted them with bowls of steaming soup.

"What kind?" they asked suspiciously, almost in unison.

"House special. Chicken."

The waitress, startled by their immediate groans, retreated to the kitchen. Dave looked at Lillian. They had to smile.

Dave pushed aside the bowl and reached for Lillian's hand. "It isn't exactly Detroit, is it?" he asked softly, still smiling.

"Not exactly."

The sun had nearly slipped out of view, taking the brilliance of the fiery landscape with it. All that remained was a blur of color, muted by the dusk.

"It's funny," said Dave thoughtfully. "When I first moved to the mountains I was convinced I was the luckiest guy in the world. I had everything I ever wanted . . . good job, good friends, beautiful country. But now, when I want to offer it to someone else, it doesn't seem like very much."

"What are you saying?" asked Lillian, looking at him earnestly.

He stroked her small hands with his large, rough ones.

"That I want to marry you. That I do love you."

She started to speak, but he held up his hand.

"I know what you're going to say, and you're right, Lill. It would be a different kind of life for you. But that wouldn't be so bad, would it? At least think about it. Take as much time as you need. Just think about it."

"No," she said.

"No?"

"I don't need to think about it."

"You don't?"

"Yes."

"Huh?"

"That's my answer. Yes."

He looked at her steadily. Slowly a broad grin spread across his face.

"Are you sure?" he asked. "You need to be absolutely sure."

"I've never been more certain of anything."

"Sometimes it gets lonesome up here. In the winter . . . ."

"I'm a Parker, right? Parkers are strong."

"Even one who changes her name to Thompson?"

She smiled and squeezed his hand.

"Let's go home," she said.

They left a very large tip, two bowls of untouched soup, and a totally confused waitress. Hand-in-hand they walked to their car.

"You look a little tired," Dave said on the drive home.

Lillian leaned against his shoulder. "I am," she admitted, "but it's a *relief* kind of tiredness, not real exhaustion. I'm suddenly beginning to realize that I don't have to be tense anymore. Scotty's home now and in good hands, Roderick has gone his own way . . ."

". . . and you've got a new life ahead too," finished Dave, reaching an arm over her shoulder. "You really think you can domesticate an ol' mountain critter like me?"

"Who says I want you to be tame?"

In spite of himself, Dave blushed.

They had finished their salad and steak before the walkie-talkie had squawked and Dave had been called out to search for three stranded backpackers who hadn't been seen since lunch.

"I'm sorry, Lill."

"Don't worry about it. I'd better get used to it. I was too full for dessert anyway. You can drop me off at my place on your way."

Dave located two lanterns, a battery lamp, and two spare windbreakers.

"Let's get married soon, okay?" he said, kissing Lillian. "It'd be easier to go off on these late-night treks if I knew you'd be waiting here when I got back."

Lillian closed the door behind them as they left.

"Tell you what I'll do," she said. "I'll write a letter tonight to Pastor Mead and tell him to get that church of his in order. We've got some business for him."

"Ask Scott if he'll be best man," said Dave.

"Are you kidding?" countered Lillian. "He'll be the one giving the bride away."

"Oh, yeah. Well, no problem. I knew that guy Kent would come in handy for something one day."

They both laughed.

Lillian finished the letter to Scott and the Meads. She sealed it and laid it on the table. She would mail it in the morning.

She yawned. Bedtime. Long past, in fact. Rufus had been asleep near the fireplace for hours.

Before going off to bed she reached toward the table and picked up the old Bible that had belonged to her father. She gently touched its age-softened cover.

God has a plan for each of us. A wonderful, beautiful plan. Sometimes it takes time; sometimes we have to be patient; sometimes we have to endure pain and disappointment. But if we just have faith, His plan will unfold and it will be perfect.

She lifted the Bible into her lap. Rather than opening it at random and leaving the choice of Scripture to chance, she carefully turned the tissuelike pages and sought out the special passage in Second Corinthians that she now fully understood.

"Our light affliction. . . is but for a moment. . . ."

She knew there would be other moments and other afflictions, but she would never have to face them alone. She had Dave, Scott, and most of all her own faith. She was strong.

She was a Parker, wasn't she?